# Praise for
# the Southern Beauty Shop Mysteries

## "WILL HAVE READERS BITING THEIR MANICURES AS THEY TRY TO FIGURE OUT WHODUNIT!"
*—Fresh Fiction*

"Well written, suspenseful, and well paced, with a killer twist!"
*—Fresh Fiction*

"This mystery is first-class . . . So, enjoy!"
*—Once Upon a Romance*

# *Polished Off*

"Terrific . . . A fast-paced whodunit. This is a winning Georgia peach mystery."
*—The Mystery Gazette*

"This first-rate mystery is well written, with smooth dialogue, plenty of action, and numerous suspects."
*—RT Book Reviews*

"Lila Dare . . . once again delights her new legion of fans with a lively, hilarious mystery that will have readers biting their manicures as they try to figure out whodunit. Add in a touch of romance . . . and you've got a cozy mystery that sizzles like the Georgia heat in summer. I can't wait for the next book in this series."
*—Fresh Fiction*

*continued . . .*

"So many twists and turns and side stories are sure to keep the reader engaged in an interesting whodunit. As a bonus, organic skin-care recipes are included. A fun read all-around!"
—*The Romance Readers Connection*

# *Tressed to Kill*

"Fans of the themed cozy will rejoice as new talent Dare debuts her Southern Beauty Shop series . . . Dare turns this off-the-rack concept into a tightly plotted, suspenseful mystery, and readers will love the pretty, plucky, smart, slightly damaged heroine and the rest of the charming cast."
—*Publishers Weekly* (starred review)

"Humor, heart, and a first-class whodunit . . . Readers will be anxious to make the return trip to St. Elizabeth, Georgia, to check in on the adventures of the girls from Violetta's."
—Casey Daniels, author of *Supernatural Born Killers*

"*Tressed to Kill* sparkles . . . Stylish, swift-paced, and charming. An endearing heroine, delightful characters, and an authentic Southern setting."
—Carolyn Hart, author of *What the Cat Saw*

"Enticing and eccentric Southern characters combined with suspenseful tension and twists."
—Linda O. Johnston, author of *Oodles of Poodles*

"[A] nicely plotted and well-executed mystery. With its uniquely Southern setting and snappy characters, this mystery is an exceptionally good addition to the cozy genre."
—*RT Book Reviews*

"Loaded with Southern charm, Lila Dare's first mystery is full of warm, eccentric characters and hometown warmth."
—*The Mystery Reader*

# Wave Good-Bye

## LILA DARE

**BERKLEY PRIME CRIME, NEW YORK**

**THE BERKLEY PUBLISHING GROUP**
**Published by the Penguin Group**
**Penguin Group (USA) Inc.**
**375 Hudson Street, New York, New York 10014, USA**

USA / Canada / UK / Ireland / Australia / New Zealand / India / South Africa / China

Penguin Books Ltd., Registered Offices: 80 Strand, London WC2R 0RL, England
For more information about the Penguin Group, visit penguin.com.

WAVE GOOD-BYE

A Berkley Prime Crime Book / published by arrangement with the author

Berkley Prime Crime Books are published by The Berkley Publishing Group.
BERKLEY® PRIME CRIME and the PRIME CRIME logo are trademarks of
Penguin Group (USA) Inc.

For information, address: The Berkley Publishing Group,
a division of Penguin Group (USA) Inc.,
375 Hudson Street, New York, New York 10014.

ISBN: 978-0-425-25781-4

PUBLISHING HISTORY
Berkley Prime Crime mass-market edition / March 2013

PRINTED IN THE UNITED STATES OF AMERICA

10  9  8  7  6  5  4  3  2  1

Cover illustration by Brandon Dorman.
Interior text design by Kristin del Rosario.

**ALWAYS LEARNING**        **PEARSON**

*For the real Corina Coffinas—*
*Thanks for making me look good!*

# [ACKNOWLEDGMENTS]

My deepest thanks and appreciation go to my agent, Paige Wheeler, of Folio Literary Management for her guidance and her faith in me. My editor, Michelle Vega, has made this project great fun because she was a joy to work with! Lynn Speno, National Register and Survey Specialist at the Historic Preservation Division, Georgia Department of Natural Resources, was kind enough to answer many of my questions. Any mistakes in that regard are my own. Yes, there really is a Corina Coffinas, and she has been an invaluable resource, giving me insight about the world of a stylist. Finally, I'd like to thank beauty professionals the world over for making all of us look good!

# Chapter One

✂

FOR AS LONG AS I CAN REMEMBER, HOMECOMING IN St. Elizabeth ranks as one of the busiest days at Violetta's, the eponymous beauty salon that my mother, Violetta Terhune, runs out of the front half of her Victorian home. This year was no exception. The phone rang repeatedly. There was just one problem: customers weren't calling to book appointments; they were calling to cancel.

Marking yet another X through a booking, Mom shook her head sadly at the schedule. She ran a hand through the short salt-and-pepper hair she gelled into fashionable spikes, and tugged at her earlobe, a habit that returned whenever she felt stressed. Then she slowly raised one hand to her head and massaged her temples.

"Still got that headache?" I asked. When she nodded, I

added, "Mom, that's been bugging you for a week now. I'll get to cleaning up that mold. That should help."

"Nothing's wrong with your mama except that another rat jumped ship." Althea Jenkins, our part-time aesthetician, lifted weary brown eyes from the crossword puzzle in her lap, and smothered a cough. Althea's hacking cough worried me the most because the sudden explosions from her throat shook her entire body with violence.

In a way, we were lucky that business had slowed, because none of us seemed up to par, physically. Althea in particular seemed tired out. Usually, she tried to squeeze in twelve facials before a special event like homecoming. But today, she had only three on the books and two of those already cancelled. I hoped she'd go home and get some much-needed rest.

"Oh, hush. They aren't rats. Just misguided lemmings." Mom smiled at Althea. They'd been friends for two decades and started the business together after their husbands died and their children were young. "Not to worry. Mrs. Everly will be here at four for her regular Friday booking. Thank heavens we've built such a following of loyal customers."

After stacking yet another shining tower of foils, I found myself with nothing to do. Usually when homecoming rolls around, I'm so busy doing highlights that I run out of foils. Then I'm forced to make them as I go, and folding foils is a job I totally despise. But today I managed to stockpile enough supplies to get me through a week's worth of coloring. In fact, I'd folded enough of the shiny silver stuff to build a life-sized replica of the Tin Woodsman.

"I might as well shift into Mrs. Clean mode. I'll take down all those knickknacks and wipe out the corner cupboard." I didn't want to tell Mom that I was also feeling dizzy. Maybe if I was on my knees, and the ground was closer, I wouldn't feel quite so discombobulated.

"Good idea, Grace Ann. Best to do it now before we get busy again, and before that man comes to inspect for mold," said Mom, pausing as she rubbed her neck to smile at me. I can depend on my mother's upbeat outlook on life, no matter what happens. Even if a hurricane hits. Which it had.

In the aftermath of Hurricane Horatio, the whole town had played catch-up with repairs. Because St. Elizabeth is on the southeast coast of Georgia, our town sustained both wind and water damage. The magnolia tree lost a limb, the veranda roof was crushed, and one of our plate glass windows was smashed, but other than the mess, the old Victorian house that Mom had inherited from her aunt had escaped unscathed. Or so we thought. Turns out the salon was full of hidden damage. Since we reopened, Althea has been coughing, Mom has had headaches, and my nose has been running. When I knelt down yesterday to retrieve a dropped hairclip, I discovered the cause—black mold growing behind our supply cabinet. Now I was determined to scrub every inch of our shop and eradicate the yucky stuff, especially before the inspector from the health department arrived.

I didn't expect the process to take too long. Mom and I had identified a couple of spots where the greenish black stuff was growing. I'd purchased a spray guaranteed to kill mold. Now all I needed to do was spray and wipe, and the nasty stuff would be gone, baby, gone.

The cupboard was half empty and I'd started washing the shelves when the front door flew open. In clomped Mrs. Everly, leading the way with her metal frame walker. Despite the fact she must be near eighty, Mrs. Everly has been blessed with an enviable head full of white hair. Usually by the time her regular appointment rolls around, that hair is mashed flatter than roadkill, but today her coiffure looked freshly styled. Instead of taking a seat at Mom's station, she and her aluminum frame stopped in front of a chintz chair in our waiting area.

Even from six feet away, Mrs. Everly's lilac perfume filled the air with a sickeningly sweet fragrance. The way the older woman worked her mouth told us all that she was fixing to make a pronouncement. I paused in my work to listen.

"Violetta? Out of courtesy to you, I decided to stop by rather than make a phone call. I won't be needing my appointment today. I plan to attend the homecoming festivities, as I always do. But as you full-well know I'm on a limited budget. A flier arrived in the mail advertising Snippets, that new beauty shop that opened over yonder." She gestured with her head to a spot down the street.

My stomach twisted into a knot. Snippets was a nationally recognized chain of hair salons, owned by Eve Sebastiani, whose father Arturo started the business two decades ago. While our town struggled to clean up after the storm, the Snippets real estate expert swooped in and bought up a prime location, a damaged commercial building three blocks from our salon. Faster than you could say "split ends," Snippets' corporate office also brought in a construction crew. The commercial building—formerly an eyesore—was refurbished, decorated, furnished, and ready to go in no time. The finishing touch had been a huge pink and black sign featuring the Snippets logo, their iconic scissors image, and touting "Affordable Style."

At first we didn't worry. We've had competition for years. Peter Wassil owns Chez Pierre, a swanky "spa" on the other side of town. Their prices are higher than ours, but their stylists aren't any better. Even if I do say so myself.

But after Snippets opened, one by one, our customers started cancelling. When we queried them gently, each woman related how she'd been enticed by a special offer tailored expressly to her needs. So, if you liked facials, you received an invitation with a coupon for a free facial. If you had your hair cut, washed, and styled here, the coupon offered a hefty discount on those services. It was uncanny. Almost as if Snippets had read our customers' minds.

"I love manicures, but I never spend that kind of money on myself. Well, I did once when Ricky and I got engaged so I could show off my ring," said Vonda Jamison, my best friend since second grade. "We're breaking even here at the bed and breakfast, but there's no wiggle room for pampering. I hope you won't mind if I use the Snippets coupon."

"Coupon? What coupon?" I had asked.

After that, we heard plenty from our customers. Although they were apologetic, they were eager to cash in their coupons for a free service or discount.

I couldn't blame them. St. Elizabeth suffered the same economic downturn as the rest of the country. Then along came Horatio, and *poof*! Things went from bad to worse. I expected our customers to try Snippets, take advantage of the savings, and then come back to Violetta's, but so far that hadn't happened.

"It's almost like they're buying our customers. Trying to run us out of business," groused Althea, her mocha cheeks flushed hot pink with irritation. She was mixing up a batch of one of her fabulous exfoliate creams made of oatmeal, aloe, and avocado. "First they offer one special and then another and another. You'd think they had an inside track on our business. They sure seem to know who likes what."

I knew Althea was thinking about those offers—and how to compete with them—as she watched Mrs. Everly, who was standing there smack-dab in the middle of our waiting area. She said, "I'm not much for coupons, but I tried the place, figuring if they made a mess of my hair, I'd have you fix it. As you can see, they did a credible job."

Mom's lower lip trembled, but I'll hand it to her. She kept a sweet smile plastered to her face. "They certainly did. You look lovely as always, Mrs. Everly."

"That lady manager over there threw in a free manicure, too. And a foot massage. Even gave me a sample of a new perfume with roses in it."

"My, my." Mom's voice retained its polite tone. "Wasn't that nice of them?"

"Being a good church-going woman, I'm bound to ask you—how come you've been overcharging me all these years? If they can cut, wash, and style up my hair for half price, what do you mean handing me a big bill the way you do? You know that since poor Geoffrey died, I've been pinching pennies!"

"I have always charged my customers a fair price," said Mom quietly.

Although her voice was pleasant, I knew her feelings were hurt. I swallowed hard and dipped my rag in a mixture of lemon-scented Mr. Clean and hot water. But the swallow didn't dislodge the lump in my throat. How dare Mrs. Everly suggest my mother ripped her off! I wanted to remind her that when "poor Geoffrey" died, Mom went to the funeral home and styled his hair for free. When Mrs. Everly's sister, Jeannie Rae, was laid up after a bad fall she took while visiting, Mom made a house call to fix both women's hair at no extra charge.

I guess I took my anger out on the furniture, because a china statue of a shepherdess on the top shelf tumbled down and hit me smack on the top of my head.

"Ouch!" With my free hand, I rubbed away the pain.

Stella Michaelson, our manicurist, closed the cabinet that housed her rainbow-colored bottles of nail polish. "I'm out of here." She hoisted her purse over one shoulder. The *squeak-squeak-squeak* of her sensible shoes echoed sadly on the wide heart-of-pine floorboards as she headed for the back door.

Over the course of the day, four of Stella's customers had cancelled their appointments at the Nail Nook. Stella took it pretty well, but Mrs. Everly's mention of the "free manicure" pushed her right over the edge.

Beauty, Stella's white Persian, stepped off her blue velvet pillow to wander over and take a swat at the fallen porcelain figurine, sending it spinning like a hula hoop across the pine floor.

"I suppose being a single mother with two little girls, you did what you had to, so you could keep a roof over your head and food on the table," said Mrs. Everly, her voice softening a bit.

"A widow," corrected Mom. "Not a single mother. If you compared the cost of my services to those at any other area salon, you'll see that we were less expensive until Snippets came along. But you have to understand, Mrs. Everly, it's not unusual for a big chain like that to come in and undercut local merchants. They have the financial backing to go for years without making a dime. Once they run small salons like mine out of business, they'll be free to charge whatever they want."

"Harrumph. That's what they told me you'd say. Not that it matters. I'm switching my business." Mrs. Everly moved her walker in a half circle so she could leave the way she came.

Rachel Whitley, our seventeen-year-old shampoo girl, rushed to hold the door open for the elderly woman. What a contrast they made! Mrs. Everly with her short white hair and Rachel with her shoulder-length jet-black hair.

"Mrs. Everly, if things don't work out," said Mom, "and

you decide to come back, I'd be happy to welcome you as a customer again."

"Will you do my hair for half price?" the old woman asked over her shoulder.

"No, ma'am."

"Then don't hold your breath!"

# Chapter Two

✄

"I FOLDED THE REST OF THE FOILS FOR YOU, GRACE," said Rachel, an aspiring beautician, who wore her black chunky motorcycle boots with the silver buckles and chains on them every day, no matter how hot the weather got. As she handed them over, the "cracked" black nail polish on her hands gleamed menacingly. Rachel alternately experimented with Goth and grunge, frequently surprising us when she came into work.

I didn't have the heart to tell her about the pile of foils I'd already folded and put away in my workstation.

With a nervous finger, Rachel twirled a lock of her hair. Usually she's busy all day shampooing our clients in the sink of our former powder room. Today there'd been plenty of time to sort through and toss old magazines, wash and fold towels, prep foils, and address the birthday cards we always sent our customers.

"Um, I suppose this is as good a time as any to tell you . . . I've been offered a job over at Snippets."

I rocked back on my heels in shock.

"Yeeow!" wailed Beauty.

"Sorry!" I'd caught her tail under one of my tennis shoes. She streaked past me and took shelter under a styling chair. There she made a big production out of licking her toe pads.

"But I told them no! I'm not taking it. No way! I mean, I went for an interview. Just to check them out. Kind of like a covert agent. Wow, is that place ever cool!" Rachel's kohl-rimmed eyes grew wide, and her fingers plucked at a run in her jet-black tights. "I mean, it's so modern and sleek, and like, big city. They've got this big saltwater fish tank smack in the middle of the shop. I could have stood there all day and watched the fish. And you'll never guess who's working for them. Lisa Butterworth. Yep, she's, like, their manager."

"Crud," I whispered. "That explains it."

Mom and Althea exchanged glances. My face burned red and I looked away. Suddenly, I felt sick, like the time I ate spoiled potato salad at the church picnic. But this wasn't anything I gobbled down. It was something I'd done.

For months I'd bugged Mom to start using social media as a marketing tool. "At least e-mail our customers with special offers," I pleaded.

"Don't have the time or the know-how," said Mom.

One day Lisa Butterworth walked in and pitched us on hiring her as a part-time consultant. She had been two years behind me in high school. Obviously she was a late bloomer, because in high school, she'd been nicknamed "Mrs. Butterworth" for her matronly figure, dumpy wardrobe, and bad hair. The woman who sat across from Mom and me wore a lovely gabardine pants suit with a silk blouse, tasteful pearls, and her hair had been professionally styled.

"I know the beauty industry. I graduated from cosmetology school after high school. I also have experience in marketing small firms like yours. I went back to GSU and got my degree in marketing."

That was impressive. I went to UGA for two years, hopped from subject to subject, before dropping out.

"First I'll compile an e-mail list of your customers." Lisa ticked off a to-do list on her fingers. "Next I'll separate them into categories. All the facial customers go in one group, the mani and pedi customers in another, and so on. Last but not least, I'll craft messages that appeal to them and the services they use. Finally, I'll send them e-mail blasts and check the click-through numbers."

"I'm not sure that our customers will appreciate getting spam from us," said Mom. She didn't know much about social media, but she recently learned to use Outlook and retrieve her e-mails.

"You got that right," said Althea, looking lovely in the dashiki she belted over black tights with a pair of ballet flats. "Kwasi gets two hundred e-mails a day. He swears he's getting carpal tunnel from hitting the delete key over and over."

Ever since she started seeing Dr. Kwasi Yarrow, a professor over at Georgia Coastal College, her conversations are sprinkled with "Kwasi this" and "Kwasi that." The way she goes on about him, you'd think she was fourteen instead of sixty-three. But maybe I'm just jealous. I've been seeing Marty Shears, a political reporter I met when he worked for the *Atlanta Journal-Constitution*. Since then, he'd taken a job at the *Washington Post* up in DC. Carrying on a long-distance romance is the pits.

Lisa defended her plan. "When it's a service people

want, when they've given you their e-mail addresses to stay in touch, it's not spam."

"I doubt I can afford your services," said Mom, eying Lisa's well-tailored gabardine suit. I noticed how sleek her hair was. Either someone else was giving her a great blow-out, or she'd mastered the skill of doing it herself.

"Actually, I'm incredibly reasonable." Lisa named a figure so low it shocked me.

Mom still wasn't convinced, but I nagged her. I called Lisa's references, and they had glowing comments about her work. Finally Mom phoned Lisa and signed on. For a month and a half, Lisa entered all our customer data into her computer. We've always kept good records, filling out a card for each customer and taking notes on our services. Now Lisa transferred all that into a spreadsheet.

Watching her attack the mountain of forms, day after day, I couldn't believe her industry. Nor could I understand why she charged us such a piddling amount. She worked hour after hour, making less than minimum wage. But she never complained. Never seemed anything but dedicated.

"Once you have all that data, what do you plan to do with it?" asked Mom one day as she looked over Lisa's shoulder.

"We'll run a few test messages to determine the bounces."

"Bounces?"

Lisa nodded. "Addresses that are wrong, no longer current, or no longer in service. By running a test message, we clean up the list. Think of it like sending out your Christmas newsletter. A few come back, right? Then you call and find out your friend has moved. This is the same procedure, but we do it through e-mail."

She sent the test message. Made a few calls. And disappeared.

"At least she didn't charge us much." Mom shrugged

and spread her hands wide in a "what are you going to do" gesture.

Now we knew why. Lisa had scammed us. She'd hired on for the sole purpose of stealing our customer list. Once she finished the job, she left. The piddling amount we paid her would have been chicken feed compared to what Snippets offered her to steal our customers out from under us.

"So that's how they knew how to reach our clients," mused Althea. "And what to suggest for them."

Mom pulled off her rimless glasses and pinched the bridge of her nose. "Excuse me," she said, "I need to use the ladies' room." And walked away.

I sank down onto the floor and buried my head in my hands.

What had I done?

# Chapter Three

WHEN MOM CAME OUT, HER PUFFY RED EYES AN-
nounced that she'd been crying. That got me all shook up,
because my mother isn't the crying type. When my dad
died of pancreatic cancer, leaving her a young widow with
two small daughters to raise and no particular education to
speak of, she grew a backbone of pure steel. She's also a
paragon of practicality, a woman who believes that when
life gets tough, you pull up your big girl panties and work
a little harder. Given all she's been through, she's pretty
hard to rattle.

Walking over to the appointment book, she ran a finger
up and down the listings. "Hmm. Grace Ann, we've only
got two people coming in tomorrow. I know you have
plans. Why don't you take Saturday off? You, too, Rachel."

"Sick! Totally sick!" said our shampoo girl.

I translated for Mom. "She means she's thrilled. I am, too."

Althea opened the cabinet by her workstation and grabbed her car keys. "Since I don't have anything in the appointment book, I think I'll hit the highway and see y'all on Monday. Kwasi's taking me out to eat at that new barbecue place, then we're going to the football game. After that, he's going to read to me from a new textbook he's working on."

Dr. Kwasi Yarrow was six years younger than Althea, but his gravitas made him seem older. He was a professor, and he wore an air of self-conscious intellectualism around him the way most men wear cologne. Of course, he drove a Prius, watched CNN, and read the *Atlantic Monthly*. I don't think Althea was attracted to him for his looks, although he wasn't a bad-looking man. Althea described her beau as "passionate," and I would add after seeing him in action with a student group that he was also persuasive.

The tall African American woman picked up her purse, a mesh sack that Kwasi told her was hand-woven elephant grass made in Ghana. It looked exactly like ones they were selling at South of the Border, that kitschy tourist place on the state line between Georgia and North Carolina. Althea stored her bag on one of the upper shelves because Beauty liked to use it as a scratching post. The design on the front was already missing two beads, and Beauty had been happily batting at something small and round earlier this morning.

"A textbook he's writing?" I stopped wiping down the baseboard. "Sounds exciting."

"What of it?" Althea stiffened and gave me "the look." I've seen grown men quake in their Nikes when she levels those powerful tractor beams on them.

"I'm just sayin'," I backpedaled.

"What are your plans for the weekend, Grace Ann? You and Marty going to the bonfire and the big game? Especially since you've got tomorrow and Sunday off?" Althea raised an eyebrow. This was a direct challenge, and I knew it. Althea and Mom both thought I was nuts for putting up with Marty's erratic schedule and vague promises. Last weekend, we were all set to spend a romantic couple of days in Old Town Alexandria, Virginia, when he called at the last minute and cancelled. "Big, big story," he said, but he was eating at the time, so it sounded more like, "Ig, ig, ory."

"Naw, I'm not much of a football fan." The real reason I wasn't going is that I refused to show up at the festivities without a date. This summer we had our ten-year reunion, and I was depressed for days. Seeing all my high school friends married with kids reminded me that the clock was ticking. For years I'd kept my desire to have children a closely guarded secret. After my failed marriage with Hank Parker, I acted like being a career woman was exactly what I wanted. Of course, pretending got a lot harder when Alice Rose married Wade Willard in a beautiful June ceremony. My baby sister and Mom spent months planning every intricate detail of the wedding, down to the pink and white tulle party favors on the tables at the reception. Three months later, Alice Rose and Wade announced they were having a baby. Six months later, that baby became twins. Nine months and two days after their wedding, Alice Rose gave birth to two boys, Owen and Logan.

While I loved being a doting aunt, lately it had become harder and harder to keep up the charade that working nine-to-five was my fantasy life. When the holidays rolled around, and the Willards sent out their carefully posed family photo, a sick tension gripped my gut. On Thanksgiving when we gathered around Alice Rose's Martha Stewart–perfect table, I tried to count my blessings. Mainly I succeeded, but the taste of loneliness grew sharper as the years went on.

"But is Marty coming? He was supposed to be here tonight, wasn't he?" Althea locked on me and wouldn't let go, those deep-set eyes of hers flashing a warning. She didn't like the way Marty stood me up over and over, and she'd made no bones about it.

"Marty has given me his word he'll be here Tuesday. He'll spend next weekend with me. We're planning to have dinner at Enchanté." I purposely got on my knees with my butt stuck up in the air before going back to work on the baseboards.

"Grace, wasn't he supposed to be here tonight?" Rachel looked up from the sink bowl she was sanitizing. "I'm only asking because you're welcome to come with us to Angelini's and have spaghetti before we go to the game."

I grunted.

"Grace Ann?" Mom prodded me.

"Fine!" I threw down the sponge. "Okay, pile on, everyone. Let's all pick on Grace Ann! Yes, he had a major development in a big story, and he had to cancel for tonight. After all, it's only a small-town homecoming, and goodness knows he's seen plenty of them. But he promised—"

Althea walked right up to me, fisted her hands on her hips, and said, "Of course, he promised. Men like that always promise and never deliver. You're old enough to know that by now. Girlfriend, you need your head examined."

After she left, Mom picked up her car keys, shouldered her purse, and headed toward the front door. "Walter has a coupon for a two-for-one meal over at Denny's. We have to use it tonight or it'll expire."

She giggled. "He called to say he bought me a mum corsage. Isn't that sweet?"

While Kwasi reeked of high-brow elitism, Walter

Highsmith cut a low-brow comical figure. He was short and pudgy, with a goatee and full moustache that he waxed into rigid loops. This was in keeping with his Civil War regalia, in Confederate gray, of course, and the sword that clattered at his side as he walked. Frankly, I thought Walter was a bit of a loony tune, but a nice loony tune. Mom seemed to like him well enough. He owned the Civil War memorabilia shop called Confederate Artefacts, two doors down from Violetta's, a proximity that made it easy for him to pop in and chat with my mother. Lately, he'd been stopping in at least twice a day. I'd always suspected he was sweet on Mom, but it hadn't been until recently that she seemed to return his affection.

I changed positions to sit cross-legged and work for a while. From my spot on the floor, I watched my mother walk out the front door. A sick feeling started in the pit of my stomach. Mom always gives me a hug or kiss and says, "Love you," before we say good-bye. But not tonight.

"Okay, I'm done here," said Rachel, closing a cabinet door. "You ready to go? I'll walk out with you."

"No, I'm going to stick around and finish up these baseboards."

"You sure? I bet they can wait until Monday. It's not like we're going to get busy again. Not soon, anyway. I've been going to this site called Scissors in Hand. It's this chat room for stylists?" She hitched one hip up over the arm of a shampoo chair. Looked mighty uncomfortable to me, but Rachel is young and super flexible. "They were all talking about what happens when a Snippets comes to town. Everyone says that their business goes south"—and to emphasize this, Rachel made a swooping gesture with one hand, starting at her shoulder and gliding down to the floor—"for at least twelve months. It takes about six months to start getting customers back, but that's only after you slash your prices to match theirs."

Honestly, I thought I'd puke.

"Oh, really?" I said. I was trying not to sound overly concerned. "Did they share any strategies for winning back customers? I mean, something we can do right away?"

"Nope. Although most of those shops didn't give away their customer list, either. I know because I asked."

A slow burn started at my neck and worked its way to my cheeks. "You asked?"

"Yes, but don't worry. They didn't know it was me. I mean, I didn't give away where I work or anything."

"Right," I croaked. "What else did they say?"

"Oh, they said that if you gave away your customer list, you were toast."

"Toast."

"Yeah, but I figure you'll think of something. You wouldn't let your mom's business go under, would you?"

# Chapter Four

✂

AFTER RACHEL LEFT, I SCRUBBED THE BASEBOARD so hard that I lost two of my press-on fingernails. I attacked the moldy molding around the doorframe with such a fury that the paint started peeling off. Seeing how black the water was in the bucket, I decided it was time to dump it and start over. On my way to the sink, Beauty got underfoot. It took some fancy footwork to keep from stepping on her, and in the process, I dumped half the bucket on the floor. It took me five towels to mop up the mess.

Beauty jumped up on the wicker chair in the waiting area and supervised my work.

I'd promised myself I wouldn't be one of those girlfriends, the kind of grasping women who don't know when to back off. I'd made a deal with myself not to bug Marty, especially within forty-eight hours of a visit, but I couldn't stop myself. I grabbed my cell phone out of my purse and called him.

"Grace Ann? What's up?" He sounded out of breath.

"Well, I'm having a bad day, and I just—"

"Hang on."

I could tell he'd put his hand over the phone. In the background I heard a high-pitched woman's voice, and then I could hear Marty saying to another person, "Yeah, just give me a sec here."

I heard the sound of a zipper being zipped up. At least I assumed it was going up and not down.

"Sorry about that. Just needed to get my briefcase closed. Right? You were saying?"

"Who's there with you?" I could have slapped myself, but the words tumbled out.

"Caitlyn, my new intern." He covered the phone again, and I heard a muffled, "Yeah, I'm coming. Hey, don't do that!" and a smothered laugh.

Then he was back again. "You remember Caitlyn? I showed you her picture."

"Right, Caitlyn. Tell her I said, 'hi.'"

Caitlyn was five foot ten, weighed 110 pounds, with long blond hair, and was all of twenty-three. I am five foot six, weigh 135 pounds, and every minute of thirty and ten weeks away from thirty-one. Don't get the wrong idea: I don't have a bad body image. Growing up in a beauty salon, I've always taken good care of my looks. I'm not a ten, but I'm a respectable eight and a half. That said, I'm not stupid. I know how younger women idolize older men, and, yes, it's true: Blondes do have more fun. The statistics show that.

"Look, do you mind if we talk later? Tomorrow even? I mean, can this wait? I promise I'll be there this coming Tuesday. Go ahead and make reservations at that new restaurant you e-mailed me about. But I've got to go now. Caitlyn and I were almost out the door. We've been working on that new story all day and we're both starved."

So they were going to dinner together. Big deal. Colleagues often did that.

"Sure," I said. "Sure thing. See you Tuesday."

"I'll call you before then."

THE CLOCK CONFIRMED WHAT MY STOMACH ALREADY knew: time for dinner. I couldn't stop by Denny's and use my coupon because I didn't want to run into Mom. Besides, the deal was a two-for-one special and I didn't have anyone to share it with. So I ripped it into teensy, tiny pieces and tossed them into the recycling bin.

I didn't want to go to Angelini's because I knew I'd run into Rachel and her mom, and I wasn't in the mood. Not tonight.

I had a taste for barbecue, but I knew if I showed up at B-B-Q Heaven, Althea and Kwasi would think I was stalking them, and I didn't want to hear another lecture from Kwasi about imperialism and the economy of Africa.

I would have given my eyeteeth to go to Enchanté, the new, hot French restaurant that got rave reviews in the Savannah paper, but I was saving that as a romantic treat for Marty and me to share.

When it came to going out to eat, I was out of luck. There was nowhere to go without running into someone from work. Or seeing someone from my high school who was happily married or at least engaged.

Heck, I couldn't even order carryout because all the restaurants in St. Elizabeth are zoned for what we locals call Restaurant Row, so you can throw a stone from one eatery to another. Even if I managed to dodge my friends inside the restaurant by ordering ahead and picking up my food, there was a good chance I'd run into at least one of the

Violetta crew in the municipal parking lot that all the restaurants shared. Especially tonight when people would eat
early and go to the bonfire at seven.

That left only one option: Walk-Inn Foods, a convenience store that's kitty-corner from Enchanté.

Now, I don't know who the marketing whiz is that came
up with the name Walk-Inn Foods, but he or she should be
shot at dawn without a blindfold. Every time I see that sign,
I get this visual of food stuck to the bottom of my shoes.
Weird name aside, they have a perfectly respectable hot
food counter that satisfies all my nutritional needs. It's
cheap, it's fried, and it's fast. I usually go for the Southern
Fried Chicken Bucket, which gives me three pieces of
chicken. I couldn't tell you what those three pieces are
because they don't resemble any part of any live chicken
I've ever seen. With the Bucket, you also get two handfuls
of greasy fries, a big piece of cornbread, and a foam cup full
of overcooked green beans. Tonight I planned to knock that
gourmet meal back with a Bud Light or two, so I grabbed a
six-pack. Nothing cuts grease like a beer. After I picked up
my Bucket, I tossed into my hand basket three of those
individual fried cherry pies, a box of Good & Plenty, a Goo
Goo Cluster, and two Snickers bars. I was deciding between
pork rinds and Doritos when I noticed a familiar head of
hair over in the personal items aisle.

Mom always says that my younger sister, Alice Rose,
would walk a mile to stay out of a fight, whereas I, Grace
Ann, would walk ten miles to get into one. Ever since Hank
and I got divorced three years ago, I've worked really hard
on controlling my flash point. Right before he and I filed
the papers, I visited a marriage counselor over in Savannah. I guess I wanted to assure myself I'd done everything
I could before I called it quits.

The therapist's name was Mrs. Klaus. She looked exactly like Santa's wife, I kid you not. "Grace Ann, sounds to me like your marriage is already over and has been for a long time."

I nodded.

"Then why are you really here?"

"I'm worried that if I leave him, I'll just make the same mistake over again. I've seen my friends do that. I mean, maybe this is the best I'll ever have—and he's the best I'll ever choose. Relationship-wise. If that's the case, why bother getting divorced?"

She smiled at me. "There are no guarantees that you won't make a mistake again. You can't change your spouse, that's for sure. But you can change yourself. Here's an important question to ask: What is it like to be married to me? Answer that honestly, and it will point you in the direction you need to go."

I nodded and thought about what she said. "I do have a nasty temper."

"Then see this as an opportunity to work on it," she said. "May I make another suggestion? Be yourself, Grace Ann. My sense is that you are trying too hard to be perfect. Stop trying to be what everyone else wants you to be. Be yourself."

I'd pretty much ignored that last suggestion until recently. Vonda gave me a set of self-help books for Christmas. I brought the books into work with me and put them behind the counter so I could read them when it got slow.

"I'm pretty happy with the old Grace Ann," said Mom. "I like you just the way you are."

With that, she and Althea launched into a karaoke version of Billy Joel's iconic song.

It was nice of them to say that, but even so, I figured Vonda was onto something, so I started reading and tried to put into practice the principles. Mainly, I asked myself,

"What do I really want?" rather than just going along with what everyone else wanted or expected.

Right now, what I really wanted was to strangle Lisa Butterworth. My fingers itched for the chance to grab her by the throat and squeeze until her eyeballs popped out. The fact that I'd been complicit in helping her steal our customer list just made me all the more angry.

So when I spotted her standing in the personal care aisle and reading the back of boxes, I marched right up to her and tapped her on the shoulder. "What the heck did you think you were doing? You worked for us under false pretenses. You stole our client list. You're a cheat and a crook! I trusted you!"

A couple of other customers turned around at the sound of my raised voice.

"Excuse me? I have no idea what you're talking about." Either she was wearing eyelash extensions or she'd been ladling on the Latisse, because I could barely see her irises when she batted her eyes at me, feigning innocence.

I have to admit, despite the fluff around the eyes, she looked terrific. While I was in my wet, lemon-scented, anti-mold-solution-soaked cruddy jeans and a tired tee shirt, she wore a form-fitting blue dress the color of the ocean on a stormy day. My tennis shoes were grubby, but the flashing red soles on her sky-high, flesh-colored heels screamed Christian Louboutin, a designer whose work I'd only ever seen in magazines. Yes, she was definitely dressed to impress, and I looked like the neighborhood bag lady. But I didn't care. I was loaded for bear and ready to take her on.

I set down my basket and crossed my arms over my chest, intending to look menacing, because I was good and mad. "You know exactly what I'm talking about. You were hired to manage a social marketing campaign, and instead, you stole our client list! How can you live with yourself?"

She tucked the box she was carrying under her arm and jabbed a bright red fingernail at me. "Actually, I'm rather pleased with myself. It's called business, Grace Ann. I'm the manager at Snippets, a *real* salon, not some rinky-dink little pretend salon that a bunch of untrained women run out of their home. Which, by the way, is a travesty! How zoning ever agreed to let you mangle that perfectly beautiful, historic Victorian house, I'll never know."

"Rinky-dink? We've been in business—" And then I noticed that people were watching us.

A small crowd gathered on the other side of the aisle. We were providing great entertainment at a reasonable fee—free!

"Yeah, yeah, blah-blah-blah. Talk to the hand." And she waved five beautifully manicured nails at me.

Self-consciously, I hid my own pathetic dirty hands with their broken-off press-on nails behind my back.

"And you'll be out of business in no time. Snippets will mop the floor with you and your pathetic group of losers. And it's all thanks to you! You gave us a wonderful start. Oh, and a real career boost for me. The company already sings my praises because we've done triple the projected business since day one because of my innovative marketing ideas."

"What?" I screeched. "Innovative—"

"Ladies?" The pimple-faced young man behind the counter craned his neck all the better to see us and scold us like we were a couple of naughty school kids. "Could you keep it down? Better yet? Take it outside? I really don't need a hassle here tonight. If you keep it up, I'll call the cops."

Exactly what I didn't need, getting my ex-husband involved in my no-good, horrible, terrible bad day.

"No problem," sang out Lisa. "She's just leaving. Do you have any Feline Feast? My cat won't eat anything else."

"Try the pet store next door, miss. Look, you're welcome to shop here," said the boy behind the counter. "I just don't want a conflict, you dig? You-all make nice, okay?"

I ignored him. I wasn't done. Not yet. No, I was just getting started. "There's nothing innovative about stealing. Ever heard of the Ten Commandments? Probably not! And let me make you a promise, we are *not* going out of business. Violetta's is a staple in this community. We have loyal customers who—"

"I really don't have time for this." She cut me off. "I have a date at seven tonight with Wynn Goodman."

I felt my jaw drop. "Wynn?"

She might as well have punched me in the gut.

"Yes, that's right. Wynn is in town to do staff development. I told him you were working in your mother's salon. He was shocked. Absolutely shocked. 'What a total waste of talent,' he said. 'Of all the stylists I've trained, Grace Ann is the one I thought would go the distance.'" She smirked at me. "Of course, I had to give him the bad news. You didn't go the distance. In fact, you certainly didn't go very far, did you?"

I stumbled backward, nearly tripping over my basket as some of the items popped out onto the floor. "Wynn," I said.

"Uh-huh. We've been seeing each other for several months now. In fact, I need to get going. He's taking me to Enchanté, that new French restaurant everyone's raving about."

She sniffed and looked more closely at the spilled contents of my basket. "Poor you. Looks like dinner alone. Again. See you around, loser!"

# Chapter Five

✂

AT THE CHECKOUT COUNTER, I THREW IN TWO whoopie pies, a bag of peanuts in the shell, and a couple of bottles of RC Cola just for good measure. You never know when there's going to be a shortage of major food groups.

Then I dragged my sorry self home to a converted carriage house two blocks from where Mom lives.

The fried chicken was cold and more batter than bird. The French fries were soggy, and there was a piece of cob in the green beans. I dragged down my secret photo album, the one with pictures of Wynn and me. On the cover was a handwritten note: *STOP! Do NOT open. In case of emergency, call Vonda.* Drawing on my tremendous willpower (not), I put the album back in its usual place at the bottom of my undie drawer.

I unlocked my smart phone and gave my BFF a call.

"Magnolia House Bed and Breakfast, now booking for the holidays. Please stay on the line, because we really want to talk to y'all!"

After three rounds of that cheery message I gave up. I cracked open a Bud Light, finished it, and felt even sorrier for myself. The album beckoned. I turned on the TV, cruised the channels, and finally watched ten minutes of *The Real Housewives of Atlanta* before I couldn't stand any more. I picked up the latest adventure of Stephanie Plum and flipped it open to my bookmark, a tired Chinese takeout menu.

After having a rough time tracking down criminals, Stephanie was feeding Rex, her hamster, who lived in a Campbell's tomato soup can. Empty, of course.

"That's it!" I bounced up off my sofa. "I need a pet. That's what's missing from my life."

Of course, in the back of my mind, I knew it was nearly seven o'clock and that Pet Emporium was right across the street from Enchanté, but if you would have asked me, I would have looked you straight in the eye and said, "Really? Do tell?"

Downtown St. Elizabeth proper comprises three city blocks square, with a municipal parking lot sandwiched smack-dab in the middle. I pulled my Fiesta into the only empty space, a spot by the Denny's, and crossed the street to Pet Emporium.

"You fixing to close?" I asked yet another pimply faced young man who was standing behind the checkout lane counting dollar bills. I made a mental note that if I ever had any extra money I would buy stock in Proactiv. On second glance, his name sprang to my lips. "Petey Schultz? You're Ray's younger brother, right?"

He grimaced and nodded.

Ray Schultz had been a year behind Vonda and me in high school. Ray was one of those troublemakers who mainly makes trouble for himself. Several times he'd been caught pulling stupid stunts like spraying graffiti on the Highway 40 overpass, gunning his motor at stoplights, and smoking dope under the bleachers during football games. Once his rap sheet got too full, he decided to enlist and join the army. Two months after boot camp, a roadside bomb killed him. His mother claimed she had a vision of his death before it happened and knew her son was being called to his glory. Or so she claimed. Since she was a known drunk, most of us murmured our sympathies, shook our heads, and walked away.

"We're open until nine, most nights, but I'm closing a little early tonight."

"To see the game?"

"Nah. Got to check on an installation we did for a business. A real whack job." Petey rocked from side to side, with his face twisted into a frown. "If I'm done with her in time, I'd like to go to the homecoming game."

"This shouldn't take long. I'm looking for a pet."

"No kidding? You do realize this is a pet store."

"Right."

"Any certain type of pet?"

"A hamster. Stephanie Plum has a hamster named Rex. That would be a good pet, wouldn't it? Loving, sweet, easy to keep."

"I don't know about Stephanie Peaches, or her hamster, but our hamsters? They bite." And he held up a bandaged finger.

"Fish. Fish would be good."

"You know anything about setting up a tank?"

"No, but I'd like a saltwater aquarium." Rachel had been so impressed by the one at Snippets. Why not get one for my apartment?

With a jerk of his head, he motioned me over to a display featuring a wide variety of tanks. I leaned over and looked at the price of a combination tank, filter, and light. "Yikes!"

"That's just for the tank. Check out the cost of the fish."

I did and couldn't believe it. A couple of them cost as much as one week's after-tax pay for me.

"Ix-nay on the ish-fay."

He picked at a scab on his neck. "Considered a kitten? Those are always popular."

I thought about Beauty. I like her, and even though she's officially Stella's cat, she's sort of the shop cat, so it would feel like cheating on her to bring home a smaller, cuter version. Thanks to my ex-husband, I knew exactly how that felt. "No cats."

The paper bag he'd been carrying moved.

"What's in there?"

"Parakeet."

"Don't they usually live in cages? Bird cages?"

"Not if you're going to kill them." He shrugged and walked back over to the checkout area.

"Kill them?" My voice went up an entire octave. "Why would you do that?"

"It's kinder than letting his friends peck him to death." Setting the bag on the counter, he studied it, picked up a bag of marbles, hefted it, and appeared to calculate the arc of the wallop he'd need to flatten the sack.

"Peck him to death?"

"They've already taken out his eye. If I put him back in the big display cage, they'll finish him off."

"What were you planning to do with him? I mean, how were you planning . . . ?"

"You don't want to know."

"Look, I'll take him."

"You haven't even seen him."

"I know. And since he's only got one eye, he probably can't see me real well, either. So we're even."

We spent the next ten minutes gathering everything I needed to make my new friend feel at home: cage, water and food cups, bird seed, cuttlebone, perch-cleaning tool, and a mirror.

"Um, maybe not the mirror." I was trying to be sensitive. "But let's add that bell inside the ball. That might be fun for him. Rolling it around would give him exercise."

"Right. You might want a book on budgies, being a beginner and all."

I agreed, and the kid rang everything up. I looked over the receipt. "You charged me for the parakeet."

"Yup."

"But you were going to kill it."

"Still can." He sighed. "I'm saving up for a Fender guitar. Loss control is a high priority for the company, and I want to get my bonus. Had a little setback recently. Okay, a big setback. I'd really rather sell the bird, but if you insist . . ." He lifted the bag of marbles menacingly and let it hover over the restless paper bag.

"No. I'm fine. We're fine. Really." My bill resembled the debt of a small nation. I handed over my credit card.

"Better hang on to the receipt. I'm not entirely sure he's going to make it."

# Chapter Six

✂

FROM UNDER THE COUNTER, HE PULLED A COLORFUL box with the printed legend, "I'm going home!" With a deft move, he dumped the contents of the bag into the box. I heard a faint, "Cheep? Cheep?"

The kid studied the box. A cartoon of Tweetie Pie stood out against the bright blue background. It smelled faintly of feathers and seed. "Might as well give you the ointment the vet suggested for his eye." He tossed me a slender tube.

"Thanks."

With the colorful box under my arm, and the cage loaded in my car, I turned over the engine on my Fiesta. By then, it was seven thirty, and I knew I should go straight home. But it wouldn't hurt to drive around for a few minutes, would it? I could leave through the nearby exit or I could drive

over to the exit closer to Enchanté. Sure, I might see Lisa
and Wynn, but what were the chances really? I mean, Lisa
Butterworth was probably lying just like she'd told a big
whopper to get ahold of our client list. Slowing down to a
crawl, I drove along the line of cars.

Wouldn't you know it? There under the security light
stood Lisa and Wynn. The years hadn't changed him. His
sun-streaked blond hair was still gorgeous, his shoulders
broad, his hips narrow, and his legs long. I got woozy just
seeing him from afar.

Better yet, he and Lisa were fighting under a streetlamp
in the municipal parking lot. You could tell from their body
language.

With a smile on my face, I forced myself to drive to the
parking lot exit. I planned to go home. But now, that I was
feeling better, I thought I'd drive past Snippets. After all, I
wouldn't run into either Lisa or Wynn. Besides, Rachel's
description aroused my curiosity.

I pulled out onto Reynolds Street and turned right instead
of left. Slowing down, I spotted the well-lit pink and black
sign with a pair of scissors slicing the word "Snippets" into
"Snipp" and "ets." Much smarter than dividing it at "Snip"
and "pets," I thought. Mostly the salon was dark, but there
was a little light coming from the back, probably a night
light or security light. Pulling my Fiesta into an empty parking space, I slipped the car into park.

Should I? Or should I not?

We have always had a great working relationship with
Peter at Chez Pierre. I'd been in his shop hundreds of times.
Once, he ran out of a certain hair-coloring formula, and I
ran a bottle over to him. I had hoped we'd have a similar professional affiliation with Snippets. In fact, Mom and I really
should have gone over and said hello after they opened.
That would have been the neighborly thing to do.

Now that pretty much seemed out of the question. But I did want to see the salon for myself.

"You stay here," I told the box on the passenger's seat. The parakeet's feet scrambled along on the slick surface, scratching against the cardboard. I bet he'd be happy to get back up on a perch. I don't know a lot about birds, but I know they aren't designed to walk on flat surfaces.

First I grabbed a flashlight from my glove compartment and did a quick recon, scouting my way around the building from the street and side lots. The flashlight bulb flickered but it didn't matter. I hardly needed it because there was an orange glow to the sodium-vapor security light illuminating the front door, another at each side, and one at the back of the building. Once I felt certain no one was around to notice me, I walked down the sidewalk toward the front door, enjoying the heady sweet fragrance of petunias in the window boxes and planters. If anyone asked, I planned to say I was checking out their hours, which I was. Kind of.

Three feet from the front door, I stopped. I could see the various lights of appliances and electrical outlets. I could also make out a watery-looking light. Moving closer, I could tell it was part of the fish tank, but I couldn't see any fish. Even from my vantage point outside, I could tell it was ginormous.

Next, I walked around to the back of the building. I wasn't sure what I'd say if I was spotted en route. Maybe that I was looking for a shortcut back to the parking lot.

Really, from every vantage point, Snippets looked super. Totally inviting and keeping with the Southern charm of our town. The clapboard siding was white, the shutters black, and a passing set of headlights illuminated petunias in a riotous shade of pink. A sign in the back noted spots for employee parking. One even announced, "Employee of the Month!" By now, I was feeling pretty good about my expedition.

So good, in fact, that if someone was inside, I might actually knock on the door and introduce myself. The place seemed that friendly and welcoming.

A newer model Toyota Camry with Georgia plates sat by itself taking up a space. From inside the building, a light glowed, and I could see someone hunched over a desk, one hand on what looked like a calculator. His or her back was to me.

I decided not to disturb him or her, but I did set down my flashlight, cup my hands over my face, and lean really close to the window for a better look.

My feet slipped off the edge of the sidewalk—and I started falling toward the glass. Windmilling my arms frantically, I struggled to stop my fall. The glass came toward me. I was going to crash through the window! I could imagine the sound, the embarrassment! With one last grunt, I threw both my hands forward—and my palms slammed into the pane.

I waited, sure that the person inside heard me hit.

But he or she didn't.

Looking harder, I noticed the white cord from a set of earplugs. Whoever was working was also listening to an iPod. No wonder he or she didn't hear me!

With effort, I did the first reverse push-up of my entire life. My skin made a sucking sound as I popped my palms free from the glass.

My heart was still pounding wildly as I squatted to pick up the flashlight. For a minute or two, I rested on my haunches, counting my lucky stars. When my breathing returned to normal, I stood up, tiptoed back around the building, and climbed into my car.

"Oh, buddy," I said to my new pet. "You missed all the excitement. Lucky you!"

The parakeet whistled twice and his little toenails scrambled along on the cardboard.

"I bet you'll be happy to settle into your new digs, right? No one's going to peck at you at my house. Excuse me. Our house."

My bird seemed to know I was talking to him because he chattered merrily.

"I think I'll call you Sam. As in Sam I Am. How's that?"

He whistled in approval.

Getting a pet had been an absolutely perfect idea!

Like a kid at Christmas, I couldn't wait to open the box and see my new bird.

Once we got home, I quickly lined his cage with newspaper, washed and dried his seed and water cups, clipped the cuttlebone to the cage, and inserted the perches. For good measure, I tossed in his ball with the bell. Finally, I filled his seed cup and his water cup.

"Come on out," I said, prying one end of the box open with my fingers. That allowed me to slide the parakeet into his cage.

*Thump!*

"Eekkk! A rat!"

But it wasn't. It was a pink creature, devoid of all but a few feathers on his body. The feathers on his wings stuck out at odd angles. A scab covered one eye.

"You look like a dog with a bad case of mange."

Turning around and around on the bottom of the cage, he tried to get a good angle on me, working out how to get his good eye—his one eye—aimed in my direction. We looked each other over.

"Whoa, buddy. You really are in bad shape."

With a flutter of wings—and what few feathers he had left—he aimed for the perch, hit it with his chest, and bounced onto the newspaper. After a quick shake of his head, he tried again. This time, he snagged the perch with one foot—and promptly swung upside down.

His one eye blinked at me in surprise.

He let go.

And fell on his head.

With another quick shake, he made a third attempt, and this time, he barely succeeded, wobbling back and forth on the perch before regaining his balance. Puffing up his scant feathers, he preened and pooped, seeming very proud of himself.

"Right. Nothing says home like a pile of poop on the floor," I said to him. "All the best decorators agree."

Still, I admit that I admired his can-do spirit. Talking gently, I reached into the cage and wrapped my fingers around him. His little head swiveled this way and that. His scabbed eye looked like it needed some attention.

"You poor little booger." I carried him to the bathroom, dampened a cotton swab and gently dabbed his eye. Next I administered a small dab of ointment. "I hope you make it."

Once I released him into his cage, he continued launching himself at perches, alternately falling and succeeding, until finally he attacked the seed dish with gusto.

"Oh! They didn't let you have any food, did they?"

In response, he chirped at me. In fact, he paused in his eating enough to chatter loudly with what I assume was a litany of complaints about being bullied by his friends.

Leaving him to settle in, I decided to read my new book about parakeets. According to the author, sexing a budgie is a job for experts. Not something for an amateur to try at home. Not that I would. It sounded faintly inappropriate for me to turn him bottom-side up and dig around in his feathers. Certainly not a way to make a new friend.

However, according to the bird experts, there were behavioral clues one could observe regarding a bird's sex. Males are more active, more likely to sing, more into head bobbing, and more social. Also a physical marker, the cere, the band of flesh over the bird's nose is blue or purplish.

My bird had a distinctly blue cere.

"Are you a boy bird?" He turned his good eye toward me and, I swear, he winked.

I laughed. "All right, Sam I Am. You have a good night, little guy. Sweet dreams." And I covered the cage with an old sheet.

# Chapter Seven

I WOKE UP THE NEXT MORNING BRIGHT AND EARLY in a good mood. When I took the bedsheet off my parakeet's cage, he hopped around happily. Early on my mom had decided that all of us needed Sundays off as a day of worship and rest, so Violetta's was always closed on the Sabbath. But getting a Saturday off was rare, especially in the fall when we were usually busy.

After puttering around the apartment and doing a load of laundry, I picked up the phone and called Vonda Jamison, my best friend since fifth grade.

"Hi, whatcha doing? I tried to get you last night."

"Of course you couldn't get me, silly. Ricky and I went to the bonfire and then the homecoming game. I was surprised not to see you there! Guess what? We won! Can you believe it?" Vonda's good mood was infectious, even over the phone. I don't know how she sounded so bright-eyed and bushy-tailed, because she got up at the crack of dawn to fix breakfast for her guests.

I found myself smiling. "Maybe we're lucky I didn't go. Maybe I would have jinxed the team."

"Don't be silly. Hey, have you had breakfast? Come on by. Ricky's making those pancakes you love."

She didn't have to ask twice. I hopped in the car, drove over, bounded up the stairs to her front door, sprinted past guests sitting at the dining room table, and ran into the kitchen. After receiving my requisite hug from my BFF, I let Ricky—her on-again, off-again husband—load up my plate. After sliding two pancakes on for me, he stuffed a broken piece in Vonda's mouth as he poured more batter into the sizzling pan.

They made a cute couple.

"I think I'm ready for a change," said Vonda. This week her hair was black. Of course, I'd colored it myself before giving her a nifty, edgy Goth cut. Vonda liked to change up her look. "That way I don't get tired of the woman in the mirror," she said.

"What're you thinking about?" I asked.

"Red. A good color for autumn, right? As long as I don't look like a pumpkin face."

Despite the fact that RJ, her son, was nearly eight, she hadn't lost the baby fat she'd gained when he was born. On her, it looked good, because Von's face turned gaunt when she was at her thinnest, but she was very self-conscious about the extra pounds.

"You'll look great, Von," said Ricky as he flipped over the steaming hotcakes.

Ricky had been our class clown, a geeky boy who grew up to be a nice-looking man. Of course, one reason was my haircuts. Until he graduated from high school, his mother put a bowl over his head and hacked away at his gorgeous auburn curls.

"Thank you kindly, sir," I said as he slid a second helping onto my plate.

"Grace Ann, you need to find yourself a man who cooks," said Ricky, as he carried a heaping plate of hotcakes out to their guests.

"Or one who can afford to take you out to eat often. Dear Lord! You're attacking those pancakes like you were starving." Vonda shook her head. I noticed a new piercing in her left earlobe. She'd added a tiny, delicate pearl. That was so like her, a study in contradictions. Von could wear lace and ruffles with a black leather skirt. Her housekeeping was impeccable, but her handwriting was atrocious. She loved beer and barbecue, but kept issues of *Victoriana* magazine next to her bed.

Their bed and breakfast, Magnolia House, also reflected contrasting styles. Built in 1874, the house itself was old, but the interior had been totally updated and modernized. Its romantic piazza, a long open porch with a white balustrade running the full length of the house, made a stunning first impression. Located in the heart of downtown St. Elizabeth, the building sat close to the street. Ricky compensated for the lack of privacy by installing a white picket fence, behind which Vonda grew amazing roses. The huge pink and white blossoms made a stunning contrast against the deep coral siding.

Inside were a dozen guest rooms, each with a private bath and big-screen TV. Vonda had lovingly decorated each room individually, each in a slightly different style, a touch her guests appreciated. The sheets were Porthault, but the quilts pure Appalachian, handmade to her specifications. Every detail, from fresh flowers on the bedside tables to the choice of magazines and toiletries, was perfect. In short, she'd created the penultimate romantic hideaway. I always felt a bit sorry for myself when I visited because I wasn't a traveler with a reason to stay overnight and let her baby me!

"Come on, Grace Ann. Time for girl talk." She gestured with her head toward the front parlor. That way Vonda could keep one eye on the front desk, but we'd have a little privacy. I grabbed my plate and she poured us two glasses of the honey-sweetened fresh lemonade that Magnolia House is famous for.

"Guess what? I bought a one-eyed parakeet!" I said.

"You bought a what?" Vonda reared back in shock.

I kept stuffing my face with German apple pancakes. I mean, if you visit Magnolia House and you don't order the German pancakes, you ought to have your head examined. "I bought a parakeet with one eye. Turquoise wings. His body mainly pink. See, they plucked off most of his feathers. But he's a chatty fellow. Likes to hop on and off his perches. Falls every now and again, but he's getting better. I think it's a depth perception problem he has to work out. I named him Sam, as in Sam I Am."

"Sam I Am what? Defective?"

"Hey, that's not nice. Just plain Sam I Am. He's actually kind of cute. Or will be when his feathers grow back."

Vonda stared at me. "One eye and no feathers? Why didn't you name him Lucky?"

"Ha, ha, ha. Although that would have fit. The guy at the pet shop was going to, you know."

"You know, what? Mark him down for a quick sale?"

"Kill him."

"Ugh. So you're telling me you have a rescue parakeet? That's a new one. By the way, it's Will.i.am, and you sure know how to pick them." She rolled her eyes and took a sip from her frosty glass. "Where'd you buy it? Fur, Fin, and Feather? I mean, if you were at the pet shop, you were right there where it happened. Only a half a block away."

"Half a block away from what?'

"The murder."

"What murder?"

"Lisa Butterworth."

"What!"

"Remember her from high school? She's dead."

"Lisa Butterworth? You're sure?"

"Uh-huh."

"Oh my gosh. I can't believe it!"

Vonda stared at me. "Why don't you believe it?"

"Well, she's the one who stole our client list."

"You're kidding!" Vonda's eyebrows shot up to her hairline. "You never told me that!"

"Yeah, she is—or was—because now she's dead!" Suddenly, those pancakes were dancing the rumba in my tummy. "And I just saw her! I bumped into her at Walk-Inn Foods, where we had a little, um, tiff."

"A tiff? As in a fight?" Vonda's face clouded with concern.

"Before I bought my parakeet, I stopped in the convenience store."

"Where you had a fight." Vonda dropped her head into her hands and groaned.

"Sort of. Not a big fight. We argued. That's all. The manager told us to keep it down. Then, I bought food for dinner. And after that, I sort of cruised through the municipal parking lot. I saw her outside of Enchanté. Talking to someone. I decided to take a peek in the Snippets window before I went home."

I didn't mention who that someone was—or that Lisa bragged to me about having a relationship with Wynn

Goodman—because Vonda would go completely nuts if she knew he was in town. After what he did to me, and how miserable I was for months afterward, Vonda had taken a vow to personally turn Wynn into a soprano, and I don't mean a mobster.

My friend sighed and gave me a sorrowful look. "How can you 'sort of cruise through a parking lot'? And then wind up peeking in the Snippets salon window like a stalker? Hmm? How does that happen, Grace? Is it like being abducted by aliens? I mean, your story makes about as much sense. Did your Fiesta navigate there without you? You do realize what this means, don't you?"

I was still hung up on the fact Lisa Butterworth was dead. I couldn't follow what Vonda was saying. "No, Von, what does it mean?"

"You must have been in the parking lot of Snippets around the same time she was killed."

# Chapter Eight

✂

"COME ON. DON'T BE SILLY. HOW COULD YOU KNOW that?" Okay, that caused me to stop eating. Vonda's news shocked me.

She shot me one of her "duh" glances. "It was all over the radio this morning."

"You know I never listen to the news. Or read the paper. Especially not since Snippets started running those huge ads for cheap haircuts. I got up, dressed, did laundry, called you, and came right over when you mentioned pancakes."

"Pathetic." Vonda pushed her chair back, walked to the front desk, and came back with a newspaper that she tossed down on the table. "Read it and weep."

## LOCAL WOMAN FOUND DEAD IN HAIR SALON

*Police responding to an anonymous caller claiming to have heard an altercation around 9:15 P.M. last night were directed to the Snippets Hair Salon, 255 Reynolds Street, where they found the body of a local woman. Lisa Butterworth, 29, 3111 Park Street, was pronounced dead at the scene. A homicide investigation is underway.*

*"We've set up a hotline and we're asking any citizen who was in the area last night to come in and talk to us," said Officer Hank Parker, responding officer at the scene.*

VONDA RUBBED HER EYES AND SIGHED AGAIN. "THE one night I turn on the answering machine so Ricky and I can make whoopee, and that's the night my best friend has a total mental breakdown and does really, really stupid things."

"Geez, she must have been killed shortly after I looked in the window."

"Are you out of your cotton-picking mind, Grace? You're their competitor. They could have called the police on you for sneaking around like that. Hank would have loved the chance to get you in handcuffs."

She grabbed the newspaper out of my hands and reread the article. "Dead. And only six blocks from here. But we have nothing to fear, right? Good old Hank's on the case."

Hank Parker is my ex-husband. Six foot three and beefy as a linebacker, the position he played in high school. Also the reason he took a lot of blows to the head. In the twelve years since we'd graduated, Hank had put on a couple of pounds per year, leaving him with a Dunlap, a belly that done lapped over his belt. My ex lives for the day he gets to shoot someone. The closest he's come is tasering a couple of drunk college kids back when we lived in Atlanta.

When Hank first applied to the police academy, a sense of pride bubbled up inside me. To hear Hank tell it, he wanted to do good in the world. I wanted to believe he was finally on the right track, that after years of flipping burgers, dropping out of University of Georgia, and knocking around at odd jobs, he'd found his passion.

And, he had. Sort of. Because Hank Parker's life lost its thrill the day he graduated from St. Elizabeth High School and hung up his Sabertooths letter jacket for the last time. Becoming a cop was his way of getting the ongoing respect and recognition he craved, even if it meant taking shortcuts. Before long, he'd collected phone numbers of cop groupies. Women who needed him to "check on" their houses because they were "afraid."

At first I chose to look the other way. After all, I was working full time at a small salon in Atlanta, saving money for my time at beauty school, since my income would be cut dramatically, and Hank was still in the academy. But the late-night phone calls from giggling female voices grew harder and harder to ignore. After a while, I couldn't pretend anymore. The scent of perfume on Hank's clothes, the lipstick, the fact he'd suddenly taken to washing his own boxers, and his strut told me my husband had gone astray.

But I didn't want to admit my marriage was a disaster. Especially not when my sister fairly glowed with maternal pride and her husband obviously adored her. So I took to pretending, to making excuses, and I got pretty good at it until the day I forgot my checkbook and came home early. I turned the key in the lock of our small apartment and immediately, every particle in my body stood at attention.

Something was wrong. The stereo Hank insisted on buying was turned down low, with Marvin Gaye growling, "Let's get it on," and from our bedroom came a rhythmic squeaking.

"Hank?" I said. His utility belt, his revolver, and his coat draped over the cheap leather recliner he loved.

The noises continued. I followed them down the hallway, past our small bathroom, and when I stepped into our bedroom, I saw Melissa Littleton, his firearm instructor, and my husband doing the nasty.

Of course, Hank blamed it on me. "You don't understand the stress I'm under. As an instrument of the law, I walk into all sorts of danger every day!"

I rolled my eyes. "Right. You haven't graduated yet. In the classroom, flying chalk could decapitate a brainless wonder like you."

By noon the next day, I'd found my own studio apartment, with a foldout sofa for a bed, a bathroom the size of a telephone booth, and a hot plate for a kitchen. None of that mattered. What did matter was that I could finally quit pretending my marriage was working.

For the past three years, Hank and I have been happily divorced. At least I am. Hank doesn't see it that way. To hear him tell it, we're still married, just taking a break. A long time-out formalized by a judge in a courtroom, and after that, I mysteriously took back my maiden name. Go figure.

The last time I saw Hank, he suggested we get together for dinner, lunch, breakfast, or just plain sex. Take your pick. I said, "No, no, no, and never ever. *Ever.*"

He laughed. "Sugar, you don't really mean that. We were so good together, Grace." And to illustrate, he clenched his fists at his side and gave a few thrusts of his pelvis to the tune of corresponding grunts.

What was I thinking when I married him?

I was thinking I would love to have a family.

"Grace Ann? Hello? Earth to Grace Ann." Vonda tapped me on the shoulder, bringing me back to the here and now. "You do realize the trouble you're in, don't you?"

"Right," I croaked. "Lisa Butterworth is dead, and I'm Suspect Numero Uno."

# Chapter Nine

✂

SINCE MARTY WASN'T COMING UNTIL TUESDAY, there was no excuse for me skipping church services. News of Lisa's death dominated all the local radio stations. I'd tried to call Mom, but we'd been playing telephone tag. Pulling into the lot at First Baptist, I spotted my mother's car. Didn't take me long to find her inside, because she always sits in the same pew, the third from the front on the right-hand side.

She'd already heard the news. "That's a shame, isn't it? I still don't like what she did, but I would have never wished that on her." When Pastor Kohler added a special prayer for the grieving family of Lisa Butterworth, Mom reached into her purse, pulled out a handkerchief, and wiped her eyes.

"Yes, it's awful. See you Monday," I said, as I gave my mother a hug.

"Pardon?"

"I said I'd see you Monday."

"Oh."

"Something wrong?" I asked.

"A lot on my mind," she said.

"Want to talk about it?" I asked, although I hoped she didn't. I was afraid she'd mention how disappointed she was in me. After all, I was the one who insisted on hiring Lisa Butterworth. Everyone at the salon had good reason to be put out with me.

"Not right now." Her smile was forced. "Maybe Monday. I need time to think."

We said good-bye, with me feeling unsettled and down. I stopped at the grocery store to pick up supplies for the week. In the checkout line, I glanced at the Sunday paper. Lisa's face grinned up at me as I put my eggs, turkey sausage, English muffins, OJ, milk, and lunch meat on the conveyor belt. At the last minute, almost as if it had a mind of its own, my hand reached out and grabbed a copy.

After making myself a grilled cheese sandwich for lunch, I brewed a new cup of coffee and sat down to read.

Turns out Lisa had done pretty well for herself, what with her cosmetology degree and going back to school. She'd worked for Snippets for five years, moving up the ranks. Her parents still lived here, but she'd moved all over the eastern seaboard. I guess she'd used her vacation time, and folks' address, to pull a fast one on us.

Snippets had taken out a quarter-page ad to mourn Lisa's untimely passing. They would be closed today, Sunday, but open for business as usual on Monday.

Since I'd already ruined my nails, I decided to clean my apartment. The Spic and Span in my bucket had turned brownish with dust and dirt when my doorbell rang.

Alice Rose stood on my front steps, her soft linen pants

in cobalt blue and matching sweater set a stark contrast to my torn jeans. Her blue eyes were dark, a sure sign she was troubled. Whereas I'd inherited our father's light brown hair, which I spruced up with highlights, Alice Rose was born a platinum blonde. After she had her boys, her hair darkened slightly, so she dropped by the shop for regular lightening treatments. Recently, she decided that long hair was too much trouble, and she demanded that Mom give her a pixie cut like Emma Watson wears. The effect was stunning and brought out her tiny little nose. If Alice Rose had put on ten pounds, it didn't matter. She was taller than I, so the weight was distributed evenly.

Glancing at the clock, I realized she must have stopped by on her way back from the early service at First Methodist. We'd been raised Baptist, but she switched to the Methodist Church because Wade went there. "Hey, you," I said and I gave my little sis a hug, inhaling the gardenia perfume she favors.

She embraced me back, although reluctantly. "What is that you're wearing? Good Lord, Grace Ann. You look like a bag lady and smell like a janitor."

"Not all of us are lucky enough to have a cleaning lady." I moved out of my doorway to let her in. Alice Rose had one favorite seat in my house, an old slipper rocker with a cane bottom that had been in our family since the days when genteel Southern women took a seat on the rockers to pull on the slippers they wore indoors.

Running a hand over her face and scrubbing it hard, she rocked furiously, back and forth, as if working off steam. "Don't start, Grace Ann. You chose a career in hair and mine is in raising two boys. You made your bed and so did I. I'm not in the mood for you to rag on me. Not today."

# Chapter Ten

✂

"WHAT'S UP?" I ASKED MY SISTER.

Sam had been watching Alice Rose carefully, quietly, but she hadn't noticed him. With a loud squawk, he decided to break into the conversation.

"What on earth is that noise?" Alice Rose jumped to her feet.

"That's Sam. He's a rescue parakeet. Sort of." I explained about his near-death experience. As if to emphasize that he was well and truly on the mend, Sam showed off for Alice Rose, chattering and fussing with his wing feathers.

"He's precious! Look, Grace Ann, I'm sorry I snapped at you. It's my fault. I shouldn't have made that crack about what you're wearing. It's obvious you're cleaning, and when you're scrubbing, any old thing is good enough."

"Can I offer you a glass of tea? Coffee?"

"Iced coffee?"

"I can make that for you. I bought Truvia. I know you like that."

Her nod was grateful and her smile tremulous. "Thanks, big sis."

"You're welcome, little sis. Let me put the kettle on to boil. All I have is French vanilla instant coffee, and the granules dissolve best that way."

Alice Rose got up from the rocker and took a stool at the counter that separates my kitchen area from my living room. Her eyes reddened as she watched me bustle around. "I'm worried sick about Owen."

The eldest of my twin nephews. "Why? What's up?"

"His teacher says his vocabulary isn't as expected for his age. They want us to take him for testing."

My heart plummeted. I knew that Wade was a good dad, but one with high expectations and a truckload of pride. If they found a problem, would he be able to adjust? Would he accept his son or forever be disappointed?

"I'm sorry to hear that. I suppose the bright side is that if they catch a problem now, they can help him before he goes to kindergarten. That would be good, right?"

"Ye-es. I guess. I mean, I hope so. If it's something they can fix."

I stopped stirring the hot water in the granules. "You think it might not be."

Her mouth twisted and she fought a sob. "I don't know. You never know, do you? I mean, you have a kid. You pray over them every night, and you hope for the best."

I handed her a box of tissues, and she dabbed at her

eyes. "Let's change the subject. There isn't anything I can do for Owen, after all. Not until I know more. Mom told me about Lisa Butterworth. That's so sad. We ran around together. You remember, don't you?"

"No. Oh, wait! Was it Lisa who used to sneak out with you to go over to Beth Black's house and watch MTV?"

Alice Rose laughed. "Guilty as charged. Hard to believe she's dead. Mom also told about her stealing your client list."

Handing over the iced coffee, I poured myself a cup of hot water and added the instant mix. "I feel sick about it, Alice Rose. Really sick."

"About her dying or her cheating Mom?"

"Both. Friday night I ran into her at Walk-Inn Foods. I sort of had a fight with her."

Alice Rose snickered. "You never were one to back down."

"Well, she honked me off big-time. I trusted her, Alice Rose! When she came to the shop, she looked like a million bucks. Very professional. She'd really grown into her features and learned to do her hair. And education? Shoot, I was impressed. Never in a million years did I think she'd run a scam on us. She was your friend, right? How do you explain what she did?"

"I can tell you exactly what happened to her. I mean, I can at least explain why she's so ambitious," my sister said. "Wow, this smells great."

"I added vanilla to the creamer. Is that what you call someone who tricks other people? Ambitious?" I took my coffee pot and rinsed it out at the sink.

"That's not what I would call ambitious, but I think Lisa looked at herself that way. Yes, I'm sure she did. We've had our problems with sibling rivalry, right?"

I squirmed. "Yeah."

"I suspect deep down that you'd like to have a family.

I see how you are with my boys. I wish I had a career. There are times when I think that if I have to wash another load of clothes, I'll go screaming and naked into the street. But Lisa's older sister, Eliza? She's an attorney up in New York City. Married to one of those Wall Street financial whiz kids. I ran into Lisa and her mother in the grocery store, and all Mrs. Butterworth could talk about was Eliza this and Eliza that. Never mind that poor Lisa was standing right there looking terrific and hurt. I mean, you could see it in her face. But her mom kept going on and on. Finally, I asked Lisa how she was doing, and Mrs. Butterworth laughed and said, 'Still messing with hair.' Can you imagine?"

"That's just so mean!"

"You should have seen the expression on Lisa's face. She nearly cried."

A pang of sympathy hit me hard in the solar plexus. "We've been lucky. Mom's never compared us to each other. Never pointed out that you're happily married and I'm an ink blot on the family tree."

My sister finished her iced coffee. "Mom loves us both, and we know that. Always has and always will. Sure, there're times that I get mad at you. And, yes, sometimes, I wish I was her favorite. Bet you wish you were, too!"

"Of course I do, that's human nature, but you know Mom. She'd rather have bamboo splinters rammed under her fingernails than create friction between us. Like you said, she loves us both, and we know it. We've always been there for each other as a family. Remember that when you get to worrying about Owen. He's got us. He'll be okay."

She stood up, walked around the counter, and hugged me tightly. "And you remember it when you think about the shop. You'll figure out a way to save it, or to help Mom move on. Maybe now's the time for her to finally get her cosmetology license. Who knows?"

After she left, I finished scrubbing the floors and my cabinets. The water swirled round in the sink, leaving a thin film of dirt. Very satisfying.

Sam had watched all my efforts with intense interest. "You need a little exercise, buddy?"

As an experiment, I unlatched the door on Sam's cage. He had a blast flying through the apartment. He perched on the dish drainer as I rinsed out Alice Rose's glass, and after eying the stream of water suspiciously, he treated himself to a quick bath. The sight of him trying to flutter dry tickled me.

I made a mental note not to run scalding hot water while he was out of his cage. I spent the rest of the day researching parakeets, learning the ropes of bird ownership, and reading a book I'd started weeks ago.

# Chapter Eleven

ALTHEA BREEZED IN THROUGH THE FRONT DOOR
and tossed the local newspaper down on the counter. "Did
you see this?"

"Old news," I said. As usual, I'd been scrubbing away at
the black mold inside the storage cabinets. From my kneel-
ing position, I paused to look up at her and did a double
take at the vision of loveliness standing next to me.

Before dating Kwasi, Althea was your typical J. C. Pen-
ney shopper who favored polyester knit pantsuits and cotton
shirtdresses, which she protected by wearing her aesthetician's smock. Nowadays she chose more exciting en-
sembles. Today she wore an orange, green, yellow, and
black tunic top over leggings. From her earlobes hung
bone-colored hoop earrings. With her full lips, broad nose,

and jaw-length Afro, she looked positively regal and totally exotic.

She tapped a finger against the newspaper. "A woman is murdered in our little town and you call it 'old news'?"

I nodded. "Because it happened Friday, yes, it's old news. But if you're asking what I think, I think it's tragic. I didn't like her, but it's still a shock, and I especially feel sorry for Lisa Butterworth's family."

"Morning, Althea." Mom joined us, carrying a big mug of coffee in her hands. Her favorite is hazelnut, and the wonderful scent preceded her as she came into the room. Mom's usually all sunshine and smiles in the morning, but today her expression was dour. "Grace Ann? I'm so glad you're doing that. I totally forgot that the mold inspector is coming by today. I guess I better get down there with you."

In a way, it was lucky we didn't have any customers on the books, because both of us scrubbed baseboards for an hour, her in the waiting area, and me in the salon. The work was slowgoing, but it looked to me like we'd made fine progress. All my press-on nails had fallen off, but I couldn't see a speck of the green black menace on the woodwork.

I took a break and plopped down on one of our wicker chairs. Mom pulled off her rubber gloves and joined me. "I can't help thinking about that poor girl. She was so young. Same age as Alice Rose. I hadn't realized that until Walter turned up the radio this morning."

I bit my lip. So that's how it was. He was staying over these days.

My mother turned red-rimmed eyes on me. "It didn't really hit me Sunday morning, but as the day wore on, I couldn't stop thinking about her. I can't imagine what I'd do if something happened to you or your sister. To think that happened in downtown St. Elizabeth, too! Right off our main drag!"

"The tourism bureau isn't going to like this one bit." Althea took a break from mixing a new batch of oatmeal–egg white face mask paste. "Kwasi says it's going to cost local businesses thousands of dollars in lost revenue. The longer they go without an arrest, the worse the downturn will be."

No one added that our business was already in the tank.

"How's the mold cleanup coming on your side of the salon?" Mom asked me.

"I'm done and it looks pretty good," I said.

"Good." Mom smiled at me. "Now we're ready for the man from the health department. Can I talk to you in my office?"

"Sure thing."

Mom's "office" is a tiny nook, a former closet, fitted with a Formica desktop, a filing cabinet, and two office chairs. Over the desk are two shelves packed with three-ring binders containing all the rules and regulations for running a shop like ours. There are also a couple of binders dedicated to formulas for hair coloring, troubleshooting, and so on. To the right of her desk is a family photo taken at Sears when I was five and Alice Rose, my sister, was three. Dad stands proudly behind Mom, who is seated. On her lap is Alice Rose, and I'm on her right, snuggled close. Every time I look at it, I get a little teary-eyed. Mom's managed to make a good life for herself since Dad died, but I can't help wondering how it would have been different if he hadn't gotten cancer.

"Have a seat." She closed the door behind me, leaving behind the trail of a strawberry scent from the body wash she likes to use. The space felt slightly claustrophobic, but I have to admit, I liked the feeling of intimacy. This little room is like a clubhouse. Mom and I would come here for what we called our "war councils." Whenever we had a problem, like when a customer bounced a check, we'd adjourn to her office and close the door to discuss how it should be handled. I think Alice Rose envied me this. Working together, talking things through like this built a bond between Mom and me, a shared interest that she and Alice Rose didn't have. It wasn't that Mom didn't love my sister. She did and Alice Rose knew it. It was just that Mom and I could finish each other's sentences. We could take one look at each other and know what the other person thought. When you spend as many hours as we did with each other, you either found your rhythm and moved in sync or you were constantly bumping into each other. Kind of like those couples on *Dancing with the Stars*. We had practiced so long, learned to communicate so well, that our footwork was seamless, and we moved like one person—at least when it came to anything that concerned the shop.

"What's up?"

"Just a couple of things." She rearranged the papers on her desk, and then she rearranged them again. Finally she sighed and looked at me over the lenses of her rimless glasses. With her gray white hair and twenty pounds of extra weight, she looks motherly and nurturing, which she is. She's also very straightforward . . . usually. I wondered what was on her mind. I suspected she'd ask me my opinion on getting more customers into the shop.

"A letter came on Saturday from the historical society. Seems that someone—they wouldn't tell me who—filled out the paperwork to have this house listed as a historic property. The St. Elizabeth Historic Preservation Committee is meeting next week to consider the proposal."

"That's fabulous! Why didn't you tell me sooner?"

She gave me a quivering smile. "I really wasn't in the mood to discuss it."

"But that's terrific, isn't it? I mean, this place will be in the historic register!"

"Ye-es, it's terrific that the house will be recognized, so it's good for the house and for the city. But for us? Not so much. I'm not sure, but I think that if the proposal passes, the house will have to be gutted and restored to its original floor plan."

# Chapter Twelve

"WHAT? HOW CAN THEY DO THAT?"

"Hang on and I'll explain what little I know. But don't hold me to any of this because I'm not an expert—and I haven't had the chance to get the details. See, someone sent a lot of paperwork to the National Register of Historic Places. Again, I don't know who did it or why someone decided all of a sudden to initiate this documentation. Whoever it was did a lot of research and digging. A copy of all the paperwork was sent at the same time to the Georgia Register of Historic Places. The house could be put in the national list and not in the Georgia list, or vice versa, or qualify for neither or both, as I understand it. Once it's in that list, I would have to fill out an appropriateness application. If the changes I've made don't pass muster, that is if they deem them inappropriate, I might need to fix what I've done. Or not." She bowed her head and rubbed the back of her neck.

"But isn't there grant money? And why would they shut down a going concern?"

From that position, her voice was muffled but surprisingly peevish. "I just don't know! Walter says there is, but I haven't had the chance to do any research yet. The point is I'm not sure what this means to me. To the salon. To all of us."

"But you didn't know this was a historic building! So why would you be in trouble for making changes?" I squirmed in my chair. Mom usually wasn't a worrier. Instead, she was a take-it-as-it-comes type of person. The fact that she was worrying had me worried.

"I don't know. Of course, I didn't realize it was a historic building. I knew it was old when I inherited it. My grandmother told me it had been built shortly before the War Between the States, but I surely did not know it has or had special significance. I didn't make any changes except to keep a roof over our heads. Opening the salon brought in enough money that I could hang on to this place. A house this old always needs something or another. But I'm not sure that any of those repairs was up to historical standards. I did what I could, the best I could, with what money I had."

"Mom, don't second-guess yourself. You did a great job. You kept a roof over our heads, you employed three other people, including me, and you raised two girls. Is it possible the house won't qualify?"

"From what Walter says, there's a very good chance this place will pass muster and have a place in the national historic register."

"Why? Because it's old? St. Elizabeth is full of old houses."

"That and it turns out that Cyril Rothmere built this place for his mistress. Can you believe it? I would have never guessed it of old Cyril, but I guess it's true."

St. Elizabeth sits in the crook of a backward L bordered by the St. Andrew Sound to the east and the Satilla River to the north. Cyril Rothmere chose the long side of the L as the perfect site for his Greek revival home. On a bit of high ground, he constructed a house with an expansive view of the river. Some say he was a man who loved beauty and his choice of the Satilla River reflected that. One of the state's fourteen major watersheds, the Santilla provided a picturesque setting, especially in the early spring when the swamp cyrilla and azaleas turned its white sandbanks ablaze with reds, pinks, and oranges. Others, more cynical, suggest he wanted to keep an eye on the commercial river traffic so he could make wise investments when tall ships from all over the world off-loaded their merchandise in St. Elizabeth's exceptional harbor.

The Rothmere home has since been turned into a museum, sheltering and preserving all things Rothmere as well as any items with historic ties to St. Elizabeth. Oh, and it's supposed to have a ghost. That makes it perfect for tourists and locals to visit at Halloween.

"So much is up in the air. How is this all going to turn out?" I wondered out loud. "I don't mean to sound heartless, but since Lisa was murdered inside Snippets, I imagine that some of our customers are bound to want to come back. Stands to reason, doesn't it?"

Mom opened her arms to me, hugged me across the desk, and held me surprisingly tight. "Honey, I don't know what they'll do. People sure can be funny. They might find the whole situation intriguing. I used to think I knew my clientele pretty well, but not anymore. Everything is all upside down now. Frankly, when it comes to the historic preservation situation, I don't even know what to do first. Or whether I need to do anything at all. Things are just happening so quickly."

She let me go and ran nervous fingers through her hair with its cute spikes held in place by a generous application of gel. When she finished, she quickly tucked her hand under the desk. "You see, this thing with the historical society isn't the only thing on my mind. Something else has come up. Recently. Just last night, in fact."

"What?" I couldn't imagine any more on our plate.

With her right hand, Mom neatened the edges of a stack of papers. "While we were at dinner, Walter told me he's planning on selling out. Seems he's got a buyer who's interested in his whole inventory. A collector. Then a friend called, another Civil War reenactor, and offered him a great deal on his Winnebago. Walter always teased him about wanting to buy it from him one day—and last week the man decided he wanted to sell. The upshot is that Walter wants to travel all around the country. He's planning to go from historic battlefield to battlefield."

"I'll be sorry to see him go. It's kind of nice how he's been popping in all the time lately."

A small smile played at her lips. "Yes, that has been nice. Actually, I've grown quite fond of Walter. Really fond. Um, he asked if I'd like to come along with."

"And what? Fly back from some of those places? Sure. I can hold down the fort. It's not like we're overrun with customers."

"No, honey." She positioned her left hand on the desk so I could see the sparkle of her new ring. "He's asked me to marry him."

It's always hard to imagine your parents did "it." Harder still for me, after all these years without a dad, to realize that my mother was still interested in "it." But the blush on her cheeks told me everything I needed to know. She might be sixty-something years old, but my mom was still a girl at heart. Anything else would be too much information, or TMI as Rachel put it.

"Where are my manners? Congratulations!" Now I reached across the desk and hugged *her* hard. She giggled as I did. "Does Alice Rose know? Or Althea?"

"No. You're my firstborn, so I wanted you to hear it first. Walter even asked if he needed to get down on his knees and propose to you, too, but I told him I thought you might take a pass. Seeing the commotion his proposal caused at Pizza Hut, I wasn't sure I wanted to go through that again."

I would have liked to have seen that but I wasn't about to spoil the moment by saying so.

"When's the date? I mean, have you set a day for the wedding yet?"

She shrugged. "Everything's up in the air."

I sank back into my seat. "What do you mean? You are going to marry him, right? You're wearing the ring."

"I've accepted his proposal, but we have a lot of details to iron out. Of course, I also have to tell Alice Rose and Althea. Stella and Rachel, too."

"Althea'll want to be your matron of honor. Or would it be your maid of honor, since she's a widow?"

"I don't know! I figure she'll let me know what she wants to be and I'll go along with it!" She paused, acting unsure what to say next. "Grace Ann, Marty is coming down Tuesday night for sure, right? I guess as a reporter, he works odd hours. Kind of hard to get used to, isn't it?"

"He promised me that he'll be here."

"Have you given any more thought to his suggestion that you move up to DC with him? Go work in a salon up there?"

A hailstorm of emotions battered me. Did I want to

move in with Marty? Was I willing to make that commitment? Had he been serious when he suggested that it would be easy for me to find work in a DC salon? Was that the same as an invitation to move in together? Or was he simply pointing out that it would be a lot less hassle if we didn't live a half day away from each other?

Other than the two years I lived in Atlanta while attending UGA, I'd lived in St. Elizabeth all my life . . . so far. Moving would mean saying good-bye to Vonda. I hadn't particularly enjoyed the traffic and noise of Atlanta. I liked the fact I could get anywhere in St. Elizabeth that I needed to go in fifteen minutes. I'd heard about beltway traffic. Seen it with my own eyes a few times when I went up to visit Marty. The thought of driving in that mess made my heart pound and my mouth go dry.

Mom was waiting for my answer.

"What if I stay here? I mean, Marty and I have only been dating on weekends for four months. I'm not sure I want to make a commitment. I could still run the shop, right?"

Her eyes filled with tears and her voice grew husky. "Grace Ann, hon, that's what I'm telling you. There might not be a shop."

# Chapter Thirteen

WAS SHE REALLY PLANNING TO CLOSE THE DOORS ON Violetta's? Or just decided to sell the house? Victorian homes like this had become increasingly fashionable, especially with young couples from Savannah, looking for a place in a small town. These houses were bringing top dollar, even in the tough economy. With business so slow, and liable to be this way for a long time, selling the house might be a good idea. We could always rent a space if she decided she wanted to stay in the beauty business.

The question was . . . did Mom want to keep working? Or was she ready to call it quits?

Suddenly, I saw everything differently, a bit like Dorothy did in *The Wizard of Oz*. The overstuffed shelves above Mom's desk filled me with a new affection, as did the crayon drawings by Owen and Logan that she'd pinned up on her bulletin board. On the thin carpet behind me was a yellow streak, leftover from a botched attempt to paint the office yellow, Mom's favorite color next to periwinkle. I ran my hand over the seat cover on my chair, a quilted pad that a customer had created especially for Mom.

Truth to tell, I couldn't imagine a world without this shop. I'd grown up here listening to women talk about their lives while Mom shampooed their hair with lavender-scented suds. The hanging ferns, the cozy sitting area, the wide heart-of-pine floorboards made this seem more like a home than a salon. The array of African violets in the windowsills spoke to a time when simple pleasures like sharing a plant cutting were true signs of friendship. Even the dust motes that danced in the early morning sunshine seemed magical to me.

As a girl, I would sweep the floor between customers, making sure to get in every nook and cranny so that no stray curls were left behind. One of our regulars, Mrs. DiSilverio, thought my industry so cute that she even bought me a child-sized broom and little dustpan to use. How I enjoyed taking the towels out of the dryer and pressing their warm, soft surface to my face! The smell of perm solution always made me cheery, because with it came the delighted cries of "Oh, I love it!" after the rods were removed and the hair was styled.

If you took a survey, I'd bet that more than three-quarters of the women in this town had come through our doors at least once in their lives. I remember one bride who insisted on having her picture taken in her white gown standing under the figurehead from the *Santa Elisabeta*, a Spanish galleon that sank off the Georgia coast in the 1500s. The wooden carving provided benevolent supervision from a wall behind the counter. Since this bride's name was Eliza-beth, she believed that her name saint was responsible for bringing her the man she would marry. Unbeknownst to us, Elizabeth had been lighting candles at church and praying to St. Elizabeth. Maybe I should have followed her lead, because that Elizabeth was happily wed after all these years later, and my marriage to Hank had been over for three years now.

In short, I loved everything about Violetta's, and the thought of turning the key in the front door one final time and walking away from all this, and all these memories, made me want to bawl like a baby. After Mom's pronouncement, I didn't trust myself to speak. I kept swallowing and swallowing, but nothing would dislodge the lump in my throat.

"Y-Y-You're honestly thinking about quitting? Closing the shop forever?"

"I'm getting older." Mom spoke in a whisper. "My back used to hurt at the end of a day. Now it starts aching around ten and keeps paining me until I crawl into bed. My hands are arthritic. Have you noticed I can barely get my fingers into the handle of my good scissors? I've got a lot less patience than I used to have. Once upon a time, if a customer like Mrs. Everly told me I was cheating her, I would have laughed it off. But yesterday, I went into the bathroom and bawled my eyes out. The truth is, Grace Ann, I'm tired. Maybe it's time for me to retire. I never did get my cosmetology license, and maybe there's a reason. Maybe in my heart of hearts, I knew I didn't want to do this for the rest of my life."

With the back of my hand, I flicked the tears out of my eyes. It took all my strength to hold back, to keep from breaking into sobs. Mom handed me the box of tissues she always kept in her top drawer. "I don't know what to say," I stuttered.

I was mopping my eyes when the door flew open and Hank Parker, my ex-husband, walked in.

# Chapter Fourteen

"GRACE ANN? I NEED TO TALK TO YOU." HANK hitched his thumbs in his utility belt, all the better to show off his nightstick and his gun. Behind him stood his partner, Officer Ally Qualls, a short, dark-haired woman about my age, who seemed interested in Hank romantically. I wanted to tell her she was welcome to him, but I hadn't figured out how. Today, Officer Qualls stayed in Hank's shadow, giving me the impression she wasn't totally on board with his visit.

Her hair needed cutting and styling. Badly. She also needed a good exfoliant, because her skin was muddy and rough.

"You ever heard of knocking?" I stood up and faced him. "You can't just barge in here like you own the place.

Didn't your mother teach you any manners, Hank? Wait don't answer that." His mother was one of the reasons I divorced him. She'd spoiled him beyond all reason. Betty Parker was a major pain in the backside. Truth to tell, Hank couldn't have learned manners from Betty because she didn't have any.

"I'm here on official business." Hank narrowed his eyes in his best Clint Eastwood imitation.

"I don't care if you are here on orders from the president of the United States," said Mom, adding her voice to mine as she stood up. Even though she's only five foot two, she could stare Hank down in a heartbeat. "You can still knock when you're on my property. Are we clear, young man?"

"Yes, Mrs. Terhune." The tips of Hank's ears turned pink.

"What is it you need, Hank?" My mother crossed one arm over the other and glared at him.

"I'm conducting a murder investigation."

"I thought only homicide detectives conducted homicide investigations. Or marshals from the GBI." After living with a cop for three years, I had naturally absorbed a bit about law enforcement protocol.

"Right. I was the first responder. I'm following up." In a low voice, he added, "This could make my career, Grace Ann. I plan to crack this baby wide open."

"Good for you. You want a medal or a chest to pin it on?" I said. Because I still had tears in my eyes from Mom's announcement, I was a bit grumpier than usual with him. Not that he didn't deserve it. Hank seems to think I'm his private property.

"A medal or a chest to pin it on? Ha, ha, ha. That's so old, even my grandmother knows that one. Nice try, Grace Ann. But I'm not here for fun and games. I'm taking you down to the St. Elizabeth Police Station."

"What? Why there? Why not to the GBI office?" Mom and I had been there once before when we found a woman dead in a parking lot.

"They've got mold. It's closed until they get it cleaned up. You can come with or without handcuffs."

No way was I letting horny Hank put a pair of handcuffs on me. Not if I could help it.

"Mom, I'll be right back." I leaned in to give her a kiss. "Don't worry about me."

"I won't. You haven't done anything wrong, darling. Call me if you need a ride home."

Officer Qualls adjusted her utility belt meaningfully, as if to issue a reminder that she was ready, willing, and able to take me down. With a sigh, I grabbed my purse and headed through the salon.

"What in the blue blazes?" said Althea as we paraded past.

"Be right back," I said, with more optimism than I felt.

Hank's police-issued Crown Victoria was right behind my Fiesta. My ex craned his neck toward my vehicle and said, "Hang on. I think you've got a tire going flat."

After walking over, he ducked down, slapped a hand on the rubber, stood, and pronounced it, "Fine."

"Get in," said Hank, opening the door and gesturing toward the backseat of his car. He took great pleasure in planting a big hand on my head to guide me into the car. Totally unnecessary, since I wasn't cuffed. True to his usual crude style, he also tried to cop a feel.

"Get your hands off me!" I yelled at him.

"Calm down." He snickered and hopped into the driver's seat.

Qualls rode shotgun. I spent the trip itching to suggest a good moisturizing shampoo to her. No one said a word the whole way there. Fortunately, Hank loves to ride with the window down, and the breeze felt good on my skin. Of course, we didn't have far to go because the station is across town, but any ride in a cop car is a long ride.

The St. Elizabeth Police Department occupies a concrete block building designed to serve as a shelter when a hurricane blows through. Squat, ugly, and unfriendly on the outside, it's not much better inside. Institutional green paint covers the walls and a rubber baseboard runs along the flooring, a gray-flecked linoleum that needs to be replaced. The smell hits you right away, a combination of burned coffee and men's cheap cologne.

"Hey, Grace Ann! Long time no see," said Officer Shep Shepkowski, stepping out from behind the front desk to give me a big bear hug.

"How's Mary Louise? And the kids?" I smiled up at him.

"Aw, she's fine. I'll tell her you were asking after her. Is this a social call?" Shep's gap-tooth grin matched his wonky haircut. Mary Louise did it herself with dog clippers, I reckon.

I shrugged. "You'd have to ask Hank. All I can say is I didn't come of my own free will."

"Suspect in the Butterworth murder." Hank rocked back on his heels, with his thumbs tucked inside his utility belt, and smirked. His shirt barely buttoned over his big belly, and his belt rode low around his hips rather than at his waist. Meanwhile, Officer Qualls stood there and glared at me.

"Right," I said. "I look like a natural-born killer, don't I, Shep?"

"What a kidder," said Shep, as he slapped his thighs and howled with laughter.

"You won't be laughing when I solve this and end up a hero!" Hank grunted as he took me by the elbow into an interview room. Officer Qualls brought up the rear.

"You aren't actually going through with this, Hank, are you?" I rolled my eyes.

"Make all the jokes you want, Grace Ann. This is my job. Time you realize it. I am a law enforcement professional, and I'm on the way to a big promotion. Better grab a chair, because we're about to begin an extensive interrogation." Officer Qualls took a seat at the farthest corner of the room possible. My ex pulled out his Miranda card and started to read me my rights. I nearly fell off my chair.

He was serious. Totally serious.

You learn a lot about law enforcement when you're married to a cop. Most of what I learned those three years with Hank was depressing. Stuff like how dangerous domestic disputes are, how it feels to wonder every day if your husband will come back alive, and how truly evil the world can be. I did take note of one vital piece of information, one lesson that I had promised myself I'd never forget: never, ever talk to a cop without a lawyer.

"I know my rights, Hank. Call Dooley Jenkins."

"Aw, crap, Grace Ann. Don't do this to me! I'm just going to ask you a few simple questions about where you were last night. See, we've got this credit card slip from Walk-Inn Foods that puts you there at the same time as Lisa Butterworth, and the skeezy kid behind the counter says the two of you got into a shouting match."

"Call Dooley."

"Did you know Lisa was dating Wynn Goodman, hmm?" Up until now, Officer Qualls had maintained a neutral expression on her face. With this tidbit from Hank, she struggled not to show her surprise—and dismay. Shoot, everyone knew he shouldn't be such a blabbermouth. Everyone but Hank.

"Call Dooley."

With a snarl of frustration, Hank shoved back his chair.

"Call him yourself, Grace Ann. You've still got your cell phone on you."

That's exactly what I did. While I waited for him, I climbed another level in Angry Birds after managing to knock down all the pigs with one volley from the slingshot. I also downed an entire can of Coke Zero and ate two bags of pretzels. I offered to share and Officer Qualls said, "No, thank you." Later she did nibble a couple of pretzels. I pretended not to notice.

Dooley showed up fifteen minutes after my call.

# Chapter Fifteen

"HEY, DOOLEY, THANKS FOR COMING." I STOOD UP
and gave him a hug. Dooley sat behind me in study hall for all
four years of high school. Back then he was the pimple-faced
kid. Today he's an okay-looking guy with a big Adam's apple,
a great haircut (I do his hair, natch), and a partner named Phil
who works in a men's clothing store. Dooley always looks
and smells great. Some people whisper behind his back
about his sexual preferences, but Dooley has come into his
own. He's a confident man, a successful lawyer, a partner in
a long-term relationship, and he's happily out of the closet.

Hank stomped back into the room and slammed his
chair against the table as he sat down. My empty Coke Zero
can went flying off the table, and bounced twice onto the
floor. I picked it up and gently put it in the trash can.

"Ya'll should offer recycling," I said. "Set a good example for the rest of us."

"I agree," said Dooley. "Being a government entity, you have a responsibility to the community."

"In fact, I insist that you recycle this," I said, retrieving the Coke can from the trash and handing it to Hank. "Go put it in the recycling bin outside. We'll wait."

Hank didn't know what to do. Glancing from the can to Dooley to me to Qualls, he finally got up and left the room with my can. Upon returning, he read me my Miranda rights, turned on the tape recorder, and asked me my name. I turned to Dooley, who gave me the thumbs-up.

"Grace Ann Terhune."

Next came my address and place of employment. Dooley approved all that.

"Where were you last night between the hours of eight and nine?"

Thumbs down.

"What was the nature of the altercation between you and Lisa Butterworth when you ran into each other at Walk-Inn Foods?"

Thumbs down.

"Is it true you were stalking Lisa Butterworth? We have witnesses who saw you driving your Fiesta through the municipal parking lot last night at seven thirty P.M."

Thumbs down.

I exhaled. At least someone had spotted me in the municipal parking lot and not in the parking lot of Snippets.

After fifteen minutes of thumbs down on Dooley's part and silence on mine, Hank stood up, and slammed the chair against the table one more time. "Thanks a lot, Grace Ann. Thanks a heap. This isn't over. Not by a long shot."

"If you are done with my client, we'd like to leave," said Dooley.

"Just don't leave town, Grace Ann. Hear me?"

"You haven't filed any charges. You have no reason to keep her or to impede her travel," said Dooley, drumming his fingers on the tabletop. "Let's call it a day, Officer Parker."

"She's not leaving until I say so!" His face was red as Hank slammed the chair once more, but this time he got his finger between the chair and the table. "Ow!" he yelled. "Son of a gun!"

The door behind Hank flew open and in walked John Dillon.

# Chapter Sixteen

✂

SPECIAL AGENT IN CHARGE JOHN DILLON OF THE
Georgia Bureau of Investigation and I met last May when
he'd investigated the death of Constance DuBois. Once he
was sure that neither Mom nor I stabbed the woman, the
sparks flew between us. He'd asked for my phone number,
but never called me. That might be for the best. John Dillon
was the kind of man that I could fall hard for. I didn't need
that sort of complication in my life. Drama and I don't play
well together.

I'd taken to calling him Marsh—short for Marshal
Dillon—and couldn't bring myself to think of him as John.
While Hank was taller than Marsh by a couple of inches,
the GBI man held himself ramrod straight and exuded an
air of command that said "soldier" or "cop" or certainly

"guy in charge" in a way that Hank would never have. Even though Hank was wearing the uniform issued to all thirty members of the St. Elizabeth County Police Department, and Marsh was dressed in street clothes, my ex did not look nearly as official or as menacing as Marsh did. John Dillon had a chiseled jaw and a longish nose marred by a lump that suggested it had been broken at least once or twice. His deep blue eyes contrasted with his tanned skin and neatly cut dark hair that was graying at the temples.

His brows rose a fraction as he surveyed me and asked, "Officer Parker, what's going on here?"

"Interviewing a possible suspect, sir." Hank wiggled like a schoolboy caught misbehaving.

"I thought your supervisor made it clear that this is my investigation. What part of his instructions didn't you understand?"

"Uh, no, sir. I mean, yes, sir. I understood, sir. I mean, Officer Qualls and I canvassed the neighborhood like you said and learned that Ms. Terhune here had been seen in several places nearby so naturally—" Hank's face turned bright red.

"Naturally you should have talked to me or written it in your report and made me aware of that finding. That's procedure, right?" Marsh eased down into a chair and leaned back against the doorjamb, with his hands in his pockets. Even though his posture was relaxed, he still managed to look ticked. Hank shuffled his feet. Qualls shivered.

"Yes, sir, but this case—" Hank sputtered.

Dooley cleared his throat.

"Special Agent in Charge John Dillon," he said as he extended a hand toward Dooley.

Dooley took it, returned the shake, and introduced himself, adding, "Ms. Terhune's legal representation."

"Ms. Terhune? Nice to see you again. Not particularly

surprising, either," said Dillon. He didn't offer me his hand. I was glad. I didn't want to turn into a puddle on the floor.

"Parker? Qualls? Don't you two have more canvassing to do? Interviews? Statements to take? What are you waiting for?"

They scampered like a couple of gray squirrels when the neighborhood cat is loose.

"Ms. Terhune, may I talk to you? In private?" Marsh asked. As his eyes locked on mine, my heart sped up.

I looked at Dooley and shrugged. He looked at me, back at Marsh, and back at me again. "You okay with that?" he said. "You two look like you, um, know each other."

"I'm fine with that." I reached up, put my arms around Dooley's neck, and gave him a big hug. With my arms still around him, I looked up into his eyes, and said, "Thanks so much for coming. The haircuts are on me for the rest of your life."

Marsh's eyes turned steely hard, and a muscle twitched in his jaw.

Dooley let go of me, stepped away, and laughed. "Anytime, Grace Ann. That was fun." As he picked up his briefcase, he ran slender fingers down his purple silk tie to straighten it. "I remember what a jerk Hank was to me in school. Kind of nice to get his goat. Call me if you need me. I hope you won't, but if you do . . ."

Dooley's exit left me alone in the room with Marsh Dillon, who promptly pulled out the chair next to his and gestured for me to sit down. Unlike Hank, whose belly bumped the table's edge, Marsh was trim, lean, and . . .

I grabbed my imagination by the ponytail and yanked her back into some semblance of restraint.

"Nice to see you again, Grace Ann." His tone was husky as he smiled at me. I gave him a nod of hello.

A five-o'clock shadow rimmed his jaw, his eyes were

ringed in tired circles, and his normally crisp shirt draped limply on his body. But he still looked good. Really good. And smelled even better. There was a whiff of musk and a green, clean fragrance in his cologne.

But suddenly, there wasn't enough air for me to breathe, and it had nothing to do with the fragrance Marsh was wearing. For one sick moment, I thought I would hyperventilate. Or suffocate. My body couldn't decide which. I also couldn't decide where to look. I knew I didn't want to stare into those cold blue eyes, so I made a big production out of tracing a pair of initials someone had carved into the wooden tabletop years ago.

"You always so affectionate with your attorney?" Marsh sounded gruff.

"Yes."

"Natty dresser."

"I think so."

"Doesn't exactly look like he belongs. Here, I mean."

"No."

"Can I get you a Coke? Or a Coke Zero?"

"No. Thank you."

"Want to tell me about Lisa Butterworth?"

There wasn't much to say. Dooley would have told me to hold my tongue. However, I trusted Marsh. I'm not a big gut-instinct person, but I knew I could tell him what happened and that he wouldn't ever turn it against me. Even as I traced the initials with my thumb, I felt sure he'd be on my side.

"She tricked me." My throat seized up with emotion and to my horror that last word came out as a gasp.

Marsh's right hand reached across the span of wood. His index finger tapped mine. "Grace Ann? You all right?"

No, I wasn't all right.

My bottom lip trembled. I studied the carved names in

the tabletop. "Just for the record, Special Agent Dillon, I am not stupid. I mean, you're the law and I'm in here without an attorney, so . . . so that's all I'm saying." Keeping my gaze on the wood, I raised my hand to pantomime zipping my mouth shut. Then I swallowed hard. Really hard.

With a sigh, he pushed back his chair, walked over to the blinds covering the two-way window, and stood there, letting his presence fill the space between us. *Scritch-scritch-scritch* came the sound of him cranking the blinds shut. His shoe leather slapped the tile floor as he walked around to his side of the table. Once there, he reached under the table and fiddled with something, something that finally went *click*.

"It's just you and me," he said, softly. "We're off the record. What's going on here?"

"I really don't have anything to say." I repeated this to myself, as a sort of mantra. In the beauty shop business, you hear all sorts of secrets. Part of being a professional is learning to keep your mouth shut. I could do that.

He rubbed his jaw. "Right. I can't blame you. But I need a few answers."

I chewed my bottom lip.

He sighed. "Lisa Butterworth tricked you. She took all the information you'd collected over the years on your clients and—"

"Who told you that?" I nearly jumped out of my seat.

"Your mother."

# Chapter Seventeen

✂

"I STOPPED BY HOPING TO TALK WITH YOU. SOMEONE reported seeing you and Ms. Butterworth having a disagreement at the Walk-Inn Foods shop. A loud disagreement. Now she's dead. I need to know what happened so I can clear you from my list of suspects."

"My mother blabbed to you? Why would she do that?" I blinked in surprise.

"Probably because Officers Parker and Qualls had just loaded you into their car and taken you away. Your mother loves you and she was worried, so when I walked in, she told me what happened." The way he spoke, it sounded so reasonable, and indeed, it made sense, but still . . . Mom usually kept her mouth shut. Why now, of all times, had she decided to blab to Agent Dillon?

He must have read my mind because he said, "She trusts me. I hope you do, too. I bet your mother doesn't make many mistakes when it comes to judging character."

Years of working with people one-on-one, listening to them tell their stories, has given my mother excellent people skills. But even so . . . it was surprising that she'd shared Lisa's trickery with this GBI agent, because Mom has always been tight-lipped. When Alice Rose and I were younger, she used to wag a finger at us and say, "Girls, it takes a whole lot less effort to keep quiet than it does to mop up a wet spill in Aisle Six, and if you don't believe me, I've got a floor you can practice on."

"I want to clear you from the list we're developing. The one detailing people of interest. In fact, I not only want to clear you, I will clear you, with or without your help. Obviously, your help would mean less wear and tear on both of us. I could wrap this case up faster."

"And get the heck out of Dodge." I aimed for funny, but my joke landed flat. Every time I saw him, I wanted more time with him, I felt drawn to him, and the intensity left me incredibly vulnerable.

He chuckled and moved his chair so close to mine that our knees bumped. "Not exactly, but I would be able to move on. Let me clear your name." His voice was husky.

He wasn't pleading, but his tone had turned softly persuasive. Sitting shoulder to shoulder beside me, his posture fostered an odd sense of intimacy—odd because the pastel green concrete block walls and the gray brown linoleum floors magnified every human sound, of which there was a gracious plenty. You could hear everything from murmuring voices, to the clicking of heels, to the hum of office machines. The hubbub outside this little room emphasized that while the rest of the world went on about its business, Marsh and I were here together in a gathering pool of silence. He reached over and took my hand, cradling it in his.

"Grace Ann? It'll be all right. Trust me. I'll get to the bottom of this."

"You sure?"

"I'm sure. We both know you didn't kill Lisa Butterworth. All I need to do is find the person who did."

It took all my courage to look into his eyes.

"When you talked to Mom . . . did she tell you I ruined her business? That she's leaving town because of me?"

To my surprise, he gave my hand a gentle squeeze before letting it go. "I don't believe that for a second. I don't think you do, either. Not in your heart of hearts. She did tell me about Ms. Butterworth stealing your client list. How she tricked you. But I'd like to hear your version of what happened. After all, if Ms. Butterworth did that to you, she could have done the same thing to Chez Pierre."

I nodded. In fits and starts, I explained how Lisa had presented herself as a bona fide expert in social marketing, which she probably was, and as a good choice for helping us, which she wasn't.

Marsh nodded. "Makes sense that anyone would jump at the chance for that type of help. You probably should have asked her to sign a confidentiality statement, but since you two went to high school together, you had no reason not to trust her."

"How'd you know we went to high school together?"

He shrugged. "Part of my job. I've been checking out who was connected to Ms. Butterworth and how. Besides, I was the one who had to inform her parents that their daughter died."

"Oh," I said. "How . . . how awful."

"Definitely the worst part of my job. After a couple of

hours, they gave me permission to look through Ms. Butterworth's things so I could get a better sense of the woman. You know that she still lived with them? Moved back here from Atlanta recently. Saving money to buy a house. Had her eye on an old Victorian. Wanted to fix it up. She loved antiques."

A lump formed in my throat. So Lisa had been trudging down the same track I was. Even though I'd been looking for a place to buy, I hadn't found anything that both matched my wish list and my budget. Unlike her, I did have my own place, a small apartment that I rented.

"Lisa Butterworth hung on to all her high school yearbooks. I flipped through them and noticed your photo. You haven't changed much over the years, but she had."

I shrugged. "Took her a while to figure out how to make the most of her features. Style her hair in a way that was flattering. Clear up her skin. Probably had braces, too. I guess you'd call her a late bloomer."

"How was high school for her? Is it possible someone here still holds a grudge? Is that what might have happened?"

"I seriously don't remember much about her. See, she and my sister, Alice Rose, were in the same grade. I was two years ahead."

"All right. Let's move on. What can you tell me about Wynn Goodman?"

# Chapter Eighteen

I ADMITTED TO MARSH THAT WYNN AND I HAD ONCE
been a couple. I explained how Wynn trained all the new-
bie stylists, and that he'd taken a particular interest in me.
Of course, I fell for the man. Who wouldn't have? Wynn
was ten years my senior, bronzed, chiseled, and blue-eyed.
The iconic California golden boy turned hair guru. Think
Laird Hamilton with a pair of scissors instead of a surf
board. Before Wynn turned thirty, he'd been touted as one
of Hollywood's best and brightest. His movie-star good
looks added to his skill with scissors gained him a constant
stream of invitations to the hottest, hippest parties.

As a traveling stylist for Vidal Sassoon, he was a twenty-
first-century global nomad, collecting passport stamps from
exotic locations. After the head instructor at Sassoon's

Atlanta studio died of a heart attack at age thirty-five, corporate dispatched Wynn to fill the void, at least until a permanent replacement could be found.

That's where we met. Because I'd been in the hair business my entire life, my skills outpaced the other stylists'. It wasn't that they weren't good; they were. But I grew up in a salon. They hadn't. I couldn't remember a time when I wasn't a part of the beauty industry.

Heck, my mom would ask me to mix up a color formulation the way other mothers would ask their kids to pop a load of laundry in the dryer. Wynn wasn't comfortable correcting other stylists' mistakes, in part because he took a free-spirit approach and because he wasn't an organized person, so he often turned to me. "Grace Ann, can you help Marcella? All her cuts are a bit longer on one side than the other." And, "Ernesto is having trouble with texturizing hair. Any suggestions for him?" "LaReesa mixed the color wrong, and now the customer needs a correction."

Mom raised Alice Rose and me both to be helpful, but my willingness to step in and save the day was more than a by-product of my upbringing. It was a result of my raging hormones.

I had a crush on Wynn. He was an incorrigible flirt. No woman was immune to his honey-dripping smile, or his slow, sweet manner. I'd seen him turn ninety-year-old grandmothers into giggling girls. That was fine by me, because bit by bit, Wynn made it clear that I was his favorite. Once when I was in the stockroom doing inventory, he stepped inside, locked the door, and crooked a finger at me.

In seconds, he had a hand up my skirt and my blouse unbuttoned.

"I'm not good at this," I stuttered. After coming home and finding my husband "getting busy" with another woman, I'd moved out, gotten a divorce, and taken a pledge to remain celibate. So far, as a strategy, it wasn't much fun but it was a whole lot less drama.

"Babe, relax," he said as he kissed my throat. "This isn't work. Or school. There isn't going to be a grade or a quiz. This is just for you, sweetheart. Just for you. A reward you've earned by being luscious. Let a master lead the way."

Boy. He played me like a fiddle. That man's fingers were magic, and his voice had a low rumble that called to a portion deep inside me, a place I never knew existed. I mean, Hank and I'd been pretty hot and heavy before we married, but my husband had been a selfish lover, a man who concentrated on himself and his needs only.

Wynn took pleasure in seeing me melt. And I craved reassurance that a man found me desirable. While I'd never admit it out loud, I wondered if I wasn't woman enough to keep a man's interest, and if somehow Hank's cheating had really been my fault. I felt like a phony—working all day to make other women more attractive, but feeling that I couldn't do the same for myself.

Even though it had been a while, I felt warm and gushy all over when I thought back on our brief liaison. During the workday, Wynn and I were great together, considering a client's needs, discussing styles and products, reveling over the outcome of our joint efforts. At night and in stolen moments, we were passionate lovers.

His betrayal totally blindsided me. It had been a sunny, beautiful June day. I walked into the salon for the start of my shift, and immediately, I knew something was up. Usually in that half hour before opening, the shop hummed with activity, a happy buzz that said everything was going right. On this day, the place seemed unnaturally silent. No one looked up as I walked past. No one called out happy greetings.

My station was tucked in the back. To get there, you

took a twisting, turning path between other stations. Every stylist added touches to make the four-foot square space his or her own. Because we spent so much time there, the stations began to feel like "home."

Today, as I approached my station, everyone went silent. I could tell something was amiss, and I spotted the reason right away. A small stack of magazine pages rested on the seat of my styling chair. A sticky note bore a scrawled message in ink: *FYI.*

The slick pages had been stapled together, starting with the cover sheet: "Hair TODAY." Flipping the stack open, I saw a four-page color article featuring picture after picture of my best, most creative work. Accompanying the photos were accolades like "innovative, flattering, and sophisticated." I grinned from ear to ear as I gazed on my work with wonder and joy. Wow! Wouldn't Mom be thrilled? I couldn't wait to share it with her. Excited by the attention, I scanned the copy for my name.

I looked at page one, page two, page three . . . and on to the end. That's when reality set in. Nowhere, not anywhere, in that long article was I mentioned by name. Nowhere. The piece was about Wynn Goodman, the hot young talent in the hair industry. The positioning of the photos, the cutlines underneath, all touted the images as Wynn's work.

But it had to be a mistake!

I read every word, every line once, twice more.

My first impulse was to call my mother. But I quickly got over that.

No way could I call her!

She had learned her craft the hard way, being totally self-taught. She cobbled together an education, struggling to open her own shop after my dad died and left her with two young daughters. Attending a beauty school in Atlanta would have been a dream come true to her. Working at

Sassoon was a situation beyond her wildest fantasies. Every week she called and asked how things were going—and she was pleased as punch when I told her how much I was enjoying myself.

If I told her about this disappointment, it would burst her bubble. Mom wanted to believe that everyone in the beauty industry was as gorgeous on the inside as they were on the outside. Because she'd lived her whole life in St. Elizabeth, she could maintain that childlike innocent view of the business. An imaginary circle had conscribed her world; life within its friendly confines had given her an unrealistic belief in human kindness.

I wasn't about to shatter her dreams along with mine.

"There's probably some mistake. The reporter got it wrong. Wynn showed him my photos to prove how good his students are. Their wires got crossed. Yeah, that's probably what happened. No biggie. When he sees it, he'll make them print a retraction." I mumbled all this to myself as I wadded up the magazine pages and tossed them into the trash can. Then I started inventorying my supplies and getting ready for the day ahead.

LaReesa Bowens showed up at my elbow. She was a large woman with a couple of homemade tattoos on her right forearm. "Girlfriend, we talking about that man! He was on the down low, girl. He's a dog! Passing off your stuff as his. That Wynn Goodman ought to be shot, he should. Everyone knows those were your styles! Everyone! What a jerk. Especially considering the other news and all."

"Other news?" I froze.

LaReesa shifted her weight and stared at me. "You mean you don't know? I thought you'd be the first person he'd tell."

"Spill it." I crossed my arms over my chest so she couldn't see my hands shaking.

"Oh, baby girl." LaReesa shook her head. "You ready for this? That skunk. He really is lower than a cottonmouth's belly on a July day. You know what he went and did? It was all over the news this morning. That talk show on the radio? The one where they talk to all the celebrities?"

"What happened!" I was losing patience, and LaReesa had a tendency to wander off topic.

"Wynn Goodman got engaged. He's marrying Eve Sebastiani!"

# Chapter Nineteen

✂

ARTURO SEBASTIANI GREW UP IN POSITANO, WHERE his father owned an olive orchard. Early on, the boy showed great talent with his sisters' hair. Their friends started lining up in the Sebastiani kitchen where Arturo would cut, color, and curl for a small fee. Inspired by the soft skin of the farm workers, Arturo created a variety of products, all using high-quality olive oil. When the boy turned eighteen, the villagers took up a collection to send him to the States for training.

Arturo arrived in New York City, found a place behind a chair, and never looked back, although he has been a huge benefactor to the area. Once a year, he makes a pilgrimage to the village, bringing much-needed financial aid to such projects as the local library, the schools, and the churches.

Somewhere along the line, Arturo attracted the attention of a wealthy socialite who convinced her husband to back the Italian boy in a series of business ventures. Thus, Snippets was born. Arturo married a model, had a bambino, and the entire Sebastiani clan often appeared *en famiglia* in advertisements for the Snippets chain.

Everyone in the industry followed the adventures of Eve Sebastiani, Arturo's only child and his successor in the business. She helped in refugee camps in Uganda, broke ground for AIDS hospitals in Kenya, and still found time to meet the Queen at Ascot. As time went on, Eve took on more and more of the decision-making responsibilities. But when had her path crossed that of Wynn's? How long had they been an item? Was it possible my friends were reporting old news? Wynn had stayed at my place overnight just last week before flying out to Los Angeles for meetings at Vidal Sassoon headquarters.

Or so he said. The company headquarters had moved nearly twenty years ago. But I needed Wynn so much that I didn't question him. Looking back, I'd been just as blind about Wynn as I'd been about Hank, but for different reasons. With Hank, I was young and stupid. With Wynn, I was needy and hurt. Ours was a typical rebound relationship, but I was too blind to see that at the time.

"Here." LaReesa handed me her smart phone. The headline: "Eve Finds Her Adam." The story: Eve sported a sparkling diamond from Wynn Goodman. They planned a June wedding on the Island of Skorpios. They met at an industry trade show, and, yes, they were truly, madly in love.

Which left me hurt, embarrassed, and out in the cold.

My knees buckled as I eased my way back into my chair.

"Can you believe it?" LaReesa gave a loud and unlady-like snort of derision. "What a turkey. And will you look at all the clients in the waiting area! Can you believe it? They're all hip to the news. They're hoping to see if Wynn still works here!"

Our attention turned to the waiting area, where customers jockeyed for space on gray leather chairs.

LaReesa did a quick scan of our surroundings before ducking her head and cupping a hand over her mouth to speak quietly. "The HQ management team is in the back room. Working on damage control. Wynn had access to our entire client list. He was in on all of corporate's plans for expansion. Knows which markets they're considering. All their upcoming promotions and ad schedules. You can bet he'll take all that with him when he marries Eve. Snippets will make out like a bunch of bandits!"

"I-If he leaves, who will be our supervisor?" I wondered.

"They already decided to bring that mealy mouthed Jenny Farquar in from Jacksonville, Florida. I've heard her specialty is tattling on people," LaReesa said. "At least that's what my cousin Shereena told me. She works in the same district. Wonder who'll be the first to get in trouble? I sure hope it ain't me!"

And she walked back to her station.

LaReesa's cousin had been right on the money. Jenny "By the Book" Farquar was a major pain. She had no creativity at all, no common sense, and a strictly by-the-book attitude. She also lacked a sense of humor and tact. In short, she was absolutely wrong for this business, or any business that relied on creative people. I'd learned at my mom's knee that creative people needed a light hand on the reins. If you pulled too hard on the bit, they spent more time bucking you off than moving forward at a trot.

Under Jenny's "supervision," I learned not to take any

chances. The slightest problem morphed into a big deal, whether it was a change in schedule or a customer with an expired coupon. It doesn't matter, I told myself. Never again would I let myself care. I was through with being vulnerable. I'd learned my lesson, and I had the battle scars to prove it.

I grew more and more withdrawn. As the weeks passed, I missed St. Elizabeth with an emotional pang that gnawed at me like hunger. Jenny proved a miserable excuse for a boss. One day, after she chewed me out in front of a customer, LaReesa walked over and asked, "Why do you put up with this? Didn't you say your mama runs a salon? Shoot, if I had somewhere else to go, I wouldn't let the door hit me on the backside as I left. I'd be out of here in a flash."

With a jolt, I realized she was right. My marriage was over, and running into Hank caused all sorts of headaches. My new lover had dumped me very publicly for a woman with money and clout. My apartment was small and I had a forty-five minute commute to work. The hours at Sassoon were horrible, and my new boss . . . well, let's say we didn't cotton to each other and leave it at that.

What was keeping me here? Pride? Ego?

Inertia.

Then I caught the flu. Day after day, I stayed in bed, sweating and shivering. I quit answering the phone. Vonda and Mom panicked when they hadn't heard from me in days. Von hopped in the car, drove the five hours to Atlanta, and pounded on my door until I answered.

"Good Lord. What on earth?" she pushed past me, surveyed the place (which she hadn't seen previously), took stock of me, and in three hours, all my belongings were packed. Vonda bundled me into the passenger seat and drove me home. Home to Violetta's.

A month later, I started as a stylist in my mother's

beauty shop. In the back of my head, I'd always known that Mom was a fair boss, who knew instinctively how to run a salon. There was no backbiting, no malicious gossip or attempts at stealing customers. All of us pulled together as a team to help and support each other. After my time at Sassoon, Mom's salon was a cool breeze of goodness brushing away the rotten crumbs of my former existence.

Violetta's was more than a job to me. It was a balm to my wounded soul, a haven for my spirit, and the perfect place of employment.

Now I'd gone and ruined it all by inviting Lisa Butterworth to "help" us with our social marketing.

# Chapter Twenty

"SOUNDS LIKE WYNN GOODMAN IS THE SCUM OF THE earth," said Agent Dillon.

I shrugged. "He certainly used me."

"You seem to have bad luck with the men in your life. I think you deserve better."

What did that mean? Was he volunteering for the job?

I couldn't look him in the face, so I answered the rest of his questions while staring down at my feet. We went back over the timeline of my actions on the evening that Lisa died. That's when I remembered, "I saw Wynn and Lisa arguing. In the parking lot."

"Tell me more. Could you hear what they were saying? How close were they standing to each other?" Marsh asked in a soft but urgent voice.

A vise clamped my throat. I choked out the answers, but it was hard. Really hard. No matter what Wynn had done to me, I didn't think he was capable of murder, and I told Marsh as much. The law man's expression never changed, although I could read his mind. He was thinking that I wasn't over Wynn.

But I was. Sort of.

I would always have a soft spot for the man, because he reminded me that I was a desirable woman. Beyond that, I couldn't stand him.

"If you think of something or you need anything, call me. Any time of the day or night." Marsh took out a business card and wrote a number on the back. "Do you need a ride back to the salon?"

"No," I said. Realizing how terse it sounded, I added, "I need the fresh air. Thank you anyway."

He held the door open for me. "Take care of yourself, Grace Ann. And watch out. There's a killer out there. It might be a one-time strike, a personal vendetta, but once a person crosses that line they change. Give your mother my best, please."

Standing ramrod straight, he nodded at me, his tan skin a handsome contrast to the pure white of his dress shirt.

Walking back from the SEPD, I tried not to think about Lisa. Instead, I turned my mind to other pressing matters, like losing my mother. If marrying Walter would make Mom happy, that was fine by me. But I hoped she would reconsider giving up on the shop. Maybe I could talk her into letting me run Violetta's in her absence—if the historic register problem could be resolved, and I thought it could. I couldn't imagine the historic register demanding that she undo what she'd done before the house was on the protected list.

If they demanded the house be returned to its original

floor plan, we could move the salon. Then I remembered the business plan I'd drawn up last year when I briefly considered moving away and starting my own salon. The cost of lease-hold improvements had stunned me then, so what might the costs be now? In the aftermath of Horatio, every builder and contractor in town asked for top dollar. Their services were in high demand. My own meager savings had dwindled as the hurricane caused us to shut our doors in the days before and after the emergency.

My pace slowed as I realized I might not have a choice in this matter. If Mom decided to walk away and marry Walter, I might need to find another job. If she stayed, I might have to go without a paycheck or take a reduction in pay until she could fix the family home or build out a new shop. A yellow leaf drifted down from the branch of an old maple and fell onto my shoulder. Others crunched under my feet.

"To everything, there is a season," I sang. A time to grow, to reap, to rest. A time to scrub baseboards. A time to say thanks. After all, we'd been lucky that the hurricane had passed us by.

But now it felt like another storm was brewing.

# Chapter Twenty-one

THE LAVENDER AND GREEN "VIOLETTA'S" SIGN WAS barely visible beyond an old hydrangea bush, but one glimpse of the colors sent a happy buzz through me. Taking the front steps two at a time, I bounded up them, only to be caught short when I reached our front door. The "Open" sign had been flipped to "Closed."

*Maybe Mom's having a meeting. Maybe she's talking to someone from the Historic Preservation Society. Or to Walter, and they're finalizing details for their wedding.*

Using my key, I let myself in and called out, "Hello?"

Moving past the chintz love seat and chairs in the waiting area, the two styling stations and sink separated by a half wall, and past the Nail Nook, where Stella Michaelson gave customers manicures and pedicures, I continued calling out. "Mom?"

"Back here!" Mom's voice drifted toward me from the kitchen. I entered and found her watching a man, on his hands and knees, prying loose a section of wainscoting.

"Eddy, this is my oldest daughter, Grace Ann. Grace Ann, this is Eddy McAfee. He's a contractor for the state. Remember? I told you we were having our mold inspection visit this afternoon."

Eddy rolled over onto his back and waved at me. "Nice to meet you, miss." He had a Mr. Magoo type of nose and tiny eyes behind glasses held together at the nosepiece with a wrapping of dingy adhesive tape. An elastic headband wrapped around the last tufts of his grizzled hair and pinned his ears to his skull. To this was attached a light, much like a miner might wear, but dangling by a few wires. The whole contraption—glasses and headband—struck me as unreliable, as though it might fall apart at any time.

"Excuse me, miss, but I'm not going to get up. I've got a situation here." He pronounced every syllable of that long word, offered me a quick salute with one hand, then took a deep breath and scooted back under the sink.

Mom's features were drawn and tired. I tapped her on the shoulder. "What's up? You weren't worried about me, were you?"

I couldn't imagine that my interlude with Hank was causing her such distress. Mom, Alice Rose, Vonda, and I were in total agreement that my ex was some sort of dopy, overgrown kid who was playing at being a cop.

Mom gave me a little half smile and sighed. "I figured Hank was here to yank your chain. That nice Agent Dillon came by and told me not to worry about you."

I tilted my head toward our man in khaki on the floor.

Raising an eyebrow, I conveyed my question to Mom. "What gives?" She shook her head and turned away.

Eddy wiggled out from under the cabinet. First the khakis, then a smudged white Polo shirt with "EDDY" embroidered over the chest pocket, and finally his head appeared. Snapping off his light, he rolled slowly to his feet, causing his official badge—Department of Public Health / State of Georgia—to bounce on his scrawny chest. He wore the grin of a small boy back from a successful treasure hunt. "Yes, ma'am! Yes, indeedie-do! Mrs. Terhune, you've got it, and you've got it bad. *Stachybotrys chartarum*. Your place is covered in black mold."

"Wait a minute! I personally cleaned it all off the baseboards. What are you talking about?" I tried to sound reasonable, but even to me, my voice sounded an octave too high.

"You might have mopped up the mold on your baseboards, but I've been looking behind your fixtures and under your wainscoting. See, mold grows. And I bet you didn't think to look up." He pointed at the ceiling.

Mom and I followed the direction of his finger. She couldn't contain her gasp and mine was equally plaintive. The ceiling tiles showed gray, wet stains as they bowed toward us.

"Full of water. I'm certain of it," continued Eddy. "This old house wasn't built as airtight as homes today. Under your siding, they used cellulose products as insulation. That's a perfect breeding ground for black mold. Plus the fact your ground is soggy out back, because it's still saturated with water. You should have run a dehumidifier in every room after the storm. That might have helped, but your windows aren't properly sealed. Your AC system isn't properly vented. The stagnant air is helping the mold grow."

My head was spinning with all this. Suddenly I felt dizzy. Mom saw the expression on my face and pulled a kitchen chair up so I could sink back and sit down.

"Bet you've all had symptoms, haven't you? Well, that's over because I'm officially shutting you down!"

As Mom escorted the jubilant Eddy out the back door, I went to the Internet and pulled up *Stachybotrys chartarum*, or *Stachybotrys atra*, a greenish black mold, commonly known as black mold. Mold, mushrooms, lichen are all an accepted part of life on the sea coast. However, at least according to the many websites I consulted, this stuff was both toxic and deadly. It could cause difficulty breathing, headaches, coughing, nausea, memory loss, dizziness, asthma, bronchitis, and, more surprisingly, urinary tract infections.

"How long will we be closed?" were the first words out of my mouth when Mom came back after what seemed like an interminable wait.

"Eddy thinks it'll take two weeks to get the insurance adjuster here. Another week for them to make a determination. A week for haggling, he says, because they never allow enough money for the needed repairs. Then if I can come up with the deductible, and if I can find a contractor who isn't too busy to take on a small job and who'll do it reasonably, it could take as long as two months. Or so he reckons."

"That means we're shut down for, what? Three months? At least?"

She pulled up a seat next to me and took my hands in hers. "Did I ever tell you that one of your daddy's favorite songs was that Kenny Rogers's tune called 'The Gambler'? It says you've got to know when to hold them, know when to fold them. Well, this is a sign, Grace Ann. I'm not a quitter, but I know when I'm beat. I'm folding. I'm putting down my cards and walking away from the table."

# Chapter Twenty-two

"TALK WITH MARTY ABOUT WASHINGTON," MOM SUG-gested again as she walked me to my car and stood there at the driver's side. Her hug left me with a lingering scent of Youth-Dew on my skin.

"What about Althea? Stella? Rachel? Does Alice Rose know about your engagement?"

"No one knows anything. Not yet. I need a night to get my wits about me. Then I'll talk to them. One at a time," she said as she watched me key the ignition. "Try to have a good time tomorrow night with your young man. You've got a whole day to get ready. That worked out pretty well, didn't it? Time off to enjoy with Marty?"

I nodded.

"Don't look so worried, Grace Ann. You always planned to work in a big city. Maybe this is God's way of nudging you out the door."

Actually, I could feel a big boot in my backside, but I wasn't happy about it.

I rolled down my window so we could continue our conversation. "You just want to see me settled and having grandbabies."

She nodded. "Yes, I do. What's wrong with that?"

"Maybe that's not right for me." Although in my heart, I knew it was.

She crossed her arms and stared off into space, considering this. "You might be right. You see, that's the only life I know. Even though your dad died young, I couldn't have imagined any other life than being married and a mother."

"But you own a business!"

"Out of necessity. Althea and I helped each other through our grief by keeping busy. One thing led to another, and before we knew it, there was a steady stream of customers. At first, we did everyone's hair for free. It was therapy for us, don't you know? At some point, we had to decide whether to continue to wash hair in my kitchen sink or make a go of it. By then, we both realized we needed an income. Neither of us had been left with much money. We hired out-of-work handymen who took cash for making the changes we needed. I'm not really surprised to hear the materials they used were subpar."

"But you've enjoyed owning this business!" I hated what I was hearing. The words sounded reasonable and reassuring, but the fact she'd been backed against the wall caused my heart to ache deep in my chest.

"It's been good to me, but I've never had the flair for styling that you have. Sure, I can do about anything and everything, but you're a real artist. There's a difference. You could make it in any big city. I couldn't. Maybe if I'd had the training, but . . . I doubt it."

She'd never said that to me before. My jaw sagged. All these years, I'd looked up to her. Now my idol was telling me that I was actually better than she was. I swallowed hard. What did that mean?

"So, you've hated it? All these years?"

"Oh, no, honey! That's not what I'm saying at all. I've loved owning the shop. I could always take time off when you and Alice Rose needed me. I was there for every ballet recital and track meet. Home when you both had measles. It's great to be your own boss. I've been able to keep a roof over our heads and food on the table. I like working with people, most of the time. And I like the beauty industry. It's a good feeling to see someone walk out of Violetta's with her head held high because she looks her best." Mom reached inside the car and gave my shoulder a squeeze. "Besides, as soon as I realized how much talent you had, I wanted to keep our doors open for you. It's been a real blessing to watch you grow more and more confident."

"So you did this just for me?"

She sighed. "No. I did it for myself, for you and for Alice Rose, so we could have a good life. For Althea, Stella, and Rachel. For our customers. For all of us. And it's been a good run, but maybe it's over. Until we get this mold problem figured out, our doors are closed."

I left her after she promised not to make any rash decisions.

Without work to structure my life, the next day dragged on and on. I cleaned my small apartment, changed the sheets, played with Sam, watered my two ferns, tossed out

old magazines, and tried not to think about how boring life
would be if Mom decided to close Violetta's for good.

My emotions swung back and forth on a pendulum. On
one hand, I was elated by Mom's praise. I hadn't known she
thought so highly of my talent. Mom was of the generation
where you don't brag. So she'd never told me she admired
my skills. Not in so many words.

On the other hand, my heart hurt and tears threatened.
Was it really time for her to close up shop? Was I hiding out
here in little St. Elizabeth when I should be working in a
bigger market? Had I taken the easy way out? Had I let my
mother carry all the burden while I played the part of a
freeloader?

Sam chirped and fluttered around happily as I ran the
vacuum cleaner. Buying him was the smartest thing I'd done
all month. I stopped my work every so often to chat with
him. Angling his head so he could see me with his good eye,
he took in all my hustle and bustle. When I talked, he paid
careful attention. Not only was he a cheerful sort of guy, but
he was also a great listener.

As I straightened the apartment and folded clothes, I
tried to compartmentalize my feelings. There was no reason to get too upset. Things had happened so fast! Mom
hadn't had the chance to take in all the curve balls that had
been thrown her way. Why, Walter had only recently asked
my mother for her hand! She hadn't even shared the news
with Alice Rose yet.

Who knew what would happen next? Maybe the historic
preservations proposal wouldn't go through. Maybe the
insurance adjuster would pay for mold remediation. They'd
done that at other businesses, or so Eddy had assured us. I
was certain that Marty would beg me to move in with him
up in Washington. Then I'd have my choice of working

here or in the big city. Marsh would quickly figure out who killed Lisa Butterworth. Once he did, Wynn wouldn't have any reason to hang around St. Elizabeth.

I had absolutely no reason to worry about anything. Anything at all!

At least, that's what I told myself.

And I was wrong, wrong, and wrong.

# Chapter Twenty-three

I HAD BEEN LUCKY TO GET RESERVATIONS AT EN-
chanté for five thirty. The person on the other end of the
phone had explained they were booked solid for anything
later. "Fortunately for you, we have this one cancellation,"
he said in a heavy accent, so that the word "this" came out
"zese."

This surprised me since it was a Tuesday night, and not
the weekend. However, I didn't mind eating early. I was
that excited about finally getting to see the place for myself.
After rearranging all the books in my bookshelf into alpha-
betical order, I showered, blew my hair dry, and went all-
out on the makeup. Inspired by Lisa's bushy lashes, I even
glued on false eyelashes.

When I bragged to Vonda that I'd wrangled a reservation, she had stopped by and dropped off a slinky black dress with a high, straight neckline and a low plunging back. "Doesn't work for me, but you'll look great in it."

That same afternoon I found a beautiful pair of black high heels on sale at DSW. Trying them on, I admired the way they lifted my calves. The shoes really complemented the sophisticated style of the outfit. Althea had given me a pair of dangly earrings with jet-black beads for my birthday. I hadn't had anything to wear them with, but when I put them on and looked at the finished outfit in my full-length mirror, the result was pretty spectacular, even if I do say so myself.

At five, I lit a couple of nice Yankee Candles I'd been saving and turned the lights down low. Plugging my iPod into the speaker system, I selected a Lionel Richie album and adjusted the sound so it was soft and sexy, but not too loud.

I planned to read the latest book in the Kiki Lowenstein series, but it seemed impossible for me to sit still. Time seemed to drag. I called Marty's cell, but it went immediately to voice mail. Five thirty, six, six thirty, seven, seven thirty. I phoned Enchanté every half hour and explained my date had been unavoidably delayed. My excuses became more elaborate with each call—and I'll admit, I also got a little more angry with Marty. If he couldn't make it, he could at least call me, couldn't he? He knew what time our reservation was. I'd text messaged him last week and again this morning.

The sun had long gone down, and it was past time for Sam to get some shut eye, singular. I put more ointment on his wound, which seemed to be healing nicely. I changed his water, blew off the husks of the seeds he'd eaten, and scratched him a bit around the neck before covering his cage with an old bedsheet for the night.

As much as I tried to get involved in Kiki Lowenstein's life, I couldn't concentrate. Maybe it was because I felt a slow burn as I wondered where Marty was. By seven forty-five I figured I better call the restaurant and cancel. The maître d' sounded a bit miffed, but what could I do? I knew I shouldn't be so disappointed, but I was. This had happened twice before with Marty. He'd gotten engrossed in working on a story and hadn't left DC until late. Then he'd be on the phone the whole way here as he continued his investigating. His job allowed him to work flexible hours, but he never seemed to take any time off. Maybe once I moved in with him, we could work out reasonable limits.

"That's the way this career is," he explained with a cheerful shrug. "The news happens when the news happens."

Well, yes, but everyone needed a break now and again. "Work is important," I said, "but people matter, too."

"The people in my life understand the demands on my time," he said, leaving me to wonder who he was talking about besides me.

Over my reasonable internal debate, I could hear Althea's voice, telling me what a fool I was. But she was wrong. It wasn't that Marty wasn't interested. He was distracted, that's all. And up until the last few months, he'd been a pretty good boyfriend. So I'd just have to work extra hard to make him regret being late. We'd have a sexy evening together, a couple of romantic days and nights, and then he'd be eager to put his work aside. If I yelled at him the minute he stepped over the threshold, what was I teaching him? That showing up was bad news!

Instead, I'd make him happy he came. Once more I made the rounds of my place, adjusting things so everything looked just right.

I'd read in a women's magazine that if you sprayed cologne on lightbulbs, they would fill the room with scent.

I ran back to my bathroom, retrieved my spray bottle of
Pleasures by Estée Lauder and squirted a little on the bulb
in the reading lamp next to my sofa.

As I put the perfume bottle back on the shelf in my
bathroom, I heard the *drip-drip-drip* of water from the
showerhead Marty had replaced on his last visit. The old
one had sputtered water, and this one was a high-pressure
nozzle that put out a lovely stream. I turned the base of
the showerhead. And waited. The drip continued. I reached up and jiggled the showerhead. Water ran down my
arm.

There was a knock at the door. I grabbed a hand towel
to dry myself and ran to answer it.

Special Agent John Dillon stood there. He was as
shocked as I was. His eyebrows flew up to his hairline. His
jaw flapped in the breeze. Finally he said, "Wow. Grace
Ann. You're enough to make a man get religion."

I couldn't think of anything to say, so I patted my
arm dry.

"Problem?" he pointed to my elbow.

"Leak in my shower. I think the showerhead isn't on
right."

"You don't look like you're dressed to do plumbing."

"You sweet talker, you."

"I mean, you look fabulous. I mean, terrific. I mean . . .
wow."

"Thanks."

"Want me to see to the showerhead?"

Not really, but then I remembered the mold situation in
the shop. Maybe I should have him look at it. I sure didn't
need to have my home filled with toxic fungus, too.

"Sure."

I pointed him the right way. Out of my peripheral vision,
I could see him giving my place the once-over. Although

it's small, I've done a great job of decorating it. When I got my tax refund last year, I splurged on nice furniture. There's a cinnamon-colored love seat from Pottery Barn positioned across from my door. To the right, near the wall is a large recliner in black. The walls are painted a pale gray, and my coffee table is an old cart I found that had been used in a mill nearby. On the wall over the sofa, I'd hung large metal and plastic molded letters from local signs, random letters that don't spell anything.

I made pillows of odds and ends of material in gray, black, and cinnamon. These are scattered on the chair and love seat. Sam's birdcage sits on top of a low bookshelf I bought at a scratch-and-dent sale at Macy's. To the left of that is an old-fashioned cupboard, and my TV is inside. There's no dining room, so guests either pull up a stool and eat at the countertop where my kitchen opens into the living area, or we sit on the love seat.

"I like what you've done here," he said, as he paused to stare. "Elegant, but not fussy."

"Thank you."

"Not so feminine that a guy would feel uncomfortable."

I think that was an opening for me to explain about Marty's visit, but I didn't. It wasn't any of Marsh Dillon's business. He had my phone number and never called. So he obviously wasn't interested. What I did with Marty shouldn't matter to Marsh at all.

"The bathroom is this way." I pointed through the short hall and he walked past me.

On the ledge surrounding the claw-footed tub, I'd placed more candles and an ice bucket with a bottle of champagne that was chilling. The shower had been an addition to the old tub, a metal rod held up the head and a circular curtain. The effect was romantic but practical.

"Champagne." Marsh's voice dropped to a whisper.

"Here's the problem." I reached past him to touch the showerhead. Only then did I remember the cut of my dress. This was the first time I'd turned my back to Marsh.

"Yo-your dress. It's . . . backless," he squeaked.

"Not entirely. Do you need any tools?" I was sort of enjoying this. I could see beads of perspiration popping out along his forehead.

"No. Yes. No. Do you have a wrench?"

"Be right back."

I keep a little pink toolbox under my bed. Althea gave it to me as a housewarming gift. I grabbed it and headed for the bathroom.

Now it was my turn to be shocked. Marsh had removed his shirt. I was staring at a gorgeous six-pack, covered with just enough hair to be tantalizing. My jaw dropped.

"Didn't want to get my shirt soaked," he said with a shrug that caused his pectorals to flex.

OMG.

I handed him the toolbox.

"Pretty cute."

I nodded. I didn't trust myself to speak. All I was thinking was, "Hurry up, Marty! Hurry!"

He must have heard me, because the doorbell rang.

I excused myself from the half-naked man. As I stepped out of the bathroom, I turned for one last look. The backside was every bit as yummy as the front. He rippled from his intercostal muscles all the way up to his shoulder blades. I felt absolutely weak with desire, and thankful that my date had arrived.

"Hey." Marty stepped inside and gave me a peck on the cheek. "Sorry I'm late. Got tied up. Big story." He smelled like Axe body wash, spicy and young.

Marsh walked in, his shirt hanging off one finger. His eyes crinkled with amusement. "The reporter, right?"

I gave Marsh a withering look.

Marty narrowed his eyes and said, "Am I interrupting something?"

"No. All done. I left the shower in good shape for you, Grace Ann," said Marsh.

Before I could respond, the lawman swept me into his arms and kissed me on the mouth. If he hadn't been holding me up, I would have keeled right over. I think I kissed him back, but honestly, all I can remember is the jolt of electricity that traveled up my spine, down my spine, and caused tingles all over.

"You aren't planning to leave town are you?" Marsh released me slowly. Good thing because my legs had turned to jelly.

"N-N-No."

"I'll stop by tomorrow." Marsh's smile was impish. "Early."

With that, he slammed the door behind him.

# Chapter Twenty-four

"I'M STARVED. GOT ANYTHING TO EAT?" MARTY rubbed his hands together. He seemed unfazed by Marsh's behavior.

I, on the other hand, felt like I'd gone a couple rounds with a stun gun. My knees buckled, and I sank down onto my sofa. "We had dinner reservations at Enchanté. Nearly two hours ago."

"Oh. I got busy. How about if you order a pizza? I've been eating at fancy restaurants all week. Boy, does that get old."

Not for me it doesn't. I could almost feel the steam coming out of my ears.

Papa John's was one phone number I had memorized, so

I dialed it, and handed Marty the phone. He ordered a pep-peroni and sausage pizza with onions, large, without ask-ing me what I'd like on mine. Since I'm not a big fan of pepperoni or sausage, I frowned.

"What?" he asked. "Got any beer?" He settled onto the sofa and pulled me close. "You look nice, by the way."

"Nice?" I aimed a lot higher than that, but oh well.

Hadn't Marty noticed the chemistry between Marsh and me? My lips still burned and every nerve in my body jan-gled. Marty curled around me, in a warm comfortable way, the crease in his Dockers as sharp and crisp as ever. But Marsh's buzz still rattled me. If he'd been sitting with me on the sofa, we'd have gone up in flames.

I gave my head a quick shake to free my thoughts. "I have five Bud Lights, two Coronas from your last visit, and a bottle of champagne on ice."

"Great! We can toast my promotion."

"Promotion? Cool." At least I hoped it was.

"Yes. I proposed—and the bigwigs accepted—writing a feature story about commerce in the wake of the Arab Spring. I want to track how businesses will respond to the new freedoms. It'll be my first big feature assignment. Might take a year or two to do all the research."

"I have my own news, too."

He put an arm around me and pulled me close. "I heard. Dead bodies have a way of turning up in your path. Guess the good marshal was here because you're a person of interest."

"Excuse me?"

"A person of interest. It's all over the wire service." He planted a kiss on the tip of my nose.

"I don't know what you're talking about."

He reached behind my sofa, grabbed his briefcase, and

withdrew an iPad. After flipping over the black cover, and flicking his fingers across the screen, he pulled up a story:

LOCAL POLICE QUESTION PERSON OF INTEREST

*Unnamed sources in the St. Elizabeth Police Department have confirmed that Grace Ann Terhune, of 467 Calhoun Street, has been questioned in connection with the murder of Lisa Butterworth, age 29, of 3111 Park Street, last Friday.*

*"Ms. Terhune and Ms. Butterworth had a business disagreement," said the source.*

*Any person with information about the death of Ms. Butterworth on Friday night are asked to contact the local Crime Stoppers at 555-1212.*

"WHAT?" I DROPPED THE IPAD ONTO MY LAP LIKE IT was a hot curling iron. "Who? How could they?"

"You mean they didn't question you?"

"Sort of. B-B-But it was my ex-husband, Hank Parker, and once my attorney showed up, and Marsh showed up, they let me go."

"Marsh?"

"That's what I call Special Agent Dillon."

"How much do you know about him, Grace Ann?"

"Not much." I paused. I pulled back from Marty to look him in the eye. "Why?

The doorbell rang and Marty paid for the pizza. As I picked the pepperoni off my slices, he gave me a little background on John Christopher Dillon. Born in St. Charles, Missouri, but he grew up in Stevens Point, Wisconsin. Enlisted in the navy at age eighteen, and soon after became a Navy SEAL. Married Polly Noble, his high school sweetheart, who was two years younger than he, when he turned twenty.

"A SEAL, can you believe it? The best of the best, the toughest of the tough, and the most deadly killers our nation has ever sent on any mission, anywhere, anytime. Think about how they entered that compound with bin Laden. It was over in seconds. Very little collateral damage. Even after a copter crashed, there wasn't a hitch. I mean, everything you see in the movies, the SEALs are all that and more. Impressive." Marty got up and got himself another beer.

"But Dillon left the SEALs after ten years of service, citing his desire for a job that would keep him stateside. That's when he joined the Georgia Bureau of Investigation as a marshal," Marty concluded, but I didn't hear him. I couldn't focus. Two words chased each other around and around in my head: *He's married.*

Disappointment washed over me.

"Dillon has closed more cases than any other marshal. Also considered deadly with a gun. Knows martial arts. Doesn't suffer fools. Word on the street is he hates your ex with a passion."

That brought me back to the here and now. "Hank has that affect on people. He's the one who took me in for questioning. But being a person of interest wasn't my big news."

"No? What gives?"

"Um, why don't you tell me more about your promotion first?"

He laughed. "It isn't near as interesting as being named a POI in a murder investigation, but here goes. See, with the Arab Spring and all the uprisings, new businesses are springing—get the pun?—up like crazy in Egypt and the other countries. I want to trace how politics influence the growth of businesses, who starts them, what red tape they have to cut through, and what that means to America. My theory is that commerce is good for peace because people grow accustomed to a better lifestyle."

I nodded. That made sense to me. "Is it going to be dangerous? I mean, I assume you'll have to visit a few of those places."

His mouth stopped midchew on another slice and he fought a grin. "Grace Ann, I can't do this story by visiting the Middle East. I plan to go live there. In Cairo."

"Oh. I don't even own a passport. I thought we might live in DC together." I felt like the time that Vonda was on a swing and I walked in front of her and she punched me in the gut. I couldn't breathe. Then it became clear to me— clear and painful—I wasn't exactly in love with Marty, but I had held on to him like a security blanket. As long as there was Marty, I had a place to go, a way to start over. As long as he lived in DC, I could move in with him, find a job there, and either we would marry or not, but I had an exit plan from my suddenly dreary life.

"Uh, I wasn't suggesting that you come with," he said in a tone that showed he was surprised I'd even think it.

"Oh." That hurt. I guess it showed on my face.

He set down his piece of pizza and wiped his mouth with a paper napkin. "I'm not sure what to do or say, Grace Ann. I can tell you're disappointed."

"It's a bit of a shock. And you didn't tell me about your . . . proposal."

"We don't really have that kind of relationship, do we? Look, I care about you, and I want us to stay friends, but you know how much my work matters to me. I'm finally getting a shot at the big leagues—so this isn't the right time for . . . us. Heck, right now, we don't even live in the same state. I mean, when we did, that was different, but now . . .

And I never led you on. In fact, I never asked you to move in with me," he said gently.

Mom always told me that the biggest problem couples had, in her opinion, was that they took a position and quit listening. "Being right becomes more important than hearing the other person out. I get women in my chair all the time who go on and on about how mistreated they are. When you sort it all out, they aren't mistreated. They're convinced their position is right and their man is wrong. The emotion gets the better of them, and they fight instead of working together to find common ground."

Her wise words came home to me. I fought the urge to react. Instead, I told myself to listen carefully, rather than rush in with an accusation. Pushing aside the sting of his rejection was tough, but I did it, and once I did, I realized he was only being honest. "That's right. You never did ask me to move in. However, you did encourage me to come to DC and find a job."

"Right. If you want to move up to Washington, I can still help you. In fact, I still have the lease on my apartment. You could move in and live there while I'm gone. I wouldn't charge you anything. It's furnished."

"Why would I? I mean, why would I want to move to DC if you aren't there?"

"Why not? There isn't anything for you here, is there? I mean, you're marking time, bumping into your ex, not really going anywhere. I should think a smart woman like you would have ambitions."

"Whoa! I like living in St. Elizabeth. There's nothing wrong with this town. Sure, I'd love to get rid of Hank, but my mom lives here . . ." And then I stopped, because she wouldn't live here for long. "And we have a business . . ." And I stopped again, because that might be kaput, too. "Well, I have friends here."

"But it's not like you have a career. I mean, what's the best you can aspire to? Taking over your mom's small shop? Two sinks? I know enough about the beauty business to know you can't be making much money." His voice was entirely matter-of-fact, without judgment.

Worse yet, if he knew how I'd allowed Lisa Butterworth to steal all our customers, he'd know we'd gone from not much money to zip, nada, zilch.

But now my blood was boiling. Suddenly, I felt like I actually *did* have a lot to lose. I didn't want to see my mother's house sold to some pretentious young couple from Savannah who wanted a weekend getaway. I didn't want to face Althea and Stella and Rachel and tell them they no longer had jobs. Yes, I would like to have expanded Violetta's, although for the life of me, I couldn't see how.

In fact, right now, I was fresh out of options. With a sinking feeling, it came to me that I might have to take him up on the offer of an apartment. Unless Mom sold her house and split the profits between Alice Rose and me, I had no seed money. Yes, I had three months' worth of income in savings, but that was all. Certainly not enough to start my own salon. I took a big gulp of my beer and wished I had something stronger.

"There isn't much for you here, is there?" Marty repeated himself.

I let him lead me into my bedroom because I couldn't face telling him good-bye. Not right then.

As his hands slid over my body, I realized that he wasn't taking advantage of me. The comfort he offered was exactly what I needed right now . . . and I would take it.

# Chapter Twenty-five

✂

TRUE TO HIS WORD, SPECIAL AGENT DILLON BANGED on my front door at six A.M. "Rise and shine. I have a gift for you," he said to me, although he carefully avoided my eyes as he pushed his way into my living area. Or maybe he was avoiding looking at me altogether, since all I was wearing was a thin cotton *yukata*, a Japanese-style house-coat that Vonda had made for me.

"Thought you might need this. We're going down to the station." He handed over a box in the familiar pink and tan colors of Dunkin' Donuts.

"We're not going anywhere," I said grumpily. Although I did lunge for the coffee and grab the bag of donuts out of his hand. After polishing off the chocolate cake donut in two bites, I took a long sip of the java. Cream and sugar both, exactly the way I liked it.

Hearing a rustling sound behind me, I set down my brew, went over, and carefully pulled away the cloth from Sam's cage.

"New roommate?" Marsh asked in a gruff tone.

"No, Marty's on his way—" Then I realized he meant the bird. "Yes. His name is Sam. Like Sam I Am."

"Dr. Seuss. One of my favorite authors."

"That's right! I couldn't remember where it came from."

"*Green Eggs and Ham*, a classic." Marsh peeped through the bars to inspect the bird. "What happened to his eye?"

"Shh. He's very sensitive about that. Another bird pecked it out." Slowly I put my hand inside the cage, wrapped my fingers around Sam, and withdrew him so I could put a dab of ointment on his wound. "I think it's healing. I don't know that he'll ever be able to see out of it. Of course, he falls off perches occasionally. And his feathers need to grow back, too."

Marsh nodded. "He needs time to adjust to the change in depth perception. But if you can get him through the trauma of the loss of his eye, he or she should do fine. Have you clipped his wings?"

"Why would I do that?" I tugged at my housecoat. Vonda made it for me out of a pretty flowered sheet. Each year she gets stuck on a craft, and so my Christmas gifts from her are a record of her passions: a scrapbook, a crocheted throw, felted slippers, and this wrap.

"So he won't fly away. What if you accidently don't get the cage door shut and he gets out? You come home from work, he sees you, flies toward you and outside. He'd be lost."

"Oh. How do you clip his wings? Does it hurt him?"

Marsh leaned so close to me that I could see the vein

throbbing in his throat. "No." He said hoarsely. "No, because you don't damage the bird. You trim a bit off the tips to keep it safe, like clipping your nails. That's all. It's an act of . . . love. Not possession."

Marty banged around in my small bathroom.

"Got any scissors?" Marsh stepped away from me. "Guess you probably do, since you cut hair."

"Actually, I make it a point not to keep shears in the apartment."

"Why not?"

"Because when you style hair for a living, there's a tendency to hack at your own whenever you get distressed. If the scissors are in the salon, that's almost impossible to do."

"I see," he said. "Do you get in these hacking moods often?"

"Lately, yes."

Carefully transferring Sam to Marsh's big, warm hand, I went to my bedroom, rummaged through my sewing basket, and retrieved a small pair of sharps. As I straightened, I saw myself in the mirror. Sometime during the night I'd removed most of my makeup. My skin glowed with that special radiance from good sex. My lips were redder than usual for the same reason. My hair was tousled. Appealing? Unappealing? I shrugged. Who knew what men thought?

"Here." I handed him the sharps.

With delicate pressure, Marsh coaxed Sam into extending his wing. Speaking to the bird in a soothing voice as he manipulated the feathers, Marsh positioned the blades and deftly trimmed the first longest feather away from Sam's body so it was the same length as the second feather, its neighbor.

"I'm only taking enough off to hamper his flight. He can still fly, so if a cat would get into your place, he can save himself. But he can't go any distance. Notice how little I took off. I'll do the same on the other side. Like fingernails, you don't want to disturb the quick."

I sank down next to him, engrossed in his expertise. "How did you learn this?"

"Grew up on a farm. Learned a lot of useful stuff. Mainly, I learned to be self-reliant, and I got a great respect for nature."

"Is that where you learned to ride? I mean, I assume you can, since you own a horse."

"Owned a horse. I had to put Groucho down last month."

"I'm sorry."

"Me, too. He was a good horse. A bunch of teenagers were goofing around and left his paddock gate open. Groucho got out, trotted over toward the road, was nearly hit by a car, then to avoid it, darted over a cattle grid. His left foreleg snapped."

"Couldn't you have had it set? I mean, there was that racehorse that broke a leg. They put him in a sling and put a cast on the leg, I think."

His smile crinkled the corners of his eyes. "That's right. Barbaro. In the end, they put him down. A horse can't heal lying down because it weighs so much that the pressure on the internal organs will disrupt their functioning. To get a sling, well, not many places have them. And Groucho's leg was shattered. Sometimes it's better to let something you love go than to struggle to hang on to it, especially if the alternative is pure pain."

"What do we have here?" Marty stomped in, hoisting his Dockers. "Room service?"

There was a bit of a strut in the reporter's step. That ticked me off. I wasn't a prize that he'd won. I'd needed comfort and distraction and Marty had provided it.

"By the way, the showerhead works great. Thanks for playing plumber." Marty's smile stayed around his mouth.

His eyes hardened, and I wondered why. He didn't care for me—not much anyway—so what was all this male preening about?

"Marty was just leaving." I got up and walked to the door.

"Nah, I can stay awhile. Where'd the bird come from? I didn't notice last night because we were . . . busy."

I explained about Sam, as Marsh rose from the sofa and put Sam back on a perch.

Marty helped himself to a donut. "And he's only got one eye? I bet that makes him pretty ugly."

I'd had enough of Marty. Fortunately, I had a great exit strategy. Turning to Marsh, I said, "I'll get dressed and you can take me down to the station."

# Chapter Twenty-six

MARTY TRIED TO GIVE ME A BIG SMOOCH ON THE mouth, as I said good-bye, but I turned my head slightly sidewise so his kiss took a miss. "I'll call you. We can get together. I won't be leaving for another month. Caitlyn has to get her passport arranged."

"Caitlyn?" I choked on the name and started coughing. Instead of walking ahead to his car, Marsh had stayed at my side after I locked the apartment door behind us. Was he protecting me? Or escorting a criminal? I didn't know and I didn't care.

"I thought I told you. I'm sure I did." Marty adjusted his aviator sunglasses and dangled his arms over the roof of his blue Honda so he could keep talking. "She's doing her doctoral dissertation on Middle East commerce, so she's coming along. Her research will help me with my articles."

"Caitlyn," I said, as I seethed with rage.

"Yep." Marty tossed his car keys in the air and caught them. "Like I said, you're welcome to come to DC. You've got a place to stay."

A slow burn started under my collar and warmed my neck. We both knew he was talking about an empty apartment. This was all for show, to be a big shot in front of Marsh, and I was tired of it.

"Good-bye, Marty," I said, as I grabbed Marsh's hand, tugging him toward his car.

"Hey! Grace Ann!" Marty called after me, but I didn't turn around. I practically hauled Marsh to his big Crown Victoria and stood there with my back to Marty as the lawman opened the passenger-side door for me. Once we'd both buckled up, Marsh pulled around Marty's still parked Honda and we drove off a little faster than absolutely necessary.

Neither of us talked for a while. Marsh pulled into Dunkin' Donuts and ordered us both more coffee. "That stuff at the station is toxic waste," he muttered.

Somehow this visit had my knees knocking. The first visit had been a joke, but this felt serious. The "source" had called me a person of interest. You can't prove a negative, so how could they prove I'd done something I didn't do? Then I remembered that old Henry Fonda movie, *The Wrong Man*. Hadn't I been married to a cop? Didn't I know they could "find" evidence? Hadn't Hank bragged about doing just that? I told everyone that I divorced Hank because I caught him cheating on me. The truth was murkier than that. I knew Hank was a crooked cop, and his cheating was the last straw.

As Marsh pulled into a space at the SEPD and turned

off the engine, I found my voice. "Am I in trouble? Do I need my attorney?"

He shook his head. "No."

We sat there quietly.

"You sure?"

"Yes."

"Why am I here?"

"You didn't tell me about visiting Snippets. The security camera also picked up your car driving through their parking lot."

I nodded. Now I was really scared. Sick-at-my-stomach, I've-got-to-use-the-bathroom scared. "Rachel, our shampoo girl, had been inside. They offered her a job. She told me the place was gorgeous. Especially the fish tank. I figured that Lisa wouldn't let me in, so since I was in the neighborhood, I thought I'd drive by."

"Tell me exactly what you did. Don't leave anything out. Grace Ann, this is important. I need to know everything. Trust me."

I closed my eyes and tried to remember. I told him about getting the parakeet, about the light in the back office, about leaving my car and losing my balance. Touching the glass window. Seeing the light blue Toyota Camry with the Georgia plates. Driving away.

When I opened my eyes, his were soft with emotion. Affection? I couldn't tell.

"We found fingerprints on the back window of Snippets. Your ex claimed they are yours and ran them through the system without consulting me. Seems he collected your prints without your knowledge while you were married."

"What!" I gagged.

"He's a real SOB, Grace Ann. As you know, that sort of behavior won't wash. But it's enough to make you look bad. Really bad."

"So he's the source that told the newspapers I'm a person of interest?"

"I'm not sure about that. I promise you, I'll get to the bottom of this. Now try to put it all out of your mind. Can I drop you off at the salon?"

"Y-y-you aren't taking me to the station?"

"No. I just needed for us to talk. In private. You aren't working today?"

I dipped my head and studied the Chuck Taylor Converse shoes I'd paired with a pink tee and black jeans for what I'd thought of as my jailhouse rock outfit. "No."

"It's usually better to keep busy than to worry."

Plucking a loose thread on the hem of my tee shirt, I said, "The salon is closed. Indefinitely. We've got black mold. Mom has to see if her insurance will cover the remediation. Besides, we didn't have any customers left. Lisa Butterworth took all of them."

And I started to cry.

# Chapter Twenty-seven

I'M NOT USUALLY A CRIER. I HADN'T CRIED ABOUT what Lisa'd done. Southern girls learn the fine art of crying at their mother's knee. Most of my friends can sob without mussing up their mascara or having their noses turn red. Me? I'm a mess when I cry. Suddenly, my troubles piled up, tumbled down, and knocked me to my knees. Fighting my emotions took all my concentration. I was not going to give in.

A tear leaked out. One tear. Okay, maybe two.

"Let's get you home." He turned the engine over and we retraced the route we'd taken, including a stop by Dunkin' Donuts, where he bought me an assorted dozen donuts. "There isn't much in life that sugar can't fix," he said with a sigh.

At my place, he took his spot on the sofa, his deep blue eyes regarding me curiously as I mopped my face with a tissue. "What's your plan? I know it's early, but you seem like the sort of person who does best when she's considering her options."

"Right. Um, I figured I'd look at the want ads. Someone in the area has to have an empty chair. A stylist rents her chair, so I won't add any raw costs."

He nodded. "When's the last time you went job hunting?"

I thought and did a bit of calculating. "Twelve years? When I first graduated from high school, the summer before I went to University of Georgia. Why?"

"No one uses the want ads anymore. Got a computer?"

I dragged out my Dell laptop, the one I mainly use for searching the Internet or going to Pinterest.

"I suppose I could apply over at Chez Pierre. We've always been friendly with Peter Wassil."

"You could, but I've already talked to him about Lisa Butterworth. She pulled the same trick on him less than two weeks after she took your customer list."

"Oh. Just like you suspected."

"It's no fun to be right about this. Trust me. He's laying off people right and left."

As he spoke, his fingers moved deftly over the keyboard. Within seconds, he'd turned up several employment sites. Turns out no less than three salons within a twenty-five mile radius of St. Elizabeth had openings.

"This one looks perfect for you. I think you should consider it." He clicked on "Salon Manager Wanted."

"But I'm not a manager."

"Before you say that, read the qualifications. You've done scheduling, right? You deal with employees, correct? Payroll? Advertising? Customers? You've had five years or more in the business?"

"Y-Yes. I guess I have. You're right."

He stood up and smoothed his tie. "You can handle it from here. Just promise me you won't leave town. I'll deal with your ex."

I got up from the sofa and turned to face him, feeling more hopeful than I had in days. "How can I thank you? I really appreciate this."

He leaned close, so close I thought he might kiss me. Instead he whispered, "You just did."

After he left, I updated my résumé, such as it was, on my Dell and hit the "send" button, winging my way toward the ad for the manager's job. Really, it seemed way too easy, compared to the old days when I went through gallons of Liquid Paper trying to get one perfect copy of my job history. I also sent my résumé to the other places offering a chair for rent. Marsh was right; hitting the "send" button was a lot easier than printing out a résumé and addressing an envelope. So easy that I had no idea where my information was going. None at all. I quit paying attention. Instead, I just sat there and hit "send" over and over again.

As long as the salon was within a reasonable driving distance, I'd make it work.

Filled with nervous energy, and mad as hops at Hank, I couldn't sit still. I called Mom, but got her voice mail. I wanted to hear what she learned from the insurance adjuster, so I left a message. I also put in a call to Alice Rose, that perfect paragon of womanhood. She didn't answer, either. I thought I'd better chat with her, tell her what had happened—if she didn't know already—and then talk about how we could support Mom through this crisis.

I thought about calling Althea, Stella, and Rachel. I wasn't sure what Mom had told them, though, and I didn't want to alarm them unduly.

Instead, I changed into a pair of old jeans, stripped the

sheets off my bed, gathered the towels Marty had used, and started singing, "I'm going to wash that man right out of my hair," at the top of my lungs. Filling a bucket with water and Mr. Clean, the only man I could depend on these days, I started scrubbing the bathroom floor—with gusto. Pretty soon I was drenched in sweat.

That's when my phone rang.

"May I speak to Grace Ann Terhune?" a cautious voice asked.

"Speaking."

"You replied to an online employment ad?"

"Yes." I did a fist pump that caught Sam's attention. He's like that. He notices everything.

"Are you available for an interview? Today?" the caller sounded timid.

"Sure. Give me half an hour to get cleaned up. See, I've been doing housework."

"Certainly. Would an hour be better?"

I paused. What if this was a person from one of the salons twenty-five minutes away? I'd grown so accustomed to getting anywhere I wanted to go in less than fifteen minutes. Perhaps I'd better back up on the timeframe. "An hour. Right. Where should I go? I mean, what's the street address? I sent résumés to several places," I explained.

"It's Two fifty-five Reynolds Street."

OMG, that was the street address for Snippets.

"Who is this?" I abandoned any pretense at manners.

"My name is Eve. Eve Sebastiani Goodman."

"Ha, ha, ha. Nice joke, Vonda. Knock it off."

"Vonda?"

An uncomfortable silence followed.

Eve cleared her throat. "We need a manager at this salon. Badly. We've put a lot of money into our lease and building out the salon. I realize given the circumstances . . .

some people might feel uncomfortable working at this location, but we're stuck with it."

"And you couldn't transfer another manager?" I plopped down on my sofa. This was too bizarre for words!

"Yes. Yes, I could. However, as you well know, the locals are comfortable with you. Bringing you in makes perfect sense. In fact, it might be the only way we can get the business back up and running."

"How do you know I'm not going to scam you like you scammed our salon? Hmm?" My temperature was rising as I thought about the damage Lisa had done. Was Eve in favor of such high jinks?

"I deeply regret what Lisa did to your business. In fact, I owe you and your mother an apology, which is why I happened to be here in St. Elizabeth when . . . when Lisa died. You don't know me, but if you did, you would know I would never, ever resort to tricking or cheating another business person. My father worked too hard and too long to get established for me to blacken his good name. You might not realize this, but back then, being an Italian off the boat was tough. Our family certainly survived its share of dirty tricks, and so Lisa's actions are appalling.

"Grace Ann, we really should meet. At the very least, let me apologize to you in person. But I think you're perfect for the job of manager. Why aren't you working for your mother?"

"We have a small issue with mold. Shouldn't take long to resolve it." I sounded more confident than I felt.

"Even if you come to work here for a short time, I'd pay you well. Whether you come for an interview or not, I want to let you go through the names on our computer. If the client was yours initially, we won't send any e-mails to them for a period of six months. How's that? Would that be fair? And if you do decide to come work here, you can handle your old clients, which might make it easier for you to keep them until you've dealt with the mold problem."

I sat up straight. That was a heck of a concession. Why was she making it?

"You must want me awfully bad."

"I do."

There was nothing coy or sly in her voice. She certainly sounded sincere.

We agreed to meet at Subway, which was also on Reynolds. That way, if her offer didn't appeal to me, or if I didn't appeal to her, we would be on neutral territory.

After we hung up, I finished my mopping, showered, and dressed. I carefully applied my makeup, and put my black jeans and pink tee back on. I didn't want to appear too eager, but I didn't want to seem all stuffy and out-of-date, either. At the last moment, I added the dangling jet-black bead earrings Althea had made for me. The effect was studied insouciance.

I liked it.

# Chapter Twenty-eight

I COULD HAVE PICKED OUT EVE SEBASTIANI GOOD-man from across the municipal parking lot. The girl had been blessed with a great head of hair. Long, blond, it tumbled onto her shoulders in picture-perfect loose curls.

Although God had been good to her in the hair department, he'd been a bit stingy when he handed out comeliness. Her eyes were small and set too narrow, a trait she compensated for by careful application of eye liner. Also, her lips were thin. A passerby might think, "She's gorgeous," until she turned around. Her features weren't symmetrical enough to be attractive. And I wasn't sure that plastic surgery could help because it can't make your eyes bigger or set them wider apart. Oh, sure, they can plump up your lips with fillers, but that can go terribly wrong.

Beyond all that, she was taller than I, and thin. Rail thin
in fact. I remembered from what I'd read that she and I
were the same age, but the drawn lines on her face made
her look older.

This flitted through my mind in less time than it took
me to walk across the parking lot and join her on the bench
outside the front door of the Subway restaurant.

"Let's grab a couple of sandwiches," she said as she
stood to shake my hand. I couldn't help but notice the huge
honking diamond on her ring finger. The sparkle nearly
blinded me.

"Is that okay?" she asked. "I know it isn't elegant, but it
is convenient."

"Fine by me."

"I'm buying," she said.

I don't know how she walked in those high heels, but
she did. We selected our food—mine was turkey on honey
wheat bread with lots of veggies while she chose the teriyaki chicken—and she paid. Ignoring the chill in the air,
we took seats outside in the sunshine, unwrapped our food,
and dug in. She didn't eat like a prissy princess. I admit I
was a bit surprised that someone with all her money would
stoop so low as to eat at Subway, but what did I know about
the very, very rich? Not much.

About halfway through our meal, she talked with her
mouth full. "Gosh, this is good. I don't care if it's fast food
or what. I love their multigrain bread. And this teriyaki
sauce on the chicken is just to die for!"

I couldn't help but laugh, because she had attacked her
food with such eagerness. There was nothing stuck-up about
her. Nothing. "You must have been hungry."

"Yes, I was up at five, and when you eat that early, breakfast is a faint memory by the time lunch rolls around. Lately,
I've been extra hungry."

"Why so early? You're the boss. Don't you set your own hours?" I took in her lovely silk blouse with its billowing poet sleeves, the tight jeans, and the spectacular stiletto high heels. Everything about Eve was first class. No wonder Wynn had fallen for her. With the exception of natural good looks, she was a lucky, lucky girl.

She smiled a genuinely sweet smile. "I wish! I have suppliers in China, and their workday is different. But today, I was up early to talk to two prominent UK designers, Toni and Guy. I want them to come here and do training for all our staff."

"Toni and Guy!" I yelped. "They're my favorites."

"Mine, too."

We stared at each other, shocked by our mutual admiration of two other stylists.

"I wish we'd met under different circumstances," she said, her voice choking with emotion. "Wynn talks about you often. He . . . he thinks the world of you. Did you know he's agreed to go into counseling? Sex addiction."

"I haven't talked to Wynn for three years."

After studying a baked barbecue chip for a long time, she bit into it. "I don't know any other way to say all this, so I'll dive right in: You have every reason to hate everything to do with Snippets. I can understand that. I can't undo the past, Grace Ann. But I can offer you a position here and now. Who knows? You might learn a new skill or two. I can put my company's resources at your disposal. We could go into it with the understanding that you'll probably only be with us a short time." The salary she proposed made my head spin.

"Plus, hospitalization, and you have hiring and firing privileges. I'll get Carol Brockman to set everything up. She's our accountant here."

I was speechless. So much so that she took it for rejection.

"Okay, if you want to play hard to get. Here's the deal. I'll even offer a signing bonus." She tossed out a figure equal to one month's pay. I wasn't sure how much the deductible might be on Mom's insurance, but surely this could make a sizeable dent in it.

"Why? Why do you want me so badly?" I pushed the last bits of my sandwich to one side and stared at her, hard.

She shrugged. "I was raised to believe that what goes around, comes around. Lisa's death is proof of that. There were many nasty tricks she pulled, including trying to run you out of business. When I found out and confronted her, she gave me a song and dance about how you snubbed her in high school. I had very little use for the woman."

"And she was involved with Wynn," I said. I wasn't going to let it slide.

"Yes, she pursued my husband hot and heavy. Eventually, he gave in. He isn't blameless. As far as that goes, she deserved everything she got." Waving a weary hand, Eve said, "Look. Wynn is no saint. He has his problems, but she went out of her way to entice him, and he's never been very strong. You were lucky, Grace Ann. He walked away from you early in your relationship. I'm pregnant. No one knows it yet but Wynn. That's why he was breaking it off with Lisa. I am not going to divorce my husband. Especially not now. I want my baby to have a father."

# Chapter Twenty-nine

✂

"LET'S GO LOOK AT THE SALON, SHALL WE?" EVE cleaned up after herself, carefully putting her trash in the big bin.

We were only four blocks away from the salon, but with deference to her five-inch heels, I offered her a ride in my Fiesta. If the low-class wheels weren't up to her standards, she never let on. As we drove, she asked me how I liked living in St. Elizabeth, what my favorite local attraction was, and so on. The turning leaves excited her, and twice she called my attention to maple trees resplendent in shades of orange and red. When we got to the salon, she even thanked me for the ride.

I have to admit, she exuded perfection with that long blond hair and those huge Gucci sunglasses. But what price was she paying? Wynn was cheating on her, that was a given. She was expecting, which should be a happy time in her life, but how could it be with an unfaithful husband at her side? And then, there was the business. Snippets had rolled a lot of money into this salon, and now a woman had died in their shop.

Her problems made my problems seem paltry by comparison.

All heads turned as we walked into the salon. The first thing I noticed was how busy they were. Two-thirds of the twelve chairs were full. All three of the manicure stations were busy, as were all three of the pedicure chairs. A happy hum of activity filled the air, except that smack-dab in the middle of the salon, between the waiting area and the services floor, was a huge empty space where the aquarium had been ripped out. That's when it hit me: I didn't know exactly how Lisa had died. No one was saying. But that glaring empty spot told me she might have been swimming with the fishes, because why else would you remove such a huge fixture? Especially one that formed the wall between your work area and waiting area? Sidling closer, I ran fingertips along the molding. When I raised them, I saw the unmistakable black grit of fingerprint dust. So I was right: This had to be the spot where Lisa had died! Or at least where something significant to the crime had occurred.

Eve took me from station to station, introducing me to people. Besides having a kind word for all her employees, she knew all their names and a bit about their backgrounds. She also knew every detail about the salon.

The décor was midcentury modern, in shades of pink, black, white, and gray. On the walls were huge posters of models with great hair, including one of Eve. The photographer had caught her at a good angle, and she looked great. The fixtures were chrome and gleaming. Everything shouted top-of-the-line.

"The water is temperature-regulated, so there's no chance of scalding. We have a huge water heater. A big sanitizer, new washer and dryer for our towels. Of course, our pedi chairs all have massaging systems built in." We went for a quick tour of the back room, where she showed me the manager's office and the back office where Carol Brockman worked.

A spacious, well-lit hall connected the non-public space to the salon floor. Large supply cabinets lined the hallway, each door opening to the widest selection of supplies I'd ever seen except for what we had at Vidal Sassoon. Shelves were packed with boxes in neat lines, and each spot was labeled.

On the opposite side was an employee lounge complete with lockers where stylists could leave their personal belongings. There was also a refrigerator, table, microwave, a small vending machine, and an espresso machine. The midcentury modern leather sofa and chairs looked surprisingly comfortable, and the cute table with its Formica top would make taking a lunch or dinner break enjoyable. A fresh bouquet of pink carnations in a low glass vase sat in the center of the table.

On the other side of the kitchen/employee area was the massage and treatment area. The white stone water feature created a soothing ambience, positioned as it was between massage and treatment rooms. Eve stepped aside to let me go first. I took my time wandering down the hall, enjoying the posters on the walls.

Each treatment room featured a knob that rotated to show "Occupied" or "Vacant." Only one room was occupied. As I walked closer, with Eve behind me, that particular door swung open and out stumbled Wynn, with his back to us.

Following him was a massage therapist, a cute redhead with freckles, wearing a white clinical jacket. She staggered along after him, grabbing at his hand and giggling. The two were so engrossed in their private world that neither of them noticed us at first.

Wynn's hair was tousled, and his shirt buttoned wrong. I spotted a bulge under one arm, immediately recognizing it as a gun holster. That shocked me. I moved to block the way, so Eve didn't see her husband.

"Oh!" Eve froze behind me.

Wynn and the redhead wrestled playfully, still unconscious of our presence. When she dove for his ribs, he wagged a finger at her. "Don't you dare!"

"Stop it!" I said in a commanding voice.

Wynn's posture changed from giddy to shocked as he slowly straightened and turned toward us. The girl with him stood completely still and blinked. She reminded me of a stunned mouse preparing to run away when you turn on the kitchen light.

Wynn stared at Eve. I turned to see that she was slumping against a wall. Pain came off her in waves. I could feel every muscle in her body shouting with misery.

His mouth moved, but no sound came out. Finally, he said, "Eve, honey, we were just . . ."

But Eve slashed the air with her hands. "Stop. Spare me."

Her husband turned ashen, then red. Then his eyes traveled to me. "Hey, Grace Ann. It's been a long time."

"Not long enough," I said.

And he looked ashamed.

It was abundantly clear to all of us what had been happening in the massage room.

"What's your name?" I spoke to the masseuse.

"Paula. Paula Benson."

"Paula, take the rest of the day off, please. Tell the front desk to call your clients and explain that you've suddenly become ill."

"Who are you?" She pouted and shoved her hands into her pockets.

"Never mind who I am. Please do as I say. It's best you leave. Right now." My voice brooked no discussion, and the rigidity of my posture must have assured Paula that I was not a person to be trifled with, because she turned around and walked toward the receptionist.

"Thank you," whispered Eve to me. "I couldn't have handled it."

"No problem."

"I couldn't get the words out." Her mouth trembled. It must have taken tremendous self-control for her not to burst into tears.

"Like I said, no problem. I hope I didn't overstep my bounds."

"No," she said in a whisper. "I needed the help."

"Aw, Eve. It wasn't that big of a deal." Wynn ambled over to where his wife was leaning against the wall. "Come here, hon." With studied casualness, he pulled her close to him. Her eyes were cold as she stared up into his, but after a heartbeat, she collapsed into his arms.

"We were joking around, Eve. That's all," he whispered to her, and he raised his head to wink at me.

It turned my stomach.

"I hope you'll consider my offer," said Eve, straightening. "And let me know quickly, please?"

"I will. Thank you for lunch and the tour." I started for the door.

"Hey, Grace Ann!" Wynn called to me. "Aren't you even going to say hi?"

I stared at him. "No, actually I'm not. I'm going to do my best to forget I even saw you, Wynn."

Eve's laugh was short and harsh. "I knew you were a smart woman from the moment I laid eyes on you."

"Smart, but not as patient as you. Call you tomorrow."

Turning on my heel, I left them there. A part of me admired her keeping her cool. Another part thought she was being stupid. I'd forgotten how much Wynn Goodman had hurt me, but seeing the damage he did to Eve brought it all back. To my surprise, I could suddenly recall every slight, every humiliation.

As I started my Fiesta, I thought about Eve Sebastiani Goodman. I liked her. Liked her a lot.

As for her husband, he could go straight to hell.

# Chapter Thirty

✂

"MOM?" I LET MYSELF INTO HER HOUSE THROUGH the back door and onto her screened-in back porch.

"In here, honey." She and Althea sat face-to-face at a small table with a gallon of sweet tea between them. Both of them sported red, runny noses. I figured they'd been crying on each other's shoulder. "We're reminiscing. Going over old times. Like the first time you ever did foils, remember?"

I blushed. "How could I forget? I was trying to wrap foil around Mrs. Culver's bangs but my hand slipped. I stuck my finger right up her nose."

We all laughed at that memory.

"Remember the time you were rinsing Renni Stephens's hair? She was eight months pregnant, and you were trying to avoid her belly?" Althea asked me.

"I lost my grip on the hose. It whipped out of my hand like a snake gone wild, twisting and turning, and soaking her from head to toe." I shook my head. "It's a wonder she forgave me."

"Your mama and I have been having a whale of a time, cussing and discussing," said Althea with a broad grin.

I poured myself a big glass of the tea, took a big swig, and choked.

"Th-that's not sweet tea! What is it?" I coughed.

"No, it's called a Pimm's Cup. They drink it in England. I've been watching *Downton Abbey*, reading English literary novels, and I came across a reference. Kwasi told me how to make it. When your mother called, I figured she had bad news, so I brought along the ingredients. Like it?"

"Wow. It's good, but it's strong."

Mom snickered softly, before blowing her nose. "Especially if you were planning on sweet tea."

"So, how are you both?"

"Unemployed, flat busted, and drunk," said Althea. "What time is it? Five?"

"Not nearly."

"Well, shoot. Then I think I'll sit a spell longer and have another drink. Before you lecture me about drinking and driving, young lady, Kwasi promised to swing by and pick me up."

"What did you decide to do about the salon?" I asked my mother. As usual, she wore a knit top in a soft pastel pattern, with matching solid pants. Totally out-of-date, but it had been her work uniform all my life.

"There's nothing for me to decide. It's out of my hands. I called the insurance adjuster, and he's got bigger fish to fry. I'm definitely small fry, get it?" And she started giggling and Althea chimed in until they were wiping the tears from their eyes.

"How long have you two been drinking like this?" I wondered.

"About an hour. Or two. It's our second pitcher." Althea raised the big glass vessel and pointed to the slices of orange, apple, and lime mingling with a sprig of mint on the bottom. "Wh-when we finished the last pitcher, we ate all our fruit like good girls."

That fruit must have been saturated with strong spirits.

"Have you two had any lunch?"

"Just this," said Mom, slurring her words. It sounded suspiciously like "justice." That stopped me in my tracks. Was it justice for Mom and Althea and Stella and Rachel and me to be out of jobs? I didn't think so. Mom had paid insurance all these years. As far as I knew, this was her first claim. As for the mailing list, one could argue as Eve did that Lisa Butterworth "got hers." But unless I took the job at Snippets, I wasn't sure I could get our customers back or hold out against Snippets' big advertising and promotion budget. Whatever else Eve Sebastiani Goodman was, she struck me as a sharp cookie. I fully believed she was a terrific businesswoman, although I had no proof. There was a certain brisk, self-confidence and determination about her that suggested she knew exactly how to run a going concern.

And Violetta's was no longer a going concern.

"I'm going to fix you two some lunch."

I found a wedge of cheese, carrots, a cucumber, and a hard-boiled egg in the back of Mom's refrigerator. After slicing the cheese, cleaning and cutting up the carrots and cuke, I mixed up tuna salad for Mom and Althea. Between nibbling on carrot and cucumber sticks, they ate tuna sandwiches.

Once they were a bit more cogent, I sat down with them and started to lay out a plan. "Eve Sebastiani Goodman contacted me today. She's down here with her husband. Wynn Goodman."

"I know who he is," Mom said, stiffening. Forgive and forget did not apply when you hurt one of her girls.

"She offered me a job."

Althea frowned slightly. "A job?"

"As manager."

"Good for you," said Mom, although since she had tuna in her mouth, it sounded more like "ood or oo."

I nodded and took a deep breath. "Of Snippets."

"Where?" asked Althea.

"The one down the street."

The two old friends stared at each other. Althea's strong jaw twitched. "I don't know whether to congratulate you or call you a dirty traitor."

"I know, I know. I have mixed feelings, too."

Mom threw up a hand, waved it wearily, and said, "My gut says, 'No, not my baby working for my competition,' but my head says, 'Yes, my girl is big enough to run her own business.' I've known that for years."

"I'm not sure that I can. I mean, I've always relied on you, Mom. But if I can come to you for help, I could give it a try. They're promising me a lot of money. Seems that since Lisa died there, none of their managers is keen to move to that salon. Who can blame them? But that doesn't bother me. It would mean a steady income. Besides, a lot of their customers are our former customers." And I told the two women about Eve's deal with me, the one where she agreed to give me back our client list.

"Huh. She should surrender that right now." Althea wrapped angry arms around her chest. Today she was dressed in a bright green tee shirt with a handmade vest. The ensemble matched her spunky personality.

"Yes, you're right, and if I pushed the point, she just

might, but what good would that do us? We don't have any place to service our customers, remember? So moving them here doesn't do any of us any good."

Mom nodded. "Tell me about it. I've been racking my brain for a way to keep the doors open, and jiminy, I sure can't. There's so much to do to get the needed repairs made." With that she started sneezing.

"Seems to me that the first repair is to your health. We need to get you and Althea out of here, and we need to keep everyone else away until you get the all clear on the mold."

"That makes sense. Walter has asked me if I want to move in with him. I guess I'm being old-fashioned, because that seems a bit scandalous."

"Get with the program, girlfriend," said Althea. "Time's a-wasting. Why should you care what people think? I'd tell you that you can bunk up with me, but I don't have a bit of space."

Mom sipped her drink. "Grace Ann has a little bitty apartment. She doesn't have any extra room. I called Alice Rose. She said she'd make room for me, but you know how rowdy those boys are. I'm not sure I can put up with much of that."

"How do you feel about moving into Walter's? He has a big house. His Victorian's almost a twin to this one."

She frowned. "We discussed it last night. He offered me my own bedroom, since we haven't set a date. That's the only way it would work for me. I'd need to know I would have privacy . . . sometimes."

"Either of you heard from Stella? I am worried about her." Althea's voice was soft.

Stella Michaelson's Nail Nook was a popular feature at Violetta's. At first, her husband, Darryl, thought of Stella's income as "pin money," in a dismissive way, but over the years, he'd come to value how that extra money allowed them a lot of luxuries. A lot of men in the South are very traditional, with that "my wife's job is caring for our home and me!" mindset. But a couple of years ago, when Stella was off work for a month after contracting a nasty case of bronchitis, Darryl had what we call a "come to Jesus" moment. After that, he made no secret of his appreciation for his wife's contribution to the family income.

More recently, Darryl was laid off from the auto dealership where he worked in Brunswick. "You would think with the problems in the economy, folks would be hanging on to their old cars and needing a mechanic," said Stella, but so far, Darryl had only been able to find odd jobs here and there. With the loss of his wages, and the normal expenses associated with parenting an eight-year-old, Stella's contribution to the family finances had gone from frivolous to critical.

"I think I have a solution," I said. "At least I hope so. If I go to work at Snippets, I'll have hiring and firing privileges. That means I can hire all of you. I'll also control scheduling."

Althea's mouth fell open, as did Mom's. They looked at each other with raised eyebrows. "Hmm," said Mom. "That's a new wrinkle."

"Hmm, indeed," said Althea.

"Would that help?" I asked. "Because if it would, and if you think it would help Stella and Rachel, too, that's reason enough for me to take the job. At least temporarily."

Mom picked up the pair of tongs to pluck a mint spear out of the bottom of the pitcher. She chewed on it thoughtfully. "It would be like keeping Violetta's intact, only with a different address."

"That's one way of looking at it."

"But what about moving to Washington, DC?" Mom asked me.

I shrugged.

Althea was more blunt. "Did Marty bail out on you last night?"

"No. Not if by bailing out you mean did he stand me up. He was here."

"Wasn't he planning to stay a couple of days?" Althea pressed the point.

"Yes," I said, but I studied my shoes.

Althea leaned forward, resting her weight on her forearms. "And did you set him straight? None of this calling you, forgetting about you, showing up late, and then being all kissy-face?"

"Sort of. Not exactly." My cheeks turned hot.

"What exactly does 'not exactly' mean to you?" Mom queried gently.

"It means we broke up."

"So you aren't going to DC?"

"No."

"Then I think you ought to take the job at Snippets," Mom said.

# Chapter Thirty-one

✂

I TOLD THEM ABOUT HANK AND HIS DIRTY TRICK, hijacking my fingerprints and entering them in the SEPD system. "I don't know what I'll have to do to have them expunged," I said.

"That man! Wait until I see him next. I'll give him a piece of my mind. I haven't even turned on the radio or opened the newspaper this morning. If I'd seen the article, I would have been beside myself," said Mom. "You know, this was the first morning in years that I've been able to sleep in, so I enjoyed myself."

Althea raised one perfectly groomed eyebrow. "I missed the article, too. Kwasi has convinced me to get the *New York Times* online. I read that every morning instead of our local rag. I got tired of opening the paper and seeing how another one of my customers had died. Now I buy the Sunday edition and take it in all at once."

I laughed, but only a little.

"That no-good snake," said Mom. "Hank Parker is a worthless piece of trash. What does Agent Dillon say about all this?"

"I've been told by my own off-the-record sources that he doesn't have much use for Hank. Especially after this stunt. Anyone could have leaked my police station visit to the press, but the most natural person would be Hank. That's his style."

"There's nothing for you to worry about, Grace Ann." Mom patted my hand. "Not with Agent Dillon involved. He's a good man. Not like some others we know."

Her sly glance told me she was speaking of Wynn and what he'd done to me. She knew all about it, of course, because she'd helped Vonda unload me from her car. Mom had seen me struggle back to health after his betrayal and my bout with the flu. "You wouldn't have gotten so sick if you hadn't been sick at heart," she'd told me as she pressed a cool washcloth to my forehead.

I wanted to spill everything I knew about the affair Wynn had with Lisa, and how Eve was pregnant, but I knew that would only upset my mother. Wynn was already a man she despised—and there was no reason to get her more angry. Mom took a very dim view of men who played around.

Then I remembered: She'd been through my father's dying of pancreatic cancer. She knew what it was like to lose a spouse slowly and painfully.

"Well, I guess I'd better call Eve and tell her I think I'll take the job."

"When would you start?" Althea asked.

"Right away. The sooner I'm there, the sooner I can hire all of you."

The proud woman said nothing, but the way her jaw relaxed spoke volumes. Althea, too, needed the income. With that in mind, I was more certain than ever that working for Snippets was a good idea. I told Mom and Althea good-bye, giving both of them hugs.

Once I got to the stop sign two blocks from Violetta's, I called Eve. "That job? I think I'd like to try it."

"Good," she said. "I'm very, very pleased. Would seven be too early for you tomorrow?"

"Not at all."

With an afternoon to kill, but a new job on the horizon, I decided to use my time sensibly. Almost on its own power, my car headed toward Magnolia House. If I was lucky, I'd get a little quality time with my BFF.

TEA AND SYMPATHY WAS ALL THAT I WANTED. VONDA had easily provided Item #1: a pitcher of sweet tea chilled to perfection and garnished with a lively sprig of mint.

As for Item #2 on my wish list, um, not so much. "You talked to that man from the GBI? Without an attorney? Even after you knew you were considered a person of interest? I better call Dooley right this instant and arrange an insanity hearing!" shrieked Vonda.

"Don't. You. Dare." I glared at her.

"Give me one good reason why, Grace Ann. One! That's all I'm asking!" She jumped to her feet and glared at me. Her brown eyes fairly glowed with anger, as she trembled with fury. The pressure of my hand on her arm was all that kept her from grabbing the landline behind the front desk and calling our old high school friend.

"I'm warning you, Vonda Mary Agatha, do *not* call

Dooley. If I'd wanted him to know about this, I could've talked to him myself."

"Someone needs to protect you from yourself! You've given that GBI agent a hundred good reasons to think you are Suspect Numero Uno. Do you have some deep-seated death wish? An overwhelming urge to style hair for inmates on death row?" Shaking off my hand, Vonda wobbled her way back down into her wicker chair. After scalding me with a horrified look, she started scrubbing her face with both hands. When her skin had turned a rosy pink, she sighed. "Bless your heart, Grace Ann. You do beat all."

In Southern, "bless your heart" is code for "you are too stupid to live, so I hope God will watch after you, because you aren't up to the job yourself."

By the same token, "you do beat all" means (and I'm translating it loosely here, so as not to be too offensive) "there isn't a dumber person on the planet. At least not that I know of."

Maybe a Yankee would have laughed off my best friend's concerns for my intelligence/safety/welfare, but I found myself paralyzed with anger. "Excuse me, Miss Cotton Bowl Princess Runner-up."

"Runner-up? Dag nab it, you just had to throw that in my face, didn't you? Well, let me tell you a thing or two, missy. You trust him? Goody. I feel a whole lot better, I sure do. Because you are such a fine, fine judge of character in men. I mean, just look at who you married."

"That's fat bacon coming from a girl whose own marital career is a wee bit checkered. Huh, when it comes to Ricky, you're like a bad country song. You can't decide whether to love him, leave him, or sign a long-term lease with him." I glared at her.

Steam curled out the side of her nostrils. Woo-ee, was she mad. As I watched, she squinched her eyes into tiny black holes and then she sniffed at me. "Maybe I don't give up as easy as you do. Maybe I'm trying to stick it out—to actually live my vows! After all, I do have a child!"

She might as well have picked up her fork and stuck it in my brain. For as long as I can remember, I've wanted to be a mama. It's not something I share with most people. In fact, I bet Vonda and my mother are the only two people on earth who know that this has been my lifelong ambition. Given that Alice Rose has two adorable children, I don't want to look like I'm munching a mouthful of sour grapes. So I've done a pretty fine job of keeping my baby-lust under wraps, if I do say so myself.

Vonda knew she'd crossed an imaginary line. Her head recoiled on her neck like a cottonmouth draws back before it strikes.

Normally, I would have apologized. I would have nodded and agreed because, after all, she was right. I should have never talked to GBI Agent John Dillon. My problem, if I cared to admit it, was that the man made me so hot and bothered that I couldn't think straight when I was around him. A smart woman would have grunted her way through his questions and walked out that door smiling with satisfaction because she outwitted and outlasted him. But I'd abandoned all pretense of good sense by talking about Lisa Butterworth's lying ways and telling him that, yes, I had visited the store the night she'd been killed.

With all this drama about Agent Dillon, I hadn't had the chance to tell Vonda about Mom and the Historic Preservation Society or about the mold and my new job. Much less relate the big news that my mother was engaged. Nor was I likely to get to share those recent developments, because

Vonda was on a tear. When she was like this, and I'd seen it before, she was not a good listener.

"Pitiful, Grace Ann. Just purely pitiful. That's what you are." She kept talking, but I quit listening.

Luckily for both of us, a guest wandered into the parlor and asked Vonda for help. Seems his wife had a headache. Did she have any aspirin?

While Vonda went to their supply closet to dig up a foil pack of painkillers, I took advantage of the situation and slipped out. I knew her well enough to know her tantrum would blow over. There didn't seem to be much point in sticking around until she calmed down.

Blinking my tired eyes in the hazy sunshine, I drove back to my apartment. Sam greeted me with a series of cheerful tweets. After spending a little quality time with him, I took a hot bath, pulled on my jammies, and spent the rest of the day watching old movies. Around eleven, I opened my laptop, sent a brief message to LaReesa and told her most of what had transpired. If she knew any inside scoop about Snippets, I invited her to share it, because as of tomorrow, I'd be knee-deep in alligators.

After that, I cracked open a beer, picked more pepperoni off the pizza Marty had ordered, deleted his recent voice message to me, which had shown up while I was in the tub, covered the bird, and went to bed.

I'd had enough drama for one day.

# Chapter Thirty-two

✂

THE ST. ELIZABETH BUSINESS DISTRICT IS SIXTEEN blocks long and four blocks wide. Eight blocks stretch east of city hall, and the other eight point west. The police department and Vonda's bed and breakfast are on the east side near the water, while our salon is on the west. Snippets is three blocks farther from the downtown than Violetta's, and my apartment is in between the two salons.

I'll say this about living in a small town. You can't beat the commute!

Even though I'd worked in salons my entire life, my pulse definitely raced as I contemplated the day ahead. I changed clothes three times, before deciding on a simple black jersey dress and low heels. Being businesslike couldn't hurt. Some of the staff had seen me during the walk-through

with Eve, but they hadn't realized why I was there. This
morning they would meet me as their new boss.

As I brushed blush over my cheeks, I tried to put myself in their shoes. Lisa couldn't have been an effective
leader. She was too self-centered. And she was a cheat. I
had no doubt she'd also been ruthless in dealing with her
employees.

There was another consideration: These people worked
in a crime scene. That had to be tough. I wouldn't like it.
Didn't like it. In fact, changing the psychic pulse of the
place would be my first priority. Whether I needed to bring
in a priest or minister or shaman, whatever. The bad vibes
from Lisa's death had to be vanquished before any good
vibes could take their place.

Sam was doing much better at hopping from perch to
perch. As Marsh suggested, all the bird needed was time to
adjust to the change in his vision. I scratched my friend's
neck, remembering how tenderly the big man had cradled
the budgie.

*Stop that, Grace Ann! He's married.*

That reminded me. I needed to call Vonda and tell her
about my new gig. She'd be over her snit by now. I also
wanted to tell all our old customers that, for all intents and
purposes, the gang from Violetta's would be doing their
"thang" in a new locale. I would take Eve at her word,
bringing Mom, Althea, Stella, and Rachel on board.

With all this buzzing around in my head, I headed to
work.

Eve was crouched by the back door as my Fiesta pulled
into the lot.

Her face was pale, and she wiped her mouth.

"Morning sickness?" I asked.

She nodded. "That and worrying."

"I'm sorry about Wynn. Really I am."

She managed a watered-down smile and tried to stand. I offered her my hand. She wore a black print skirt, gathered at the waist and stopping at the knees to reveal a pair of bright red tights and ultra-cool boots. A short jacket in solid black topped a red formfitting sweater. A scarf in red and black was loosely wrapped around her neck. Totally adorable, although wearing a scarf in the fall in Georgia is a bit over the top. Most of us get too hot for that sort of nonsense. Even so, her look was edgy but businesslike. "Want to hear something really sick? I love him. I am truly, crazy, madly in love with the guy. As much as it hurts when he pulls stunts like yesterday, I don't want to let him go. Pretty stupid of me, huh?"

"I don't think so," I said quietly.

"What a powerful, tough businesswoman I am! I can't even manage to marry a guy who's faithful."

I couldn't just stand there. I gave her a hug. She clung to me like I was a tree in a hurricane. I realized her arms were as thin as twigs.

"Let's get you inside. This is a small town. You don't want people talking about you. Trust me, they will," I said. "Keys?"

She handed them over and I unlocked the back door. I watched as she punched in a security code, Wynn's birthday.

"We fought all night. He told me he can't help himself. Worse yet, I'm worried. The police have questioned him twice! Each time, he gets more and more freaked out. He has claustrophobia. The thought of going to jail makes him physically ill. Me, too, but for different reasons."

"Okay, you need to sit down, Eve. Come on." And I took her by the arm in a direction toward the office. "I'm going to make you a cup of hot tea with lots of sugar. My gran was from Scotland, and she always said if tea with sugar can't cure it, it can't be fixed."

Eve's mouth trembled, a hint of a smile.

Fumbling at switches as I went, I turned on the lights. In the employee dining room, I found dirty mugs. That would definitely have to change. Folks would have to be more responsible about the dishes.

I washed one, filled it with cold water, found tea bags in a box, brought the water to boiling in the microwave, and added the bag. Two heaping spoonfuls of sugar went in next, along with a spoon.

"Here you go."

"Why are you being so nice to me? Because you need this job? I know the mold stuff is worse than you let on. You are right; everyone talks in a small town."

This rankled a bit and I frowned at Eve. "I would be nice to you whether I needed a job or not. That's the way I was raised. It's also the way we are here in the South."

"I'm sorry. I didn't mean to offend you. I'm not myself. I'm so scared," she stuttered, after another sip of tea.

"About the business?"

"No. Closing our doors here would hurt, but not much. We're so big that closing a salon here and there doesn't matter. I know it sounds callous, but it's true. Although it would be nice to stay open long enough to recoup our build-out expenses. But if we can't, well, we can take the loss." She paused and stared up at me. "Grace Ann, do you think Wynn could have killed Lisa?"

# Chapter Thirty-three

✂

THAT SHOCKED ME. A PART OF ME WANTED TO scream, "You mean, you don't know?" Or, "You're a worrier?" Or, "You have reason to think he might have?"

Instead, I took a deep breath. "What do you think?"

Tears erupted, and she started sobbing hard. "I don't know!" By now, every bit of her carefully applied makeup was gone. I'll say this for Eve, she cried like a Yankee. Her nose ran, her eye makeup melted, and she blubbered with abandon. "I-I-I'm not sure what to think. He offered to meet her at Enchanté because it was a public place where it would be harder for her to make a scene. See, until there's an opening at the Santé Center in Dallas, we've been seeing a marriage counselor together. The counselor suggested that Wynn meet Lisa in a public place to say good-bye.

Lisa'd been bugging him to go to Enchanté. Ironic, isn't it? They had anything but an enchanted evening. Once she realized it was the end, she started screaming at him. The maître d' asked them to leave."

I nodded. "I happened to drive by about then. I saw him and her arguing."

"You told the police that, right?"

"Yes. I hope you aren't going to ask me to lie for Wynn, because I won't."

She raised her hands and waved away my concern. "No, no. I wouldn't ask you to. What you're saying confirms what he told me happened."

"What did he do next? I mean, after they argued in the parking lot."

"He says she kept screaming. Finally, he gave up and started toward the hotel where we're staying. The Holiday Inn Express on the highway."

I nodded. We didn't do five-star hotels here in St. Elizabeth. Magnolia House would have been a much nicer place, but the Holiday Inn Express was brand new and clean. I could see why they chose it.

"But he didn't want to leave her on bad terms. The counselor told him he needed to tell her it was definitely over, no questions. So he went back hoping she'd settled down."

"Did he talk to her again?"

Eve shook her head emphatically, no. "Wynn couldn't find her. Her car was still there, in the municipal lot, but she wasn't around. He said he drove in circles, trying to spot her because she was wearing high heels and couldn't have gone far. Then he drove through the Snippets' parking lot."

That startled me. I'd been lucky not to run into him.

"Did he see anyone in the salon? Were there any lights on? It must have been near dark." I tried to be careful not to give away the fact that I had, indeed, been through the same lot. Of course, I had seen lights in the shop. Someone had been working in the back when I had driven through.

"I got the impression he saw someone or something because he wouldn't answer my questions. I mean, he danced around them. I got the idea there was more to it."

"So he isn't coming clean with you?" I asked.

She shook her head. "No. You know how it is. He lies very easily."

That was an understatement. "Let's think this through. If it wasn't Wynn, who might the killer be?" Rummaging through the mess on the desk, I found a pen and a legal pad. At the top of the first page, I wrote: *SUSPECTS.*

"There's you. Your mom."

I put down the pen. "Aw, come on, Eve."

"But you both had cause."

"Eve, in the South, when we want to get rid of a person, we don't kill 'em in a store. We brew oleander tea and poison them. Or we hit them over the head. Or shoot them and say it's a hunting accident. Whatever we do, we always clean up after ourselves. If my mama or I had killed Lisa, we would have dumped her body where the gators are. The Terhunes are naturally neat people. Good housekeepers. We don't cotton to messes. We sure wouldn't leave a corpse out in the open where it would stink up the place. Oh, and by the way, if we wanted to off good old Lisa, we have lots of friends who would have helped us do it discreetly."

Her mouth made a perfect "oh." "Are you teasing me?"

I smirked and picked the pen back up. "Halfway. I'll leave you to guess which parts are truth and which are lies. Now let's get back to that list. Who's on it now that the Terhunes aren't?"

"Carol Brockman is our accountant. She and Lisa hated each other. Someone was stealing from us. Carol thought it might be Lisa."

"Did you tell the police this?"

She shook her head. "They didn't ask me. That big offi-cer was asking the questions, and he acted like he already knew the answers."

"Hank Parker?"

"Um, yes."

"He's my ex-husband."

Her eyes widened. "Really? It's hard to imagine the two of you as a couple. You're so much more . . . sophisticated."

"Thanks. I think. Okay, continue. Who else could have killed Lisa? Who stood the most to gain?"

She shrugged and dabbed her nose. "Okay, Vinny Torelli, one of our stylists. Lisa seemed to pick on him, from what I've heard."

"Anyone else?"

"Honestly, I don't know. I would have to say that Lisa didn't get along particularly well with any member of our staff. Except for Corina Coffinas. But Corina gets along with everyone."

"Then why did you keep Lisa on?" I tore the top sheet off the pad, folded it neatly, and stuffed it into my pocket.

Eve rolled her eyes at me. Given the smeared mascara and liner, the gesture was oddly comical. "Do you know how hard it is to fire an employee these days? It's really, really difficult. Especially if she's been tomcatting around with your husband. I talked to Steven Clifford, our attor-ney, about the situation, and I thought he was going to have a heart attack. He says Lisa could have sued us for sexual harassment, wrongful dismissal, and a dozen other charges. The fact that she'd been a good employee for years would work against us in court. I swear, Grace Ann, it was like she changed when she moved here. Maybe it was being back in the same town where she grew up. She wanted to be an important person, and she was. Sort of. Until she acted like one."

I nodded. "I've heard her mother compared her to her sister, and Lisa got the short end of that stick."

"I've heard the same." Eve sighed. "Believe me, if I could have fired her and made her go away, I would have. But as it was, I was stuck with her. Sounds crude, but whoever killed her did me a big favor."

# Chapter Thirty-four

✂

AFTER THAT, EVE OPENED THE FILE CABINET AND withdrew the contract her attorney had drawn up and faxed over. She handed it to me.

"Take your time reading it," she said. "Not that there are any curve balls, but you should always know what you are signing. If you have any questions, feel free to consult your own legal counsel."

Everything was as she had promised, so I put my John Henry on the bottom line. After I handed it back to her, Eve showed me the security code again. I didn't tell her I had it memorized, and why. Holding my copy of the store key in my hand, I examined it carefully.

"In case you are wondering, no, there wasn't any sign of forced entry. Whoever killed Lisa either had a key or was invited in. No one broke into the building." Eve put a hand to her forehead and sighed. "I can't decide if that's good news or bad."

My new boss showed me where they kept the empty cash drawer, wrote down the combination to the small safe that held each day's starting allotment of cash, and walked me around the back office where Carol Brockman worked. From a drawer, Eve withdrew the appropriate tax forms I would need.

"The schedule has already been changed to reflect Lisa's absence," she said. "Supplies were ordered last week. There ought to be enough for a week or two. Of course, I'll be in and out. We can't leave town until . . ." She stopped talking and teared up.

"If I need help, who's the best person to answer my questions?"

"Carol can answer any questions about money, purchases, petty cash, and so on. I gave her a day off, so you won't see her until tomorrow. Suzee Gaylord is our senior stylist. Been with the company three years. She's not here today, or I'd introduce you, but you can ask her any questions on procedure."

I nodded and took a deep breath. "I'd like to hire Mom, Althea, Stella, and Rachel from our shop. Mom can do almost anything. Althea specializes in facials and treatments, but can do styling, although that's not her favorite service. Stella does nails and pedicures. Rachel is an all-around helper and a shampoo girl."

"That's up to you. As long as you make the numbers, you can hire anyone you want. Here are the projection sheets."

Pulling down a clipboard from a row of them, she handed it over to me. "See all the clipboards? Notice the labels. There's one for the scheduling, one for sales of products, one for total sales projections, and one for shrinkage. Just about everything you need to know is there on its own clipboard. If you don't mind, I need to check my e-mail while you look everything over."

At first I thought the revenue projection sheet must have been for the whole company. Or for all their stores in Georgia, the numbers were so high. But once I studied the sheet carefully, I could see this place was projected to make ten times the income we had at Violetta's. Best of all, it was on pace to do so!

Next I took down the scheduling clipboard. Working Mom, Althea, Stella, and Rachel in wouldn't be hard.

The shrinkage proved negligible. I wondered why Carol Brockman thought someone was stealing, so I looked over the cash register report more carefully. One day the till was over, and the next it was under. The amounts varied. Could it have been caused by making change sloppily? I'd have to ask Carol.

The amount of products sold surprised me. For Violetta's, retail products made up a small portion of our revenue. A quick look at these numbers told me that Snippets pumped the merchandise in and out. A second sheet explained why: incentive contests. For each one hundred dollars in product that employees sold, they got a twenty-dollar bonus. Neat!

All in all, the numbers looked to be in order. But somewhere, somehow, one of these reports might point to a reason for Lisa Butterworth's death.

Hank's policing manuals emphasized that the key to solving a murder was motive, means, and opportunity. It would be difficult to figure out who had had opportunity since the crime happened after regular business hours.

Means? I had no idea how Lisa had died. None. Hmmmm. The fish tank was involved, but how?

Motive? Okay, so she was disliked. Lots of people had enemies, but they were still walking around unharmed.

Eve was on the computer checking e-mails from the other salons. I glanced over her shoulder. She had fifty new e-mails. I couldn't imagine dealing with all those! She glanced up, which gave me an opening to ask, "Eve, I heard that Lisa also sold the client list from Peter Wassil over at Chez Pierre. Is that true? If so, Peter might be a suspect."

"Yes." She sighed. "But Peter had an attorney call Lisa. She gave back the list and deleted all the names from the computer."

Why hadn't I thought to do that? Hadn't Vonda suggested that to me? I wanted to pick up all those clipboards and whop myself up the side of the head.

"So Peter had no reason to want to see Lisa killed, right?"

She nodded and put a hand to her mouth. "No. I don't think so. Oh, I forgot to tell you. If you stay long enough, you get profit sharing."

"Profit sharing?"

"Uh-huh. We match what you put into your 401(k). Because Lisa was such a good manager—income- and expense-wise, not personality-wise—everyone in this salon was on pace to add a significant amount of revenue to their retirement plans."

"What do you call 'a significant amount'? I mean are we talking about enough to buy a case of whoopie pies? Or what?"

"An amount roughly equivalent to one-quarter of their yearly income."

I nearly fell off my chair. "So let me get this straight. Your employees are the best paid in the industry, you offer paid ongoing training with big-name stylists, medical benefits—"

"And dental."

"And dental. You offer paid vacations, bonus money for selling product, and profit sharing."

"Right. And remember, this salon was ahead of projections for hitting their profit-sharing goals, in part because of Lisa Butterworth."

I whistled through my teeth. "I'd kill for a job like this."

# Chapter Thirty-five

✂

"I HAVE ONE OTHER QUESTION. ONE THAT'S REALLY bugging me. As long as you are being candid, I might as well ask." We were, after all, alone in the salon, and I wanted to get this off my chest.

Her smile flickered, a tentative okay. Her hand froze on the mouse as she waited.

"Why are you really staying with Wynn? In this day and age, you could easily raise a child without a father. His behavior yesterday with the massage therapist was outrageous! Not to mention, he could get you sued for sexual harassment."

"I told you. I want my child to have a father."

"Gimme a break. Your dad is still alive. You are young. You could remarry. Wynn would always be a part of your child's life, but you shouldn't have to put up with this ongoing humiliation. No woman should!"

"Remarry? For my money, right? Look Grace Ann, take a close look. I wasn't blessed with stunning features. I'm not as pretty as you are. Even when I'm at my best, I'm what? A six? You're an eight or nine. I'm lucky to have found a guy like Wynn."

"That's a load of crap, and you know it. As for your looks, you aren't giving yourself enough credit. Besides, there are a few tricks you don't employ that you should. Which is sort of a shock, seeing as how you're in this industry."

She shook her head at me. "I would feel weird walking into one of my salons and letting someone I hired work on me."

I waved the paperwork she'd given me around. "I haven't handed over my employment contract yet. Or a W-2 form."

"What's that supposed to mean?"

"I don't officially work for you . . . yet. Go clean your face and let me give you a makeover."

"What? I don't have time for that."

"Sure you do. It's your job to be a walking, talking ad for Snippets." I pointed to the large framed picture of her that hung over the manager's desk. She'd signed it with a hearty, "Love to all of you at my newest Snippets!"

I made brushing-away gestures with my hands. "Now go. Wash your face. This won't take long. It'll give you a chance to see if I know my stuff or not."

To my vast relief, she giggled and walked away, coming back with a clean slate for me to work with.

"Come on," I said, beckoning her to one of the workstations. "Let's have a little fun."

Blinking rapidly, she said, "You won't do something silly, will you?"

"Nope. However, I'm going to start by trimming your bangs." And I whipped a cape over her shoulders. "Let me grab my scissors. You might want to take off your scarf."

"Oh, I'd rather not. It took me twenty minutes to arrange it right," she said, as I came back with the scissors. Her reflection startled me. I've never seen a more frightened client. "Relax. I'm only going to slightly angle your bangs," I said as I combed, measured, and trimmed her hair. "Right now with them straight across your forehead, they invite the eye to calculate the distance between your orbital sockets, which is a bit narrow."

"Don't I know it," she murmured.

I smoothed on foundation, but when I got to her neck, she flinched, pulling away from me. Her scarf shifted, revealing two long scratches on her throat. Obviously, she had hoped to hide them with her neck gear. Saying nothing seemed the wisest course.

"Next I want to pluck a few of the eyebrow hairs closest to your nose. That will also help with the illusion that there's more space between your eyes."

To her credit, she didn't flinch. When we were done, I led her over to the vast makeup display and encouraged her to sit.

"Adding a few false eyelashes only to the far outside edges of your eyes will elongate them, and again, draw the viewer's attention outward." After going through a drawer, I found a suitable pair of falsies, trimmed them, put on the glue, let it get tacky, and added them to her upper lids.

"Now we'll add foundation. Notice that when I finished, I also put a dab of lighter foundation on each side of the bridge of your nose. I ran a bit of highlighter up the bridge of your nose."

She sat perfectly still with her eyes closed.

"The eyeliner should be black for maximum wattage.

I'm extending it beyond the outer edges of your eyes. I'll go over it with brown, to soften the look. The shadow I'm applying is lighter at the bridge of your nose and darker at the outside edges. As for your brows, I'm extending them outward, too."

I could have been working on a sphinx, so quiet and still was she.

"Last of all, I'll add taupe pencil under the outer two-thirds of your lower lid."

I lined her lips and added a soft shade. "Okay, take a look."

Her mouth went slack. She stared at herself. "Wow. Wow. Wow."

"Is that your parrot imitation?"

She giggled. "I've never looked this good. I'm almost an eight."

"Even if you were a one, you wouldn't deserve a man who isn't faithful."

With a sigh, she nodded. "The real reason I stay married? The one I'd never say out loud? My dad begged me not to marry Wynn. Daddy told me, 'I see how he is with other women. He will never be true to you.' But I ignored my father. Usually, I do whatever Daddy says. I've always been a daddy's girl. The one time I chose to rebel, and see what happened?"

"Rebellion. I totally get that. My mother's nickname for me when I was growing up was Rebel." I put back the brushes and tossed the cotton tips I'd used. "Did you see where I set the employment papers?"

"Absolutely. I'll go fax them to our attorney. Is there a paper I can sign to hire you as a friend?" Her lower lip trembled.

"Nope. That's a promise written on our hearts, one letter at a time."

# Chapter Thirty-six

MOST OF THE STAFF WERE AT THEIR STATIONS AND ready to go by eight forty-five, and we opened at nine. Although this salon wasn't cozy like Violetta's, I had to admit that the layout was superb, with a great flow. Each stylist had a station designed so that all the tools were within easy reach. The sinks were new, and the seats tilted perfectly at the touch of a button. Whereas we bumped into each other a lot at Violetta's, there was adequate space for walking around, but not an inch of waste.

"Everyone!" Eve clapped her hands. "Gather around, please!"

The stylists did as directed. If they looked a bit wary, who could blame them after hearing that their boss had been murdered. I studied the expressions on their faces.

While they seemed respectful of Eve, they didn't seem cowed or uncomfortable.

"As you all know, we mourn the passing of Lisa Butterworth. She did an admirable job getting this place up and running and making a profit. However, her loss means the salon needed a new manager. I am honored to introduce Grace Ann Terhune to you. She's—"

"The best overall stylist I ever trained," said a voice from behind us.

Wynn sauntered over until he stood at his wife's side. "I trained stylists for Vidal Sassoon for nearly five years. I must have seen three hundred or more come through. Not one of them held a candle to Grace Ann. She should be teaching master classes in cutting in New York. Or coloring in LA. But she's here and we're lucky to have her." With that, he led applause.

I stepped forward, keenly aware of his eyes on me. With a slight nod of my head, I said, "Look, y'all, I can't imagine what you're feeling, having lost Lisa in such a violent way. I am truly, deeply sorry about that. If I can do anything at all to make you feel better, don't hesitate to ask. And if you'd like, I was thinking that this coming Sunday we could have a moment of silence and light candles in her memory before the salon opens. I'll bring a smudge stick, too. That's supposed to dispel any bad energy. What do you think?"

Shocked expressions all around changed to tentative, "Hmm. Maybe she's okay."

I smiled. "I'll be by to say 'hey' to each of you. I'm looking forward to getting to know you. Now have a good day."

"Moment of silence on Sunday?" Eve whispered in my ear after the group dispersed. "That was inspired."

"Hey, this is the South." I cupped my hand over my mouth and whispered, "We like our comforting traditions."

With that, I straightened and caught Wynn's eye. He held out his arms to me for a hug.

What could I do? I stepped into his embrace, all the time thinking what a lying sack of horse crap he was.

"You're looking fantastic," he said. I narrowly avoided a mouth-to-mouth kiss.

"I heard your good news. Congratulations," I said, eager to put things on the right track. I was onto his tricks. His easy familiarity was the first step along the path to falling for Wynn.

He grinned. When that man smiled, tectonic plates shifted. I mean, he had this half grin that warmed the hardest hearts, unfortunately, because it often got him out of the trouble he had caused.

"You aren't still mad at me, are you?" His smile was easy, uncomplicated.

"Yes, as a matter of fact I am. I think you are a low-down, no-account, sleezy SOB, but I think your wife is an angel. She deserves better, and I mean that."

Eve's eyes teared up. "Thanks, Grace Ann. That's awfully kind of you."

"You're welcome."

"Hey," said Wynn, "I know I need help. Didn't I tell you I'd get it? Huh, Eve? Come on, Grace Ann. That was a long time ago. Can't we be friends?"

As he tried to hug me, I moved away, but not before my elbow collided with the lump under his arm. "Whoa! When did you start carrying a gun?"

"Since we were in New York and some creep tried to rob us. He was after Eve's ring," Wynn said, with a nod to the five-carat sparkler on Eve's finger. "I have to protect my wife."

"Start by protecting her from your bad behavior, buster."

"She's right, Wynn. You're the one who's hurting me now." she said, through clenched teeth.

"Ah, hon," he whined.

Eve shook her head. "Let's all go in the back. I get tired of providing free entertainment for my staff."

Once we'd moved from salon floor to private area, Eve turned on Wynn, crossing her arms over her chest and glaring at him. "Where were you?"

"Not my fault," he muttered. "That guy from the Georgia Bureau of Investigation came by the hotel and hauled me in again, right after I dropped you off here. I was on the treadmill in the workout room when he flashed his badge. The guy next to me missed a step and went flying into the wall."

Sinking down into a chair, Wynn groaned. "I thought I'd go nuts inside that police station. The walls closed in on me. I can't stand being cooped up. I couldn't stand being in the darn car! That Crown Vic he drives doesn't have any handles in the back on the passenger doors."

Eve said to me, "I told you he has claustrophobia. Can't stand elevators."

A memory surfaced of a visit we had made to a department store in Atlanta. Wynn insisted on taking the escalator even though our hands were full with packages.

"What did he ask you? Are you a suspect? You should have called me. I could still get Steven to fly down." Eve rocked a bit unsteadily on her feet. I pulled up a chair behind her knees and guided her to a seated position. She turned her face to me and explained, "Steven Clifford is our corporate attorney."

I remembered her telling me that earlier.

"I can't tell what the dude was thinking." Wynn flipped his palms up to his wife in a gesture of defeat. "The security cameras caught me cruising around the lot the night

Lisa died. He wants to know if there was anyone else on the premises."

Of course there had been. I'd seen a light on through the back window, and a person hunched over a desk. The desk belonging to Carol Brockman, actually. Thinking back to that evening and quickly glancing around, I realized this desk was not in line of sight of the window.

"Was there anyone else here? Maybe that's our killer," Eve asked, in a breathless, hurried voice.

"Yeah."

"Who?"

He shuffled his feet. "I don't want—"

"Tell me! I'm tired of playing games with you. Were you meeting someone? Another woman? Here? Was it Paula Benson, the massage therapist Grace Ann sent home yesterday?"

Wynn pulled his chair closer to Eve's, but he kept his gaze on the floor, purposely not meeting her eyes. "No, Paula wasn't here, but she was supposed to meet me here. I was going to give her money."

"What!" Eve's hazel eyes flashed bright with anger.

"Calm down. I knew she and I had to break it off, and I was afraid she'd come back on us for, you know, harassment. Or something. So I asked her to meet me here. I was going to say good-bye and give her some money to make her life easier. That's what we were doing yesterday in the massage room. Honest! I gave her two thousand dollars."

Eve's face turned alternately scarlet with rage and white with shock. Boy, was she mad. "Did it occur to you that giving an employee cash on the side might look incriminating? Did you talk to Steven Clifford first? We keep him on retainer. All you had to do was dial him up!"

"I didn't want it to get back to you."

"Everything gets back to me! That's the nature of my job!"

"Well, this time I wanted to take care of it myself!" He sounded like an eleven-year-old boy who tried to make his own breakfast and left a trail of broken eggs in the kitchen.

"Excuse me," I interrupted. "But did you meet her here? Paula Benson? I happen to know there was a person here inside the building shortly after you and Lisa fought. Was Paula here waiting for you?"

A puzzled expression preceded his slow reply. "No. I mean, I don't know. I drove away because I was so mad at Lisa. But I was almost to the hotel when I remembered about Paula, and how she expected me, so I drove back here."

"You told me you headed back because you wanted to make it clear to Lisa that it was over!" Eve put her fists on her hips.

"Well, that, too, but mainly, I had the money to give Paula. But she wasn't here. The only car in the lot belonged to that other woman. What's her name? The accountant."

# Chapter Thirty-seven

I ITCHED TO TELL ALL THIS TO MARSH AND LET HIM follow up. Last night I'd entered his personal cell phone number in my phone's directory. When I had a break, I'd text message him and ask if we could talk.

Who are you fooling, Grace Ann? You're hot on the guy!

So hot that I took a trip to the ladies' room to splash cold water on my face.

While I was in the stall, two sets of shoes came into the stalls adjacent to mine. "What do you think of her?" said the female voice to my immediate left. Her English was slightly accented. Corina was the speaker; I was sure of it.

"Country hick. What can she know?" said the stall two over.

"Oh, Taffy, you slay me. What do you think Suzee's

going to do when she hears about this? It should have been her job, you know. She was hoping for a promotion."

A toilet flushed. I lost part of the next sentence, but Taffy responded with, ". . . she thought she was home free now that Lisa is gone."

"Yeah, well, she's not going to be happy when she sees that Miss Georgia Peach is now her boss. Is it true she had a fling with Wynn way back when? I mean, he sure made a big deal of how good she was. Too much, if you ask me," said Corina.

Taffy laughed. "Bet she can't do hair for love nor money."

Another toilet flushed. "We'll see," said the other girl. "Let's give her a chance."

I gave them a few minutes to make an exit before I came out of my stall. Their conversation hadn't surprised me. Of course they'd want to see whether I was any good. I would, too, if I worked here.

Then it dawned on me: Maybe Suzee bumped off Lisa. If Suzee was in line for Lisa's job, why not hurry the process?

With shaking hands, I text messaged Marsh: *Could we meet for lunch? Interesting stuff to tell you about Lisa.*

The phone vibrated with a response before I finished drying my hands.

*Sure. Angelini's at one?* said the text.

*See you!* I messaged back.

All salons use a system of "ups," which means that stylists take turns being assigned new customers who are walk-ins, that is, who don't have an appointment with a regular hairdresser. As manager, my "up" would be the last on the list, because the goal was to build the business of the staff.

There are managers who see this rotating system of assignments as a great excuse to sit on their butts in the back room and eat donuts, or smoke cigarettes, or generally waste their time. Smart managers walk from chair to chair, greeting the clients and being available for consults. That's what I did.

"She wants her hair short," said Taffy, as I approached her chair and her client, a middle-aged woman with a very, very long face and hair down to her waist. The hair, while long, did nothing for her. Nothing at all. The weight of the hair pulled down her features, making her look older than she probably was. A lot of people get so caught up in the long-hair-is-sexy mode of thinking that they don't ask themselves, "Yes, but is long hair sexy on me?"

Taffy was obviously waiting for me to do something. I lifted the woman's hair and tried a few rearrangements to get a sense of what might work for her. Taffy glowered at me. "We can't cut more than two inches off a client's hair without an approval form. The acting manager has to sign off."

"I'll be right back." Taffy's tone had embarrassed me and a scalding heat warmed my face. Although I knew there'd be a learning curve, I had hoped my staff would be gracious as I scaled that mountain.

In the back room, Eve was hunched over paperwork while Wynn played a game on the computer.

"Excuse me. We have a client with long hair. I was told we need an approval form."

"Let me handle this," said Wynn, opening the file cabinet, withdrawing a form, and leading the way to the floor.

"Hey, I'm Wynn Goodman." He gave the woman a heart-stopping smile. "And you are?"

"Jeanette Ricker."

"Glad to meet you, Jeanette. What lovely hair you have!"

The woman preened, running her fingers through her mane, flipping it, and giving him a coy expression. "I think it's too long. Don't you?"

"I don't know. It's lovely. You're so pretty that you could wear it short or long." Wynn stepped behind the chair and went through the same contortions I had with her hair. "But I think shoulder length would be more flattering. You could still put it in a ponytail, or updo, and it would still be totally hot . . ."

The woman in the chair melted. Wynn stroked her hair as if she were a prized mare. The gesture brought back memories.

I walked away, trying to compose myself. Now I knew about the approval form. I would still have to prove myself to these people. I just wasn't sure how.

# Chapter Thirty-eight

✂

TAFFY SANDERS AND I STOOD OVER A SIX-YEAR-OLD who had butchered her hair. The small figure in the chair blinked sadly and said, "I was a-trying to be bootiful."

Her mother said, "I'm so mad I could spit. How could she have done that? Mandy Sue, I'm going to paddle your fanny good when I get you home."

I turned to the woman and smiled. "This happens every day of the year. Trust me. We can fix it. She'll look fine, and I bet she'll never do it again, will you, Mandy Sue?"

The tiny tot shook her head. "Never. Not ever."

To Taffy I said, "I think if you part her hair on the other side, the longer hair will cover the nearly bald spot."

"Great idea." Taffy nodded. "Come on, young lady. Let's

take you over to a sink so I can wash your hair. Which do you like best, strawberries or mango?"

"Berries."

"Good. We have a shampoo that smells like fresh berries."

I escorted her mother to the waiting area and showed her how to make herself a caramel latte. Once the mom had a copy of *Vogue* in one hand and the drink in the other, she settled down. "Kids are such a trial. Think twice before you have one!"

I gritted my teeth. Why did people say that? A child was a blessing. I could understand getting frustrated, but over a haircut? How ridiculous was that? Every hair follicle in my head screamed out, "I'd like to slap you silly," but instead, I smiled and said, "I'm sure you don't mean that. You two are having a bad day. That's all."

The woman snorted. "My husband had to have his little girl. We have three boys, but he wanted to keep trying."

It got harder to keep my tongue. "Uh-huh, and she'll be a treasure to you in your old age. What's that saying? A boy is a son 'til he takes a wife, but a girl is a daughter for all of her life?"

With that, the woman's face changed. "Isn't that the truth? I've been my mama's caretaker for as long as I can remember. My little Mandy Sue *is* a good girl."

"I'm sure she is." With that, I left her, intending to speak to Taffy to praise her for her calm manner with the harried mom.

But I didn't get that far. I stepped out of the waiting room, deep in thought, and walked right into Hank's arms.

"Grace Ann, sugar, I hope you aren't upset about that article in the paper." Grabbing the back of my head, he pulled my mouth toward his and tried to French kiss me, but I wrestled myself free.

Officer Qualls stood behind him, glaring at both of us.

"Don't you ever touch me again!" I snapped at Hank.

"Special Agent Dillon told me I had to."

Officer Qualls stepped up. "Respectfully, he told you to apologize, not to have personal contact."

"Same-o, same-o. You aren't going to sue the department, are you? Grace Ann, you know how much this case means to me. I was the first responder! Lisa Butterworth was floating in that tank, looking like one of them mermaids, when I found her. This is my case! He's trying to take it away from me."

"So she drowned, right?" Since Hank was being chatty, I figured I might as well take advantage of him running his mouth.

"No, sirree, bobtail. I mean, kinda. See she'd been smacked right between the eyes with something. She'd obviously been standing on one of them step stools. The blow knocked her backward into the tank. She was probably unconscious when she dove in, and that's how she drowned. Or was electrocuted. Hard to know which."

Officer Qualls elbowed Hank. "Sir! You shouldn't be talking—"

"Don't make no never mind. She's my wife."

"No, I'm not," I said. "I've been happily divorced from you for over three years."

Lisa had drowned? The news hadn't mentioned how she died, only that she had. How unusual was that? A person drowning in a fish tank? And then electrocuted?

I rubbed my chin. "So it could have been an accident."

"Heck, yes, it could have been an accident. You want to confess? You don't have a record, Grace Ann. I bet Dooley could get you off. I'd come visit you. We could have conjugal rights." His fist bracketed his hips as he gave it a bit of Elvis action.

I groaned.

There are times when I truly wonder what sort of idiot I must have been to marry Hank. This was one of them. Scenes flashed through my mind: My mother begging me not to do it. My sister telling me I was a dope. Vonda stomping her foot and saying, "Are you nuts?" And Althea shaking her head and muttering, "You are in for a world of sorrow."

Why hadn't I listened to them? Well, there was that baby thing. That desire to have a child. But if I was really, totally honest with myself, Eve Sebastiani and I wore the same stupid badge of dishonor. We both had been determined to prove other people wrong. Eve married Wynn to prove to her father that he was wrong. I married Hank because I wanted to prove Mom, Alice Rose, Vonda, and Althea wrong.

I suddenly felt even closer to my new boss.

"Hank? Hear me and listen up good: I did not kill Lisa Butterworth. Nor did I have a fight with her here in the salon. Got it? If you show your face in this place one more time, I'll swear out a restraining order."

"But this here's a crime scene," he pouted.

"Was a crime scene. You've released it. Now get out. And don't come back."

"But Agent Dillon said I had to apologize. Do you accept my apology? Say you do, Grace Ann, so I can get him off my back!" Hank whined.

"Hank, if you crawled to me on your knees, if you begged me most sincerely, if you shouted it from the Smoky Mountains, I would still not accept your apology. You know why?" I could feel everyone staring at me. All our customers, Corina at the front desk, and Officer Qualls.

I dropped my voice to a whisper. "Because you aren't truly sorry. You're only sorry you got caught."

"That's from *Gone with the Wind*, isn't it?" He frowned.

"Get. Out. Now." I pointed to the door.

Officer Qualls took him by the arm and dragged him away.

# Chapter Thirty-nine

AS THE OFFICERS WALKED OUT, IN CLOMPED A MAN wearing a khaki shirt and a utility belt. He moved past me with purpose, paused in the middle of the salon, and did a tight circle. Corina must have hit a button on the phone at the reception desk, because Eve walked out quickly, her face closed and solemn. She spoke to the man in low tones and shook his hand.

I figured she'd call me over if she wanted to include me.

Meanwhile, one look at the clock caused me to realize that Vinny needed help adding perm rods to an older woman's hair. The woman had been a walk-in, with only a scant hour to spare, but she had demanded a perm. By dividing the labor, we could get to the processing portion of her visit faster. A thin young man with acne scars and long fingers,

Vinny moved like a frightened rabbit, in jerky start-and-stop motion. Growing up in a salon, I learned to wrap perm rods before I was ten. Once I started helping him, he shot me a grateful expression, particularly when he saw how fast my hands moved.

Eve and the man in khaki moved over to the gaping empty spot where the fish tank once stood. The construction was ingenious. The stylists' area was one step up, on a platform with great lights that made everyone appear healthy, unlike most salons, where they use cheap bulbs. The shampoo sinks, dryers, and waiting area were a step down on the lower level. The tank had formerly divided the two levels up to waist high.

"I told her I needed to frame it in, to bring the wall down to meet the tank. But Miss Butterworth insisted on having it lower like this, and open."

Eve's face hardened. "That's not the spec I approved."

The man in khaki shook his head. "I know! I told her that. I showed her your initials, but she didn't want to spend the extra for a half wall coming down over the tank. She wanted it open and airy, and those are her words. I explained to her there was a safety problem. How the hood and light on the aquarium weren't really enough to keep anything out. Anyone out, either. Told her the light fixture in the hood would get wet. Reminded her that electricity and water do not mix." He stopped, rubbed his face hard, and I could see his hand trembling. "She said, 'You are working for me. I can fire you anytime I want.'"

He wiped his face on his sleeve. "I can't believe she died there! I feel like it's all my fault, but, ma'am, I begged her. I even have this in writing 'cause I told her I didn't want to be responsible." Digging in his back pocket, he unfolded a tired sheet of paper and handed it to Eve. "I told her it would never pass code, but she only laughed and said, 'My uncle is on the building inspections committee. Trust me, it'll pass.' You know it did, or I would have come back and done it my way."

"If this had been done according to our specs, she would still be alive." Eve sounded both angry and resigned. "When Suzee found her, she was facedown in the water! You were right about one thing: That flimsy hood didn't stop her when she took a nosedive."

Eve's voice rose to such a pitch that stylists turned to stare. She shook her head and huffed. "Mr. Jasper, we need to talk about this in private. Please come with me back to my office."

Suzee Gaylord found Lisa? Suzee who wanted a promotion? Wasn't that convenient?

Vinny Torelli walked by, and I recognized the customer with him as Mrs. Vernon Althorp. I knew the woman because Mom banned her from Violetta's after a quick confab with Peter Wassil at Chez Pierre. Seemed that Mrs. Althorp was a scam artist. She sat through two haircuts at our salon—and at his—before demanding her money back. Before I did anything, however, I wanted proof the woman was up to her old tricks.

"Corina? Could you pull up the records for Mrs. Althorp, please?"

"Certainly."

"What does this code mean?" I pointed to a 666 digit on the screen.

Corina leaned close and whispered, "Means she's a demon. We couldn't please her. See? We gave her a refund all three times she's visited."

"Thanks. That's what I needed to know."

I walked over to where Vinny Torelli was running a comb through Mrs. Althorp's auburn hair.

"Excuse me."

Vinny's eyes went wide as he stuttered, "Y-Y-Yes?" His skittish expression told me he expected to be chastised. Fingering his tie, he smoothed it into his vest, and then ran his palms down the seams of his black jeans.

"You're fine. Actually, I wanted to speak to Mrs. Althorp. You remember me, don't you, ma'am? My mother is Violetta Terhune, the owner of Violetta's."

Mrs. Althorp's double chins waggled as she squirmed in her chair. "Uh, yes. Vaguely."

"Ma'am, let's see if I can refresh your memory. You visited Violetta's twice, and each time, after saying you were delighted with your service, the next day you returned and asked for your check back. Which is the same scam you pulled on Chez Pierre, isn't it?"

Her mouth turned dour and she glared at me. "What of it? It's not my fault those stylists weren't very good."

"Hmm. I printed out the records for your visits here. I see you've had three washes, three colorings, three cuts, and three styles. Each time, you left saying you were delighted but you returned the next day and complained."

Mrs. Althorp whined to Vinny. "Who's she? I want to talk to your manager!"

Vinny stepped back from the chair, his fingers moving nervously to his tie. "Ma'am, she's the boss."

"That's right. I'm the person in charge. Mrs. Althorp, I suggest you take your business elsewhere. I doubt anyone here can make you happy."

"Well, I never!" She grabbed her purse, stuck it under her arm, and stood up. "Then I'll just have to find another stylist right here in this salon."

I shook my head. "No, ma'am. I believe you misunderstood. I'm asking you to leave. If none of our stylists have been able to satisfy you in your last three visits, I doubt we can make you happy now."

With a rumble like approaching thunder, Mrs. Althorp tore off her cape and stomped her way out of Snippets. Vinny and I watched her go. We didn't talk to each other until after the heavy woman slammed our front door shut.

"Thanks, Grace Ann. I mean, I think I should say thanks. I get another 'up,' right?"

I laughed. "Absolutely. Since she won't be wasting your time, you can probably squeeze in two clients in the space she would have taken."

"I hate customers like that. After I work with one of them, I'm down in the dumps the whole next week."

Putting a hand on his shoulder, I said, "Vinny, you can't let one customer do that to you. Ever. It's only hair. It'll grow back. Whether you've done a great job or not will always be subjective. I know you know that, but if the creeping doubts get to you, come find me and we'll talk."

Tilting his head slightly, he nodded. "Thanks, Grace Ann. I guess working with Lisa sort of tore down my confidence. She specialized in finding fault and assigning blame. After a while, that grates on you, you know? I would go home at night feeling like a whipped pup."

That troubled me. "You can't do your best work if you are scared. I'm sorry that Lisa treated you that way."

Putting the cape Mrs. Althorp had thrown on the floor into the dirty linens basket, he went suddenly silent. I waited. Was he okay? I hoped so.

He studied me thoughtfully. "I guess I'm ready for that next up."

"You bet. One's coming through the door right now." With a nod at the young man who needed a haircut, I gave Vinnie's shoulder a light punch. "Go, get 'em, tiger."

# Chapter Forty

BY QUARTER 'TIL ONE, I'D CONVINCED THE TWO stylists on the floor and the receptionist that I had some redeeming value. Vinny smiled eagerly at me as I walked past. So did Taffy, who must have shared her view with Corina Coffinas, because the other young woman seemed to relax a bit in my presence. Corina had to have been the person talking with Taffy in the john. Taffy was a good stylist, but she didn't have the wealth of experience that I had, and that was slowly becoming evident.

With each passing hour, I grew more and more confident. I could handle this job. So I was in a particularly good mood when I left for lunch, walked down the street, and saw Marsh waiting for me on the sidewalk outside of Angelini's. His tan slacks fit perfectly, and his Oxford cloth shirt was a sky blue that brought out the color of his navy eyes. As usual, he wore a silk tie in a conservative pattern. For the most part, he could double as a successful business-man, except for that bulge under one arm, and a certain don't-mess-with-me way he had of holding himself.

"You look nice. How's your job hunt coming?" he said.

"I am now gainfully employed."

He gave a low whistle. "That was fast."

"In fact, I'll treat."

"No, you don't. My mother would roll over in her grave."

"I insist. I want to celebrate, and I also want to thank you for helping me land a new position."

Finally, he shrugged. "If you insist. But don't expect to make a habit of this. I hate having my manhood threat-ened."

I laughed. "Okay."

Once we were seated, we ordered quickly so I could get back. I assumed he would have limited time to eat also.

"Now tell me all about it. Where are you working?" The corners of his eyes crinkled as he smiled. I never noticed it before, but there was a tiny scar in his left eyebrow.

I ignored the hum starting in my body and took a big sip of cold water to keep myself calm. "Snippets. Eve Sebas-tiani Goodman hired me to take Lisa Butterworth's place."

"What?" his whole demeanor changed. "Grace Ann, you can't do that!"

"Shhh," I warned him. People had turned to stare. "What are you talking about? Of course, I can do that. I can take a job anywhere I want."

"Not when there's a killer loose. Not when the murderer is probably one of their staff. You can't work there! It's dangerous! You could get killed!"

Whoa. Where was this coming from? Mr. Calm, Cool, and Collected seemed totally freaked.

"I could get killed? How? There are always people there at any given time. If your reasoning follows, all of them could die, too, so aren't you going overboard?"

He sputtered, grabbed his glass of water, and downed it in two gulps. "But we haven't apprehended the murderer."

"It's not like I'm going to drown in the fish tank. Or get electrocuted."

"H-How did you know about that? It's supposed to be kept quiet. Did that idiot of an ex-husband tell you about where we found her body? And, yes, she drowned, but she drowned after being smacked in the forehead. When she fell off the step stool, she crashed right through the hood and light contraption. Getting hit in the head could happen to anyone, including you, whether the fish tank is rein-stalled or not! Oh, crap," he moaned and put his head in his hands. "I can't believe I told you all that."

"Not to worry. Hank already spilled those beans. He and Officer Qualls came in so he could apologize. Instead he grabbed me and tried to ram his tongue down my throat. Your idea?"

Marsh snorted so angrily he sounded like a bull ready to charge. "When I get ahold of him . . . Look, I told him to apologize. That's the least he owes you. I wonder how he knew where to find you? I thought he'd call you on the phone."

"Probably talked to my mother." As soon as I said it, I knew that wasn't likely. Mom was too miffed at him to tell him where I was. "Or my sister. Maybe he's been following me around. Point being, I don't want to talk to him. Ever. So please forget about the apology, at least in person. I don't want Hank anywhere close to me."

Now Marsh turned red, then white, then red again. "I'll see to it he doesn't bother you again. Did he at least apologize?"

"After he accused me of murdering Lisa. Again. In front of customers."

Marsh groaned. "I need a drink."

I signaled the waiter. "Two glasses of Pinot Grigio," I said to the man in black, and then turning to Marsh, I added, "I shouldn't have a glass of wine, but seeing how this day is going, I think I will. Here's hoping I don't have to cut any hair this afternoon."

"You can't do this," he hissed that last word. "It's too dangerous for you to work in that salon. Right after lunch, I'm going to march you back to that salon and stand there while you quit."

"*What?* You are not doing any such thing! You're not my boss. You're not my boyfriend. Maybe you can treat Polly that way—"

"Polly?"

"Did you think I wouldn't find out? Or that I wouldn't care that you're married?"

"Married! That's what this is all about? My wife?"

By now every head in the restaurant had turned to watch the fireworks at our table. The waiter brought two glasses of wine, eyed us nervously, set them down, and backed away. I grabbed mine and downed it as if it were Gatorade.

When I finished, Marsh's eyes were big as bread plates. I set down my wineglass and said, "I'm done here."

I scooted out my chair, got unsteadily to my feet, and proceeded to flounce out. Flouncing, by the way, is a much-admired Southern art form. Especially when flouncing out of a restaurant. To flounce, one must first push back from the table and then stand and toss the napkin onto the chair. This is the Southern belle equivalent of throwing down the gauntlet. Then, when all eyes are on you, you flip back your head so your hair whirls just so. And finally, you stomp off.

I'm not much at crying, but I'm a world champion flouncer.

I could feel Marsh's eyes burning holes through my back, so halfway to the front door, I executed a perfect "flounce with a twist," the much-vaunted "pseudo-flounce," a move admired by many but perfected by few. I stopped, did an about-face, marched back to the table, and said, "Since being macho is so all-fired important to you, you can pay for lunch!"

The crowd gave me a perfect ten.

# Chapter Forty-one

ON MY WAY BACK TO THE SALON, I CHECKED MY phone messages. LaReesa had texted a quick message: *Call me ASAP.*

So I did.

"Girlfriend, how goes it?" her low voice always bordered on a chuckle.

"Not so good, but I'm on my way back to work right now, so I can't really bend your ear. Can I get you caught up later?"

"Got it. Let me just give you the down and dirty. You know I'm on that hairstylists' loop? Lisa Butterworth was on it, too, and she sent out a blast right before she died that she was expecting."

"Expecting what?"

"Duh. A baby."

I stopped walking to get my balance. The glass of wine on an empty stomach caused my head to spin. Surely I misunderstood. "Baby?"

"That's right."

"Oh, boy."

"I don't think she knew if it was a boy or a girl."

I didn't correct her misimpression. "Uh, I'll get back to you, LaReesa. Thanks so much."

Either her news or my empty stomach or both were causing me to feel sick.

Walk-Inn Foods to the rescue. I decided to duck in there, grab a sandwich, wash it down with a Coke, and go back to the salon. As I stood in line, I wondered if Wynn was capable of murder. He was a liar and a cheat, but—and this seemed like a silly conclusion given those other adjectives—he wasn't a bad person. I couldn't imagine him getting violent. On the other hand, he never had so much to lose as he did now.

Petey Schultz took a spot in line behind me. Under his arms, he had two bags of cat litter and a case of beer. On his left cheek, he sported a big Band-Aid surrounded by an ugly crop of zits.

"How's that parakeet doing?" he asked. Glancing down at the litter under his arm, he added sheepishly, "Ran out at the store."

I told him about Marsh clipping Sam's wings. Reciting the story increased the sharp ache in my throat. Why were all the good men taken?

"That's sick, I mean, wicked righteous. I mean, clipping his wings was the right thing to do if you don't want him getting out. There are parakeets who escape every year."

"They die?" Our winters weren't horrible, but we did,

on occasion, get down to the midforties in December and January.

"Not always. There's actually a type of bird, the monk parakeet, that's illegal to bring into the state because they are likely to compete with native birds for food."

"Is my bird a monk parakeet?"

"No, yours is the regular Australia budgie. There've also been reports of a flock of feral budgies that live along the coast of Florida, and I once heard about a flock in Illinois. They wintered over in a farmer's barn."

I smiled at Petey. "That's fascinating." Glancing at his beer, I added, "You having a party?"

He blushed. "Sort of. A going-away party."

"For a friend?"

"Naw, for me." Moving close to my ear, he whispered, "I got my bonus coming in a couple of days. Figured I should split while I could."

"I understand. I wanted to leave St. Elizabeth when I was your age, but I came back."

"Leaving might be best thing for me." His look grew pensive. "Definitely."

The clerk motioned that he was ready to ring up my goods. Mindful of the booze on my breath, I added a pack of spearmint gum to my lunch, paid the man, and told Petey good-bye. "Safe travels," I said.

For a moment, I thought he might burst into tears. "Yeah, it's kinda too late for that."

# Chapter Forty-two

DESPITE THE FACT I WENT BACK TO THE SALON feeling unsettled and upset with Marsh, the rest of the afternoon went by quickly. Since I knew the beauty-treatment business, I thought it best to learn how Snippets ran their salons. So I decided that working with Corina at the front desk would give me the best overview. My goal was to see how she did the scheduling, who was busy, who wasn't, and how fast each stylist worked.

Several familiar faces from Violetta's showed up for services. A couple had the good grace to look embarrassed about their defection. A few were so clueless, they acted confused. One woman even said, "Grace Ann, nice to see you, as always," as if I had worked at Snippets my whole life!

I did my best to smooth over any sense of unease. Changing a hairstylist can be as unsettling as getting a divorce. Your stylist often knows every intimate detail of your life, occasionally even more than a spouse does. I realized that our "old" Violetta's customers might think I'd hold their defection against them. I tried hard not to, because I knew that if I let the customers know how betrayed I felt, they would never come back to Violetta's. My fingers were crossed that the insurance adjuster might give Mom good news, and we could reopen the shop. It was one thing for Mom to decide she was tired of styling hair, and another for her to be forced out of business.

Besides the regulars from Violetta's, there were a lot of customers I'd never seen. Eve came up to where I was sitting at the front counter. "What do you think? What impressions do you have of this salon? I really want to know."

"Your clientele includes a lot of our old customers, but you also do a big business with younger, hipper women, and businessmen in suits," I said.

"The building and the décor sets the tone for the salon. As adorable as your Victorian house is, I don't think it did you any favors when it came to attracting a younger generation of clients. Or businessmen. The vibe was wrong for them. Consequently, you didn't even get a chance at their business, except if they'd been coming to you for years—or a loved one dragged them in. Unfortunately, people can't always tell whether they've had a great cut or not, especially at first, but they can tell if they like the ambiance." Eve spoke without a trace of unkindness. Nor was she being judgmental. The woman knew the hair business— and I was quickly realizing I could learn a lot from her.

She was right about our quaint Victorian house, although I hated to admit it. I had also noticed all the small creature comforts that Snippets offered, small indulgences that made a visit here pleasurable: the free hot drinks and ice tea bar, the precisely adjustable water temperature in the rinse sinks, the comfortable chairs in the waiting area, the up-to-date magazines, the extensive makeup bar, the free samples that were generously given to customers, and the terrific lights that made people look good. There was even a special type of flooring that made standing on your feet easier on your joints. That benefited both the customers and the stylists. The list of amenities could go on and on. I couldn't wait to get Mom and Althea here and give them a tour.

"I've met almost all your staff," I said, "except for Suzee Gaylord. Is she coming in later? I haven't memorized the schedule yet."

Eve shook her head. "I gave Suzee the day off. As you can imagine, she was very upset. I asked if she wanted to come back, but she told me she did. But I figured a vacation day with pay couldn't hurt. She has a six-year-old, and I know her time with her daughter is precious. Let's go in back."

Once we were in the cozy niche that served as an office, Eve's shoulders drooped. "Suzee is the one who found Lisa's body."

"You're kidding!" I acted surprised. "Poor thing."

"Yes. Suzee's been angling for a promotion for six months, so she's been coming in early and leaving late. That's how she happened to get here before me or Carol— and how she happened to discover . . . the body." Eve picked up a pen and doodled on a piece of scrap paper.

I waited.

After a bit, Eve started again. "Suzee and Lisa used to be good friends, but Lisa gradually started abusing the friendship by dumping all her grunt work on Suzee. Suzee didn't quit because she really needs this job."

"Grunt work?"

"Dealing with angry customers. Handling scheduling problems. Taking inventory."

"Are you suggesting that Suzee might have been involved in Lisa's death?"

Eve quickly shook her head. "No. I mean, I don't know! Suzee is totally devoted to our chain. She came to us as a single mom fresh out of beauty school with no experience, and now she has a well-paid career. I can't imagine her ever doing anything that would reflect badly on Snippets. In fact, Suzee is the one who told me that she thought Lisa had stolen your customer list. She also told me that Lisa was purposefully undercutting your prices so she could run you out of business. Or at least that's what Suzee suspected."

"That's true. I mean, everything we did, this salon offered for a lot less. We had customers who were furious with us. They thought we were gouging them."

"That's definitely not our corporate policy. Yes, we offer introductory rates on a client's first cut or style, but we don't try to drastically undercut our competition! That's just stupid! There's no point to it."

I told her about Mrs. Everly, and how she'd accused my mother of ripping her off.

Eve tugged at her jacket. "Darn it! I trusted Lisa. Sure, I was pleased at the great numbers she turned in, but I never realized how much damage she was doing. Trust me, I'll make sure that all my managers know that this is *not* how we do business."

"I think that's a good idea. She was on at least one loop where stylists 'talked' to each other. Who knows what she might have shared about her strategies."

Then I stopped myself. I didn't want to tell Eve that Lisa had gone on a loop to announce she was pregnant. Eve seemed more fragile as the day went on. I wasn't sure if she could take much more bad news. It was nearly four o'clock, and no amount of concealer could cover the dark shadows under her eyes. All day she'd been dealing with fallout from Lisa's death. And, of course, she was worried about Wynn.

Eve sighed. "I sure hope she wasn't bragging to outsiders about how she was undercutting local prices, but when I'm honest with myself, I wouldn't put anything past her."

"I wouldn't, either."

Looking down at her wedding band, a gold circle of diamonds, Eve's mouth trembled. "I told myself I didn't like her because she was a flirt. If I didn't like every woman that Wynn found attractive, I'd make myself miserable. And I didn't want to be miserable. I wanted to be happily married. So I ignored my gut instincts when it came to Lisa. I shouldn't have, but I did."

"You had other things on your mind."

"That's not much of an excuse. If she hadn't been killed, she might well have run your mother out of business!"

"Not to make you feel bad, but she almost did. Mom said that the mold inspection was the last straw."

"That's just plain wrong, Grace Ann. Papa would never agree to doing business like that. He remembers how hard it was for him to get started. I really need to apologize to your mother in person as soon as I can. When can I meet her? I'd like to see your shop from the inside, too. I've heard so much about it."

I hesitated. "I'll ask Mom if we can drop by tomorrow."

"Good."

"Now, you've been here all day and you looked tired. When are you planning to leave?"

"I still have mountains of work to do."

"Mom always says, 'It will be here tomorrow.' I think she's right. You need to take care of your health, Eve. Especially under the circumstances."

My new boss gave me a half smile. "Yes, you're probably right. I'm not thinking straight. Time to call it a night. It's pretty quiet here in the evenings. Taffy and Vinny can handle the traffic. Come on, I'll walk you out."

It came as a surprise to me how protective of her I felt. Eve might be a seasoned businessperson, but she was also a surprisingly vulnerable young woman.

# Chapter Forty-three

✂

THE BUZZ OF MY NEW JOB WORE OFF FAST ONCE I started driving home. A light rain was falling. Rain that we desperately needed. Knowing the roads would be a bit slick, I slowed down. The journey gave me time to think about Marsh, and thinking about him led to feeling lonely. Also to feeling frustrated. Marsh needed to know what I'd learned about the conflicts in the salon. But how could I tell him? Especially now when I'd walked out on him?

Suzee Gaylord had reason to want to see Lisa dead. Carol Brockman might be the owner of the Toyota Camry I'd seen in the parking lot. According to Eve, Carol thought Lisa was stealing. If the accountant confronted the manager, perhaps that struggle led to Lisa's murder.

Or was the contractor so frustrated with her that he did

her in? She'd bullied him into changing the plans for the salon. Perhaps he worried that Snippets would come after him and make him redo the place at his cost.

Pulling up to the curb in front of my apartment, I realized that to learn more, I really needed to talk with Wynn. Was there any clue that had been overlooked? What had Lisa said to him before he drove away? Did he know what she was planning to do next?

Did Marsh know that Lisa was pregnant? Was it possible that another man was involved? Someone local? That might have been the reason Lisa was killed.

I turned off the engine and sat for a second, gathering what was left of my energy. The rain was light but showed no signs of letting up. Fortunately, the apartment I rented from Genevieve Jones was thirty feet from the street. My little place had once been her garage, but Mrs. Jones had long ago converted it into a living space for her son, who had died of lung cancer at sixty. He had never married.

After hurrying along the sidewalk with my head down, I made it to my stoop before I noticed a yellow tag had been wrapped around my door handle. The soggy paper read: "Sorry we missed you! A gift for you from St. Elizabeth's premier florist is waiting . . ." and in a loopy script: *See Mrs. Jones.* Thanks to the rain, the note nearly fell apart in my hands. Two minutes more, and I wouldn't have been able to decipher the writing.

Mrs. Jones stepped out on her porch and waved to me, beckoning me to take the two-stepping-stone pathway from my front door to hers. "Saw you pull up! Got your flowers!" She shouted across the broad expanse of her piazza.

My landlady was a tall, cranelike woman with skin so translucent it reminded me of tissue paper. She was a busy volunteer who visited "old people" and shut-ins, with her weekly bridge games lending structure to her life. Once I accompanied her to tai chi, where her agility and balance astonished me. As she moved into the pose mimicking a crane flapping its wings, I wondered if she might fly away. The pouf of her thinning, snow white hair as it formed a halo around her head heightened her resemblance to a crowned crane.

Ducking my head again, I jogged back out into the shower, but this time, I ran up the stairs leading to Mrs. Jones's front door. She hugged me and pulled me inside.

"Aren't they lovely?" Her housedress was nearly as faded as her blue eyes, but it was neatly pressed with starch. Her pearl clip-on earrings dangled along her scrawny neck. Mrs. Jones was a real pip with those blue eyes that danced with excitement. She pointed to a beautiful bouquet of long-stemmed roses taking pride of place on her mahogany dining room table. "I didn't want them to go dry, so I watered them for you."

She'd done more than water them; she's soaked them good. The flowers were drenched, as was the card accompanying them. Her eyesight grew ever more dim with each day, and I worried that soon she'd run into a real problem getting around town in her huge, gold Impala.

"Come sit a spell, Grace. Here, take this towel and dry yourself off. I've got a fresh pitcher of sweet tea, and I want to show you what'll surely be the last blossom on my gardenia this fall. See it? There out by the roses? Now I want to hear all about you being a person of interest. Gracious, I don't know as I've ever met a person of interest before."

"Thank you kindly," I said as I took the cold glass from her gnarled hands. I am nothing if not polite, because every Southern girl has manners drummed into her from birth onward.

I'd taken just one sip when she said, "So they're trying to blame you for the death of that awful Lisa Butterworth."

"You knew her?" I shouldn't be surprised. Mrs. Jones gets around, and St. Elizabeth isn't a big town. My drinking glass clinked as I set it down on her glass-topped side table. One day I'd have to remember to buy her coasters, because the muggy weather caused terrible condensation. You could easily ruin a fine antique with a wet glass, and Mrs. Jones had a house full of them.

"Carol Brockman is my niece. Twice removed," she said with a knowing grin. "I've heard all about that terrible young woman."

In the South, familial relationships are sacred. It's common to ask, "Who's his people?" the way a dog breeder might ask about a purebred's lineage. The complicated intertwining leads to odd and strained explanations. "Once removed," "twice removed," "on my daddy's side," "by marriage," "and by blood" are everyday parlance. It's confusing, so I ignore it. Mrs. Jones was simply telling me that she and Carol Brockman were distant relatives, not kissing kin.

"That so?"

"Sure you don't want a couple of shortbread cookies to go with that sweet tea? I buy boxes of them every year from the Girl Scouts." This was a bribe. I could hear the rest of the story only if I agreed to refreshments.

"You know, I think I will."

From her kitchen, she brought an eggshell-thin plate of fine china that was loaded down with more cookies than I could eat in a year. First she handed me a damask napkin to put in my lap. "Yes, indeedie-do. Carol was fit to be tied. She sees all the receipts. That girl was trying to pull a fast one on the company. See she wanted to recoup the money they spent for that big fish tank. Guess how much it cost. Just guess."

I named a figure.

Mrs. Jones chuckled and hiked her thumb toward her ceiling. My eyes followed the gesture and noticed cobwebs hanging from the light fixture.

I raised the figure.

Mrs. Jones hiked her thumb again.

Surely that tank hadn't cost more than a month of my salary? Well, it did. At least that's what my landlady said.

"Lisa thought it was a big waste of money. Carol caught her monkeying around with the different chemicals. Don't you know all those fish up and died? Carol came in one morning and they were all floating belly up. Lisa was happy as a pig in mud," she said as she shook her head so the crown of hair floated around her face.

"Really? But now the salon is left with a big empty space in the middle."

"Don't you know it?" said Mrs. Jones with a nod. "Carol got me an invitation to the grand opening. That was some party, I tell you. I remember precisely how big that tank was, and how much space it took up. You see, that Lisa Butterworth wanted a big empty space. Yes, it's true. She was fixing to put in a display rack for more product. Originally, she had called Mrs. Sebastiani, I mean, Mrs. Goodman, and told her what she wanted to do, but Mrs. Goodman had a fit. She was not happy. They got to hollering at each other over the phone. Carol heard ever' bit of it."

So Eve and Lisa had fought. Interesting.

"But they calmed down, right?"

Mrs. Jones smiled, those bright eyes of her lively with mischief. "No, they did not. Lisa hung up on her boss. Eve called back and spoke to Carol. Carol told her about the missing money."

"Missing money?"

"Lisa was skimming a little off the top, don't you know? Every bill that came in from a supplier, Lisa added a bit and handed it to Carol. Most bookkeepers wouldn't get wise to that, but Carol started double-checking the paper invoices against the order books. That's how she noticed the discrepancy. She's a smart one, our Carol."

"What did Eve—Mrs. Goodman—say when she learned about Lisa stealing from her?"

Mrs. Jones shrugged. "She told Carol to keep track of the dollar amount. See, when it reaches a certain amount, it goes from a misdemeanor to a felony. Mrs. Goodman told Carol, 'I'm going to make sure Lisa never, ever pulls a stunt like this again. Believe me, she'll wish she was never born!' "

# Chapter Forty-four

✂

I THANKED MRS. JONES FOR COLLECTING MY FLOW-
ers and left, walking in the light rain and picking my way
along the stepping stones. As part of our agreement, I
helped her with the gardening for a reduction in my rent.
The overgrown honeysuckle sent up a heavenly fragrance,
as did the last of the season's roses. Soon they would need
trimming and mulching as preparation for their dormancy.
What was it Mom had reminded me? Everything had its
season.

Eve had lied to me, by omission. She'd said that Carol
thought someone was stealing. Actually, she had proof that
Lisa was dipping into the till. Why hadn't Eve been honest
with me? My new boss hadn't told me that she and Lisa
were at odds, even though she had mentioned Lisa's prob-

lems with everyone else in the shop. Curious-er and curi-ous-er, as Alice said in Wonderland.

Balancing the flowers in one hand and fighting my rain-slick doorknob with the other, I managed to slip into my apartment as I wondered out loud, "What else is Eve hiding from me?"

Sam greeted me with an excited stream of chirping and general carrying-on. I shook off the rain and set my roses on the kitchen counter.

"You'll have to wait, buddy. I need a towel." After I grabbed one, the soggy card stuck in the blossoms demanded my attention. Gently extracting it from the plastic pitchfork that held it, I opened the damp envelope, withdrew the card inside, and tried to make out the message. "Sorry" and then a blur.

"Totally useless," I muttered. "But these sure are lovely." They were long stemmed, a deep romantic red like you see in commercials. Hank had sent me roses once before. Right after I found him with Melissa Littleton. Could this be his attempt at apologizing for naming me a person of interest? It would be his style. A grand gesture signifying nothing.

Squinting at the card and holding it under a lamp, I could barely make out the letter M.

I set the card down and checked my phone messages. There were three. One was a hang up. Alice Rose, my sis-ter, called to say, "Grace Ann! I can't believe what you've gone and done! Working for Snippets! If that doesn't make you a traitor, I don't know what does!"

I hit "delete." When she calmed down, and I explained everything to her, she'd apologize. Unfortunately, Alice Rose did not walk away from quarrels if they involved me. Then she was every bit as combative as I was. Her worries about Owen were probably putting her on edge. I made a mental note to call her tomorrow and ask what she'd learned.

The final message on my machine was from Marty. "I've been thinking, Grace Ann. I'm sorry about the other night. I've never been good with commitment. On the ride back to Washington, I had plenty of time to think. Why don't you—" But the message was cut short.

So that was it. The flowers were from Marty. I briefly considered tossing them, but why waste good roses? Instead, I freshened the ends and put them in a vase of warm water.

Sam had gotten noisier still, raising a general ruckus and demanding my attention, as if he was bothered by something. I reached in, let him hop on my index finger, and withdrew him carefully. He calmed down immediately. I wondered if I could teach him to kiss me, as my grandmother's bird used to do with her. Tentatively, I lifted the small bird to my mouth and touched my lips to his beak. He stared at me nervously, looking past me with his good eye, and backed away.

"No kisses?"

"I've got plenty of them for you."

I whirled around to see Wynn standing in my doorway. His hair dripping wet.

"What are you doing here? Get out!" I scolded him. Sam fluttered up and would have flown away had Marsh not clipped his wings. With a quick grab, I corralled my frightened bird and popped him back in his cage.

"Hey, the door wasn't locked and I stopped by to talk. You don't want me to stand out in the rain, do you?" He stepped inside and shook the water from his leather jacket. As usual, every hair of his fell into place, leaving him as devastatingly handsome as any male model could be.

I felt the attraction that had drawn me to Wynn in the first place, and that hormonal tractor beam made me furious.

"I want nothing to do with you. Nothing!" Without

Eve's mitigating presence, the force of my anger at Wynn hit me hard.

His shoulders dropped and his face lost all eagerness. He wiped his face on his sleeve. "Aw, gee, Grace Ann. Did I really hurt you that badly? I mean, I understand you have a reason to be upset, but geez."

"You kidding? You passed my work off as your own. You shuffled all your responsibilities at the school onto me, but never gave me credit. And worst of all, you were dating Eve behind my back. You humiliated me twenty ways to Sunday!" I screamed at him.

"Oh, babe, I never meant to embarrass you. I thought you knew we weren't exclusive." He started for my sofa, but I got between him and it. "No. Out!"

Wynn rubbed his eyes, trying to look sad. "Come on. We can talk this through."

"No, we can't. There's a huge difference between not exclusive and one person being engaged to someone else."

"I meant to tell you. Honest I did!"

"Wynn, knock it off. We both know that the word 'honest' is not part of your vocabulary."

He bowed his head and, I swear, he looked exactly like an eight-year-old boy with his hand caught in a vending machine. That was a large part of his charm—and he knew it. When he raised his eyes, tears stood in them. "Okay, I deserve all that. You're right. I knew all along I was going to hurt you. That's what I do, Grace Ann. That's what I am. I'm a loser. I can face up to that. I've told Eve I'll go into counseling, and I will, but meanwhile, I want you to know that I love her. I really, really do. With all my heart. More than I've ever loved anybody in my life. I want to do right by her. And my baby. I can't believe I'm going to be a dad!"

I didn't say a word. Either he was the world's best actor

in a leading role, or he was for once being totally candid with me.

"Right. And what kind of father are you going to make?"

"I know . . . I know."

"Eve deserves better."

"You are right. She does." He sniffed. "Did you ever read that comic book? Richie Rich, the poor little rich boy? That's Eve's story. Her dad kept her locked away. She's never had friends. He raised her to take over his business, and that's her whole life, twenty-four-seven. When we met, she'd never even gone to a movie in a theatre. Or gone flying kites. Or riding bikes. He protected her, but he also kept her away from real life."

"And now she has you," I said. "Lucky girl."

"Well, yeah. I'm not much, I know, but I can have a good time, can't I? I can make a woman feel special. I can get people laughing." To prove it, he did a silly soft-shoe imitation and ended with a goofy grin.

"Your point?"

"Look, she's wanted this baby for a long time, and I gave it to her. I love Eve more than life itself. Help me out here. I know your ex-husband is on the police force, and I heard that he came into the shop. He still cares for you. Could you tell him she didn't do it?"

I shook my head at Wynn. "What makes you think that Hank Parker or anyone else would listen to me?"

He sighed. "Okay, whatever. It's just that I know she didn't do it."

"Did you?" I stepped closer and shoved my index finger into his chest. "Was it an accident? You smacked Lisa. She fell. You thought she'd climb out of the fish tank?"

"No!" he yelled. "I didn't do it! Don't you see? That's why I'm so worried! I didn't do it and I think maybe Eve did!"

# Chapter Forty-five

FOR A MINUTE, I WAS TOO STUNNED TO SAY ANY-thing. What a jerk he was, blaming his wife! "I can't help you or her. My ex and I don't exactly see eye-to-eye."

"But he sent you those flowers, didn't he?" Wynn pointed.

"Those are none of your business."

"Okay, all right. Look, Grace Ann, all I'm sayin' is that I love Eve. I really do. More than I ever thought I could love anybody."

"That's nice to hear you're capable of deep emotion. Now go. Shoo. Get out of here." I hustled him out of my apartment.

"You've got to forgive me, Grace!" He resisted my tugs on his arm. "Besides, it's raining."

"So what? I don't got to do anything. Good night!" As

I locked the door behind him, I rested against its comforting
surface. What was going on? First Eve wondered if Wynn
killed Lisa, now Wynn worried that Eve had killed Lisa.

Who was the real culprit? If it wasn't one of the two of
them, who could it be? Carol, the accountant? Suzee, the
second-in-command? Eve told me there'd been no forced
entry, so I could assume that the killer either let himself in
or Lisa had opened the salon for her killer.

That meant that she must have known her murderer, but
that wasn't unusual. Most killers know their victims.

The more I thought about what I'd learned, the more
confused I became. I went into my bedroom and started to
undress. As I did, I found the folded piece of paper with the
word *SUSPECTS* written across the top. Pulling a pen
from my bedside table, I made notes.

1. Carol Brockman—Was definitely at the shop by herself that night. Thought Lisa was stealing.
2. Suzee Gaylord—Was in line for a promotion. Where-
   abouts unknown.
3. The rest of the staff
4. Eve?—She had to be sick and tired of Wynn's cheating. Where was she the night Lisa was killed? Any
   alibi?
5. Wynn?—If Lisa was really pregnant, could that have
   been Wynn's child, too? Was he worried about his
   marriage to Eve being in trouble if Lisa was pregnant
   with his child? He drove past the shop, but claims to
   have stayed in his car after he left Lisa.
6. Contractor—Got Lisa to change his work order. Might
   be in trouble with Eve now. Where was he?
7. Other?—Could be Lisa had gotten pregnant by another
   man. Maybe he met her at Snippets?

After standing on my feet all day, I wanted a long soak in my tub. I poured a scented Epsom salt mixture that Althea had mixed up onto the porcelain surface of the clawed basin, turned on hot water, and stirred it with my hand. The fragrance of lavender mixed with eucalyptus wafted upward, bathing my face in scent. With one hand, I twisted my hair up on top of my head and used a clasp to keep it there.

I had one foot in the water when the doorbell rang.

Pulling on my wrapper, I gave the tub a longing look and padded to the door.

Marsh stood outside. In the rain.

I debated what to do, but I did need to talk to him and tell him what I'd learned, so finally I opened the door.

"It's wet out—" He paused as water dripped from his hair. "Was I interrupting?"

"I had one foot in a hot bath."

"Go. Take it. Have you had any dinner?"

"No."

"I owe you a meal. How about if I go get you dinner from Angelini's? I promise no arguments as an appetizer. I'll pick up a bottle of wine, too. You look like you've had a long day."

"I have." I moved to the kitchen. "Here's the front door key. You do *not* have permission to copy it."

"Roger that. I'll be right back. Lock up behind me."

I went back to my bath, which was, I'll admit, heavenly. The soak did me a lot of good. By the time the water turned cold, I heard the key turning in the lock. I climbed out, dried off, and put on a pair of soft stretchy pants and a tee. I debated about whether to grab a bra, but since this was my house and my rules, I decided I had the right to go for comfort. As a compromise, I put on an exercise bra. That made me decent but wasn't as restrictive.

Marsh put two place settings on my coffee table. He'd located the wineglasses and was busily rummaging around in a drawer. "Bottle opener?"

I opened my junk drawer and withdrew the necessary item. Then, deciding that he did, indeed, owe me a meal, I sat down to watch. As far as I was concerned, he could darn well prep the food for both of us. Which he did even though he clearly was soaking wet.

Unlike Wynn, Marsh didn't whine about it.

At last, he sat down, too, next to me. "Before we eat, I want to apologize. I see you got my roses."

"You?" I took a bite of the salad. Surprisingly good. Marsh had tossed the leaves in the dressing that he whipped up with a bit of mustard and olive oil from my pantry.

"Yes. Didn't you get the card?" He speared a piece of tomato.

I got up and showed it to him. I also grabbed a towel and handed it over. His attempts at drying his hair were clumsy but endearing. Finally I grabbed a comb and smoothed it into place.

"Drat. Who did you think it was from?"

"Marty. Or Hank. Remember? I threw him out of the salon today."

"Believe me, I'm not likely to forget about your ex-husband's visit. Officer Qualls confirmed what you told me."

"Yes, she's his little sidekick. The only time I feel dumber than Hank is when I remember that I married him."

He raised his wineglass. "Here's to honesty."

I lifted mine and nearly choked. "Honesty?"

"Yes, I think it's important to be honest about our mistakes. While we're on the subject of relationships, I believe I still owe you both an apology and an explanation."

The wine went down like silk. "Shoot. Mind if I keep eating while you grovel?"

He laughed. His chuckle was low, baritone and sexy. "No, go right ahead."

For a minute he watched me attack my salad, and then he said, "I had no right to act so demanding. You, of course, have a right to work wherever you want."

"It is, of course, a free country." Sounded lame, but it fit.

A rueful grin told me he agreed. "You see, I overreacted, and it has to do with Polly."

I put down my fork. Suddenly, I regretted letting him in. I didn't want another dead-end relationship. True, this was only dinner, but I couldn't deny my feelings for the man. Most of the guys in my life had been attractive, but none had lit the firestorm within me that Marsh did.

"Polly," I repeated. "Your wife."

"Yes."

"You love her."

"Yes. With all my heart."

*Well, Grace Ann, that's that. Finish your meal and get him out of here.*

"She's been dead ten years now," he said and he hid his face behind his wineglass.

"I-I-I'm so sorry!"

"So am I. We were high school sweethearts. I joined the military so we could get married and I could support her. Us."

"Wh-what happened?"

"A creep I put in jail got out and shot her."

I sank back and shivered. The venom in his voice surprised me. The expression on his face was one I'd never seen before: raw fury. It quickly disappeared, and in its place was a pain so deep I found myself wanting to hug him, to soothe him.

But I didn't. I sat there.

He nodded and scooted a piece of lettuce around on his plate. "Right. My fault. I let down my guard. I didn't protect her. No one told me the jerk had gotten out. I had warned her, of course, to be careful. When you're involved with a lawman, you need to be, because, well, there can be repercussions."

"Repercussions."

"Right." He took another drink of wine, set it down unsteadily, and it bumped his fork, which then hit the floor and clattered.

I jumped up to get him another, because I don't believe in the ten-second rule. His fingers touched mine as I handed it over. "It wasn't your fault. You know that."

Marsh avoided my eyes and resumed eating his salad. "Who else can I blame? Certainly not her. I wish you could have met. She was wonderful. Polly never met a stranger. She was the sweetest, most open and friendly person I've ever known. When that scum showed up at our front door with a story that he'd had a flat, she let him in. It never occurred to her . . ."

He set down his fork and drank a lot of water.

"It must have been terrible."

"It was. Worse than you can imagine." He paused. "No sane human being can imagine that sort of violence."

Neither of us spoke for a long time. I stared at my plate. He stared at his. Finally, he said, "Well, I've ruined another perfectly good meal from Angelini's. Guess that'll teach me."

"Teach you what?"

"To mix business and personal. Can't be done. Never works."

"Are you saying you have feelings toward me?" I was tired of guessing games.

"Yes. I thought you knew that." He turned and took my hand.

I didn't dare look up. Instead I stared at his fingers cradling mine. I didn't want to see his eyes. Suddenly, my mouth was dry and my heart pounded so hard I thought for sure he could hear it.

The room was so quiet, you could hear Sam's feet as he hopped around his cage. I don't know how long Marsh and I would have sat there, not speaking, but a little bell rang. Once, twice, three times.

The sound was new. I wondered what it was.

I rose from the sofa to follow the noise, head turned toward it, and it took me to Sam's cage. There he was, happily chasing his tiny bell around the bottom of his cage. "Oh, look! He learned to make his bell ring! Isn't he clever?"

Marsh put down his napkin, got up, and joined me staring at the little blue bird. "He sure did."

We stood there, elbow to elbow, like two proud parents.

And then he took me into his arms and kissed me.

# Chapter Forty-six

I DIDN'T BELIEVE IN SEX ON A FIRST DATE. OR
second. Or third.

But I was ready to put my qualms aside the minute
Marsh's lips traveled down my throat and his hand slipped
under my sports bra.

Fortunately, the man has an iron will. "We need to stop.
Right now," he said in a husky voice.

"I don't want to."

"Neither do I, but this isn't a good idea."

"Why not?" I asked. I had a list, but I wanted to hear his.

"First of all, there's an investigation ongoing, and I
could compromise it by having sex with you."

That wasn't on my list. I had thought about getting hurt,
getting involved, but not about that stupid investigation.

"Right," I said and I pushed him away. "Do you still think I could have killed Lisa Butterworth? If so, you've got a lot of nerve coming here and having dinner with me."

He wouldn't let me go. "Oh, I do?" And he kissed me again.

"I know you didn't kill Lisa Butterworth. In fact, I want to show you this." From his coat pocket, he pulled a grainy photo and handed it over. "The security camera took this. Lisa is already inside the shop. This person came to the door and was let in."

All I could see was a figure in a hoodie. I told him so. "Heck, I can't even tell if it's a man or a woman."

"That's the problem. The quality is so poor, I don't know why they bothered. A cheap system. Not worth the electricity it runs on."

"Can't you fix it? Like on *CSI*?"

"I wish. That stupid TV show has raised all sorts of unrealistic expectations. There's no way we can enhance that photo and make it clearer."

"How about the FBI? They can do stuff like that."

"Right. But they have bigger concerns than one murder in small-town Georgia. Come on, let's eat dinner." He took my hand and walked me back to my sofa before sitting down himself.

"If you can't tell who that is, how come you know it isn't me?" I said as I finished my salad and helped myself to the pasta with vodka sauce. Next I took a bite of the green beans topped with sliced almonds.

"The manager at Walk-Inn Foods described what you were wearing. No hoodie. Besides, what are you? Five-six? This person is at least five-nine. That much we can tell."

Unfortunately, that didn't narrow down my suspect list much. Wynn, Eve, and the contractor were all at least three inches taller than I. As was Carol Brockman. As for Suzee

Gaylord, I didn't know. But Vinny Torelli definitely was at least five-nine.

I told him what I'd heard about Carol Brockman. "Eve lied to me by omission. She made it sound like Carol was suspicious, but possibly without cause."

He nodded. "I can't quite get a read on her."

"I think she's been overly sheltered, but she's been exposed to business at such a high level that she sends off confusing signals."

There were crinkles around his eyes as he responded. "I think you've nailed it. Most of the time, she seems very sure of herself. Very much in control. Then she seems to sort of tilt." And he turned his hand to one side to illustrate. "Like a poker player who's out of control."

"Remember, too, she's pregnant. As was Lisa."

"How did you know that?"

I smirked. "I have my sources."

"A leak in the SEPD?"

"Lisa posted news on a LISTSERV for beauty professionals."

"Incredible. People don't seem to realize or care how much information they give away."

"Is it possible she had a boyfriend here in town? Or somewhere else? Could he have visited her at the shop? Gotten angry and smacked her while she was on the ladder?"

He set down his fork and stared at me. "Unbelievable. You even know about the ladder?"

"Step stool," I corrected myself.

"Step stool."

I told him about the contractor. "But I'm not sure that he's a real suspect."

"He could be liable for wrongful death under the circumstances."

"Even though she signed a piece of paper authorizing the change?"

Marsh nodded. "That's probably not worth much. Especially if a jury gets ahold of it. When you have a big business like Snippets, people line up to sue you. At the very least, Lisa Butterworth's family might bring a wrongful death suit against the contractor and put him out of business."

That reminded me of Eve's conversation with Wynn, and his visit here. "Wynn told Eve he went back to the salon to pay off Paula Benson. She's a masseuse. When Eve was showing me around the salon yesterday, Wynn came staggering out of a room with Paula in hot pursuit. It was gross."

Marsh gave a low whistle. "Man, that guy loves to live on the edge. Do you really think he is a sex addict?"

"Something's definitely wrong with him. But I'll say this, I think he's genuinely in love with his wife. He came by a few minutes before you showed up. I told him to leave, but he's worried." I bit my tongue.

"Spill it, Grace Ann."

I shook my head. I wouldn't betray Eve. Instead, I said, "You scared him. That's all. He hoped I'd have some sway with Hank. That I could put in a good word for him."

"And you let him in?"

"I hadn't locked my front door. The roses were in my hand, and I was sort of juggling everything."

"Right." Marsh stared at me. "You need to be careful. I've promised myself I won't go all weird on you again, but you do need to be careful."

"What are you saying?" I finished the last scrap of my pasta.

"Don't let Wynn in next time. Don't trust Eve, either."

That irked me. "Why not? You don't seriously think she could have killed Lisa, do you? Surely Eve has an alibi?"

He took a sip of water. "Since you've been married to a law enforcement official, you know there are things I can't share with you."

"Really?" I hiked an eyebrow. "Hank shared everything with me. Remind me to tell you someday why I divorced him. The not-for-publication real reason."

"Besides the fact he's dumber than a grub worm?"

"Besides that."

# Chapter Forty-seven

THE NEXT MORNING PROVED UNEVENTFUL. I'D HAD a lot of trouble dragging myself out of bed. Dreams of Marsh Dillon kept me tossing and turning. I dressed carefully, pairing a pair of black slacks with a V-neck blouse dotted with small black sequins. Despite the special flooring at the salon, my feet still hurt a little from yesterday, so today I slipped on a pair of black FitFlops, sandals with a special sole that supports your foot. The faux black stones on the toe strap of the FitFlops made them a combination of dressy and casual that was perfect.

After taking care of Sam, I climbed into my car and sat there. What could I possibly do to help break the ice at the salon? An answer came in a flash. I stopped by Jergens, a local family-owned bakery, and bought scones and muffins. To my surprise, our contractor was standing there in line.

"Hi, I'm Grace Ann Terhune. The new manager at Snippets," I said as I extended my hand. "I saw you in the salon yesterday."

"Roy Jasper, GC. Right. I put in a bid to fit that open area the right way."

"I know. What's a GC?"

"General contractor." Roy Jasper was a couple inches taller than me, with a ruddy, sunburned complexion. His dark brown hair was close cropped over his ears, and a bit long on top, but nothing special. I noticed a couple of small seams in his forehead, telltale signs he'd had skin cancer removed. Most of the older adults in the South sport similar scars. They didn't wear sunblock when they were young, and now an entire generation is fighting melanoma, one ugly incision at a time.

"Oh. So will you install the new aquarium?" Of course, I wasn't interested in talking about the fish tank. Not at all. But Mama always says you can catch more flies with honey than you can with vinegar, so I thought I'd better chat him up.

"No, that's the responsibility of Fur, Fin, and Feather. They have a maintenance contract with Snippets. All the other salons have tanks, too. I build out around the tank, so I was there to take measurements my last visit. Since then I ordered the lumber and materials I'll need. Should be here in two days."

His body was stocky, and he crossed his arms over his big chest in a manner that implied he was accustomed to being the boss.

"Will your work interfere with ours?" I asked.

"Depends on what you mean by interfere. I'll tape up plastic all around the area," he said, pointing with his finger and drawing an imaginary rectangle above us. "We'll try to keep the dust and noise to a minimum, but there will definitely be plenty of both."

"Too bad you didn't do this the first go round. Would have saved a lot of hassle."

Mr. Jasper coughed and glanced around nervously. "It wasn't my fault. That woman pitched a fit and demanded that there be a clear line of sight between the chairs and the waiting area. Went on and on about how it was her salon." And he sighed.

A customer got his order and both Mr. Jasper and I moved forward a few paces.

"Now she's dead. For what? From what the cops told me, it happened because she was hit in the head and then fell in that darn tank. I warned her that could happen if there wasn't a half wall coming down to meet the hood. I begged her. Told her it wasn't safe and she wouldn't listen."

I nodded. "You know, it's weird. I'll always remember where I was the night that Lisa Butterworth died."

"Yeah, me, too. I was with my family for the whole of the homecoming bonfire and game. My son, Troy, is on the Sabertooths football team. His blocking allowed our quarterback to make the winning touchdown! It should have been a happy memory for my wife and me and my boy, but now it'll forever be overshadowed by Ms. Butterworth's death."

The young man behind the counter motioned Mr. Jasper forward.

"Have a nice day," I told him after he received his coffee and started toward the door.

He gave me a curt nod. "See you soon."

I pulled into a spot right as another driver climbed out of her car, a beaten-up green Volkswagen Passat. I figured she was Suzee Gaylord. "Hey there!" I said with a cheery wave. "I'm Grace Ann Terhune."

"I know who you are." Suzee frowned, then thought better of it, and quickly assumed a more benign expression. Even then, her eyes and her nose both tilted down slightly, giving her face a natural negativity. Her voice, certainly, did not sound welcoming, either.

I understood where she was coming from. Mom and I once found a dead body in a parking lot. For days afterward, we were both on edge. Added to the trauma of what she'd discovered, Suzee had another reason to be down in the dumps. She'd been working for Snippets for three years and expected a promotion. Every inch of the woman screamed "beauty industry professional." Her hair had been highlighted perfectly, and the cut emphasized her best features, almond-shaped brown eyes. Her makeup had been carefully and expertly applied, but that downward cast could not be totally disguised.

Before Suzee and I could move away from our rides, another car pulled in. Somehow Carol must not have gotten word that she worked in a salon. Her hair was a disaster, a helmet of too tight curls, and she wore no makeup. Whereas Suzee wore dark pants, a silver blouse with a draping neckline, and a sharp silver and black belt, Carol's clothes could have been donated to Goodwill and promptly rejected. Her sagging stretch pants bagged at the knees, and her top had a large pink stain in the center. As we say in the South, Carol looked like twenty miles of bad road.

"Good morning," I said to her. "I brought scones and muffins from Jergens."

"You're kidding!" Carol's smile lit up her face. "That's my favorite bakery. Since they're on the other side of town, I don't get their treats often."

Even Suzee smiled a little. Not much, but enough to show me she wasn't completely averse to being friendly. The three of us started toward the back door, but the sound of a big motor stopped us. Wynn drove into the parking lot, his black Porsche purring as it came to a stop. The passenger door opened and out stepped Eve. The set of her shoulders suggested trouble in paradise. With an "oomph," she slammed the car door and walked away from Wynn. If she'd bid him farewell, it might have been private or quiet, because I didn't see any indication she regretted leaving his company.

All four of us entered the salon after I unlocked the door and punched in the security code. Carol lingered until I unwrapped the bakery treats. After grabbing one quickly, she headed for her office. Suzee puttered around making herself coffee, but finally came over to examine the treats. I could almost see the indecision before she reached out and grabbed a scone. "Why not take one home for your daughter?" I suggested.

Her eyes narrowed. I stood my ground.

"What about my daughter?" she asked.

"I said you should take something home to her. I remember how I enjoyed it when women would bring my mother baked goods." I shrugged in a friendly way. "I figured your child might enjoy a treat, too."

"You don't mind?" Suzee hesitated.

"Of course not. Please help yourself."

Using a paper towel, she scooped up a blueberry muffin. She also picked out one candied ginger scone before she left for her workstation.

Our doors opened promptly at nine to a much-reduced crowd from the day before. Corina did a super job of handling the flow, and I took care of three customers before glancing at the clock and realizing it was time for Eve to meet my mother.

"Eve, do you have many women friends?" I wondered as we traveled in my blue Ford Fiesta the few short blocks to Violetta's.

"No." She shrugged. "You'd think I would, being in this business. My mom died when I was young. It's always been Papa and me. We lived in a bad neighborhood when he started his business, so he sent me to a Roman Catholic school. Those nuns were strict. They kept us busy from the first bell to the last. My aunt Maria would meet me at the gate to the school and walk me home. She cracked the whip, making sure I did my homework. By the time I made it to college, Papa was teaching me how to run Snippets, so I took business courses at the community college so I could work around the salon schedules."

"That's a shame," I said, as I parked in front of the house, next to Mom's car. "Because growing up around women has been the best part of living in a salon. It's sad to think that you missed out. Come on. I'll take you to meet my mother."

When I called earlier to see if we could drop by, Mom confirmed to me that she'd moved in with Walter, at least temporarily. She'd agreed to meet us at Violetta's a little after lunch. "I feel awkward about living with a man who isn't my husband, even if I am a squatter in his guest bedroom. So let me meet you there, all right?"

I assured her that Eve simply wanted to apologize, and that the meeting place didn't matter, but on second thought, I wanted Eve to see the salon, so we set this up. Although Violetta's wasn't swanky like Snippets, there was a cozy ambience—and I felt like Eve should see another side of this business. A warmer, more personal and intimate one.

My throat got a lump in it as I walked my new friend to the front door. I missed the snug and friendly atmosphere and wished that the salon was still in full swing so she could get a taste of the camaraderie all of us had enjoyed.

A camaraderie I hoped to reestablish starting today. I'd text messaged Althea, Stella, and Rachel, inviting them to come by in the afternoon so we could discuss their employment.

"Wynn drove me past this place several times," said Eve as she stopped to admire the last of the season's roses, the four-o'clocks, and the spicy-smelling mums in bronze, yellow, and orange that formed a broad band of firelike color surrounding the screened-in front porch. "Such a lovely setting. Almost like a Southern garden."

I laughed. "That's because it is."

Mom met us at the front door. "Welcome, Eve." And she gave my friend a hug. For a second, Eve stiffened, then she softened into the embrace, her whole body releasing its tension.

"I came to apologize, Mrs. Terhune. My papa taught me to deal honestly and fairly with people. Arturo Sebastiani would be ashamed if he knew what Lisa Butterworth did to you and your business. Not only did she abuse my trust in her, she also abused Grace Ann's trust. Worst of all, she did this while in the name of our business, and that grieves me terribly. I hope you can find it in your heart to forgive us."

Even though I'd known Eve was here to apologize, I was still shocked by her little speech. Mom's face betrayed that she, too, was surprised by how fervent Eve's words were.

"Of course I accept your apology. Welcome to Violetta's . . . such as it is."

Eve nodded solemnly. "I hope I can find a way to make it up to you for what happened. I understand that you are closed temporarily because of the mold situation?"

"I spoke to my insurance adjuster yesterday. He's going to see what he can do," Mom said, lifting her chin slightly.

She didn't mention the problem with the historic register. I guess Mom felt it was best to take things one step at a time.

"Now that you're here, may I show you around?" In any

crisis, good Southern manners will save the day. Although the slightly puzzled look on Mom's face told me she was still a bit shocked by Eve's fervent regrets, my mother had tapped her own personal default key and reverted back to her upbringing. A guest is always welcome in our home, and Violetta's had always been a home first and a salon second.

Since Snippets is so austere by comparison, I wasn't entirely sure how Eve would react, but she seemed to have a sincere appreciation for how comfy the space was. She stopped immediately to admire the wicker furniture in the customer waiting area.

"I love the hanging ferns. Oh! And look at all the potted violets! Just like your name!" Eve cooed, as she examined the purple, pink, and white floral display clustered on the windowsill.

Mom nodded. "Most of these were given to me by customers. That's one reason I cherish them."

Of course, the visit was old hat to me. As usual, the dust motes danced in the morning light as the sunbeams angled through the wooden blinds. The wide, heart-of-pine floorboards were kind under our feet, which makes a huge difference when you are standing up for hours. The magazines were newish, with corners comfortably worn by many thumbs.

"Stella is coming for Beauty later today," said Mom as the snub-nosed Persian deigned to climb off her blue velvet cushion and walk over to us. Beauty tilted her head, making a judgment, and went straight for Eve's arms. To my surprise, my boss caught her and nestled her face in Beauty's fur.

"Listen! She's purring," said Eve with all the excitement of a child.

As Mom led the way, Eve walked around as if in a

trance, while stroking Beauty. But she froze when she saw the figurehead from the *Santa Elisabeta*, a Spanish galleon that sank off the Georgia coast in the 1500s. Her gaze fixed without blinking on the statue occupying a spot on the wall behind the counter, where she provided benevolent supervision to all our labors.

"Saint Elizabeth, who was cured of her barrenness to give birth to John the Baptist, may her name be ever blessed," she said in a whisper. "I prayed to her, all during Advent. I said, 'Give children to those who ask and faith to those who are barren of heart,' and she answered me." A strange expression of ecstasy came over Eve's face as she stared up at the likeness of the saint.

"She has led me here for a reason. I know it. See? I'm getting goose bumps." Eve extended her arm for me to examine. After I nodded, Eve continued to stand and stare at the wooden likeness. Mom and I exchanged glances of surprise. Most people admire *Santa Elisabeta,* but this was beyond simple appreciation. It was as if Eve was mesmerized.

"Eve?" I touched her elbow gently, not wishing to scare her, but hoping I could bring my new boss back to earth.

With a shake of her head, Eve returned her attention to our shop. "Uh, right, I guess we better get going. It's just that Elizabeth is my patron saint. I never expected to see a statue of her, especially in such an unexpected place. I mean, if we were in a church or a museum, that would make sense, but in a salon? It's . . . it's like a miracle."

"God works in mysterious ways," Mom said, taking Beauty from Eve's arms.

This was all too woo-woo for me. I glanced at my watch. "I think we'd better get back."

Mom hugged Eve again. "I would have served you

refreshments, but with the mold and all, we really shouldn't stay here for long."

"Mrs. Terhune, I'd like to formally invite you to come work with us at Snippets. At least until you're back up and running. The offer is open to any of your staff as well. When you reopen the doors on Violetta's, you can take all your old and new customers with you. I promise."

Mom pulled on her earlobe nervously. "I don't know what to say! That's incredibly generous of you. I will talk to my staff. If they are agreeable, we'll drop by later today. By the way, please give your father my regards. We've never met, but I hope we will someday. He's an icon in this business."

Eve's face crumpled. "I'd do that Mrs. Terhune, but it won't really matter. Dad has frontotemporal dementia, a sort of Alzheimer's. The disease has radically changed his personality and his behavior. He's not at all the man he once was. He barely recognizes me these days."

"How long has he had this diagnosis?" Mom asked, the horror written large on her face.

"It's a rapid-onset disease. He was fine until about six months ago." Her voice grew soft. "Fortunately, it takes people rapidly, so he won't suffer long."

"Oh, I am so, so sorry!" Mom said.

Eve gave her a watery smile. "So am I, Mrs. Terhune. So am I."

# Chapter Forty-eight

BACK AT THE SHOP, I ASKED CAROL IF SHE'D LIKE TO join me for a quick bite at Subway. I was more determined than ever to figure out who killed Lisa Butterworth, and to clear Eve. My invitation was met with hesitation. Carol looked me over as if deciding whether I was worthy of her company or not. A part of me wanted to snap at her. After all, why not be pleasant? We were coworkers and I rented my apartment from her aunt, Mrs. Jones.

Instead, I bit my tongue and relaxed my shoulders to disguise my annoyance.

"You buying?" she asked after a while.

"Of course." I smiled.

"Okay. Let me stop in the restroom first."

Eve looked up from the reports she was studying as I

watched the woman clomp away. "Don't let that bug you. She's aloof, but she's dedicated to the salon. You're accustomed to being frugal, I bet, so you two will get along. That's her big bugaboo. That and following rules. She's a big one for rules. When Lisa decided not to let Mr. Jasper finish the salon as I had specified, Carol was on the phone with me right away."

"Why didn't you get it fixed then?"

"The call came the same day that I moved my dad into an assisted-living facility. That week was rocky." She looked away. "He was there for two weeks before they called and told me they couldn't handle him. I had to find a facility that was dedicated to handling Alzheimer's patients. Since it was short notice, that wasn't easy."

"I'm sure it wasn't. That's a shame, Eve. Why did you decide to put in such a big tank? I'm sure it was expensive."

Eve turned back toward me with a smile. "Actually, it's a cost-saving device. You see, aquariums have been shown to have a calming effect on people. They lower the blood pressure, reduce stress, and reduce anxiety. In kids with ADHD, they've been shown to settle down significantly. There's even research that shows that watching fish can reduce pain. So while it's costly at the outset, we've been experimenting with large tanks. There are significantly fewer complaints about stylists running late in our salons with tanks. In fact, we get fewer complaints overall in the salons with tanks."

"Fascinating," I said, and it was.

Carol stepped up behind me. "Of course, for some people, aquariums have been known to be lethal."

An awkward silence followed.

"You ready to go?" I said to the accountant. "Eve, do you want us to bring you anything?"

"No," she said. "Wynn and I are going to lunch together in about fifteen minutes."

With that, Carol and I left on foot to walk to Subway. "I rent from your aunt," I said, hoping to start a conversation.

"I know."

She said nothing else for a block or two. I made desultory remarks about the fall leaves and the brightly colored mums we passed. Carol's lips were sealed. Finally, I'd had enough. I stopped in my tracks. "Look, if you have a problem with me, I prefer to get it out in the open."

"I had my apartment cleaned for mold a couple of weeks ago, so I stayed over at my aunt's house. You had a man sleep over. I know because I saw him go in at night and not come out until the next morning. That's what loose women do."

"Oh." This was not what I expected. A problem with me being competition, yes, that I could handle. A concern about me taking Lisa's place so quickly. Either of those would have been expected. But to throw my personal life at me? That was bush league. I knew Mrs. Jones paid no attention to my personal life, so I naturally assumed no one else did, either.

A slow burn started at my collar and worked its way up my neck. "You have no right to intrude on my privacy, but for the record, the man who stayed over is a man I have been dating exclusively and just broke up with. It's not like there's a regular parade in and out of my bedroom."

Her mouth twisted up while she considered all this. I used the opportunity to glance at her left hand. No ring. This wasn't about her religious beliefs. It was about jealousy.

"Is that why you pushed Lisa Butterworth into the fish tank? Because she was sinful? What does that make you, huh? A murderer?"

Carol staggered backward. As she did, she misjudged the terrain behind her and fell hard on her butt. I stared down at the woman. Growing up in the South, you learn never to talk about politics or religion. This altercation reminded me why. I understood that people had strong feelings about premarital sex, but I didn't appreciate the lecture, particularly since I'd shown such admirable restraint the night before.

Her face turned petulant as she sat there. "I didn't do it! I know that ex-husband of yours thinks I did because he keeps coming round and asking me questions, but I didn't! I can't help it, but he's making me feel all fidgety."

"He has that effect on people," I said with a sigh. "Come on. Let me give you a hand up." With a grunt, I pulled the other woman to her feet. Brushing the bits of grass off her pants, she thanked me and continued with, "All I did was loan Mrs. Goodman my car. That's it, that's all. The Goodmans only have one car down here, and her husband—that awful man!—had hers."

Finally, we were getting somewhere. "When did you loan it to her?"

"On Friday afternoon, we were going over last month's figures. We know that someone has been taking money from the till, but we don't know who. We also know someone is playing with the invoices, and I'm certain that is—was—Lisa. Mrs. Goodman went over the books with me because she wanted to make absolutely certain that the person messing with the invoices had taken more than three hundred dollars."

"Why?"

"Because any dollar figure over two hundred ninety-nine dollars and ninety-nine cents, it's a felony. Mrs. Goodman was mad as heck. She wanted to put Lisa away for a long time. She even said that it would serve Lisa right if her baby was born in jail. I don't think she really meant it, but maybe she did because she'd just heard that Lisa was pregnant—and she was claiming it was Wynn Goodman's baby!"

"How'd she get that news?"

Carol's stubby fingers waved away my question. "It was all over the Internet. I think that made Mrs. Goodman the maddest. She thought everyone was laughing at her because it took her so long to get pregnant."

"So when did you loan her your car?"

"Right before closing time. Ten 'til five. She asked if she could borrow my car. Said she'd drop me off at home, and she did. Promised she'd fill up the tank for me. You know how expensive gas is. So I let her keep it until Saturday night."

I nodded. Our walk had taken us to the heart of downtown St. Elizabeth, where pedestrians filled the sidewalks, hurrying to grab lunch before they went back to town hall or the stores where they worked. "Let's postpone this discussion until we grab our food and talk in private."

Once inside Subway, she chose a foot-long sub with everything on it, an extra-large cola, two bags of chips, and two cookies. Evidently her cost-cutting methods included soaking other people for more food than she could possibly eat. I said nothing but ordered my regular turkey on whole wheat with green peppers, tomatoes, lettuce, black olives, and mustard, plus a diet Coke, and paid for everything. Carol could barely carry all the food the clerk handed her.

Lucky for us, a table opened up in the far back of the narrow restaurant. "Grab it!" I told Carol, and she moved surprisingly quickly toward the surface.

"Do you think Eve killed Lisa?" I asked as soon as we sat down.

"No. I mean, I don't think so, I mean, she could have,

but . . ." Carol's lower lip trembled. "I hate to think I'm working for a murderer."

"How did she act when she borrowed your car? Was she in a bad mood? Was that when she said she wanted Lisa's baby born behind bars?"

"No." Carol took a big bite from her sandwich. "She said that when she heard about Lisa being pregnant. That was mad talk. She said that on Thursday, and she was over it by Friday. Except for the part about checking the books. Mrs. Goodman is a very nice boss. Understanding. When I asked her why she didn't call the police right away when I told her, she said that she wanted to be sure. That anyone could come up short and borrow from the register. It happens in the other salons all the time. As for the invoices, well, sometimes there are discounts or special deals, like deducting the cost of shipping. Those can change the final payment amount. At least that's what Mrs. Goodman said. She wanted to check everything over carefully before she gave the thief a chance to pay it back."

"But that never happened, right?"

"Right." Carol smashed several chips into her mouth.

"Was it Lisa? Could Lisa have guessed that you were onto her?"

Carol shook her head no, and a piece of orange barbecue chip fell from her bottom lip onto her sandwich. "Lisa paid no attention to me. I overheard her call me 'the troll in the back who guards the gold.' I was a nonperson to her."

"Who do you think killed Lisa Butterworth?" I picked up a slice of pickle and bit into it, savoring the way it made my mouth pucker.

"I'm pretty sure it was Suzee Gaylord."

"Oh?"

"The roof blew off on her duplex when Horatio hit. Turns out the shingles had been stapled on rather than nailed on like they were supposed to be. Happened to a lot of people. The building inspectors looked the other way. Rain soaked the entire place and ruined all their appliances. Of course, all that wetness caused mold to grow. Suzee's daughter has asthma, so she has had to move out and stay in a cheap motel until a contractor can clean the mold out."

"So she's paying for her duplex and for a motel room?"

"Uh-huh. Suzee's tried to track down the builder, but he's long gone." Carol's straw gurgled as she chugged the last of her soft drink. "I know she's behind on her credit card payments. Creditors call the salon all the time and ask for Suzee. So maybe she was taking money from the till and skimming the invoices—and maybe Lisa figured it out. Or maybe Suzee just wanted Lisa's job."

"As manager? The job that Eve Sebastiani Goodman gave me?"

"Could be. That'd help her get out of hock. All I'm sayin' is that if I were you, I'd watch my back."

# Chapter Forty-nine

SUZEE HAD MANAGED TO AVOID ME MOST OF THE morning, but that was easy for her because we were both busy. At one point, she disappeared from the floor. When she returned, she was talking with Eve. Whatever they were discussing, Suzee seemed pleased. In fact, her face beamed with joy.

Mom, Stella, and Althea came in as a group to fill out job applications. Stella stood at the counter with eyes wide as bread plates, gazing in wonder at the workstations and the displays. Althea acted as if she'd had a cool infusion, disregarding her surroundings entirely. Mom glanced around and smiled. I took all of them into the back. Eve stopped her work to say hello and encourage them to join the Snippets' crew.

"But when Violetta's opens, we'll go back there," said Althea, her jaw jutting out defiantly.

Mom smiled at her friend.

Today Althea was dressed in bright green, bright red, bright yellow, and bright orange stripes broken by fields of black. The high collar on her long robe suggested a priest's clerical neckline, but the addition of a large pendant quickly set the record straight. "Can we take our customers back to Violetta's when we go?"

"Absolutely. I told Mrs. Terhune and Grace Ann as much," said Eve. "I realize this might well be only a stopgap measure. On the other hand, whether it's permanent or not, I can offer a competitive plan of benefits." Reaching down into the desk drawer, she pulled out two four-color brochures outlining the many advantages that Snippets offered their personnel.

I could tell that Althea was impressed because she didn't automatically toss the paper into the trash. She's not one for using her words when her actions will do. Stella kept swallowing, her Adam's apple bobbing like a kite in the wind. "We would get all of these benefits? You mean I can add my daughter and husband to my insurance?"

"Of course, if you decide to stay longer than ninety days. That's the insurance company's decision, not mine."

Stella's stiff posture buckled with relief. Her fingers loosened their grip on the denim skirt she was wearing.

Mom sighed. "That's a much better compensation package than I've ever been able to offer."

Eve nodded. "Mrs. Terhune, it's strictly a matter of economies of scale. If we weren't so big, I couldn't do as much. There are negatives as well as positives to a large company, as I'm sure Grace Ann has pointed out, since she worked at Sassoon."

"How come you're doing this? Being so nice to us and

all? Do you have a guilty conscience?" Althea's eyes hardened as she stared at Eve.

"Of course I do. What Lisa did was wrong. There are no ifs, ands, or buts about it. I can't change the past. I can't really make it up to you. Grace Ann took me to Violetta's today and I apologized to Mrs. Terhune in person, but that's hardly enough, is it?"

"So you're trying to make amends? And this is it?" Althea drew herself up to her full height. As a tall woman with regal bearing, she could be intimidating.

Was she planning to lambast Eve? Climb all over my new boss? Turn on me and chew me out for ruining Mom's business? Althea's loyalty was unquestionable, as was her twenty-five years of friendship with Mom. They'd been through the deaths of their husbands, raising children as single moms, struggling to keep roofs over their families' heads, and now, was this the end of the road?

"That's mighty nice of you," said Althea. "You can't be blamed for what Lisa Butterworth did."

I hadn't realized I'd been holding my breath, but suddenly, I blew out a long exhale. As I did, a movement to the left caught my eye. Special Agent John Dillon walked in on us, flashing his badge. "Eve Goodman? You're under arrest for the murder of Lisa Butterworth. Please come with me."

# Chapter Fifty

EVE HELD HIS GAZE AND DID NOT BLINK. SLOWLY, she got to her feet before turning her head toward me in that somnambulant manner of a sleepwalker. "Grace Ann, you're in charge while I'm gone. I stand by any decisions that you make on my behalf," Eve said. "Please tell Wynn what happened, and tell him not to worry about me. He should be here shortly. Tell him everything will be all right. Promise me!"

"Of course," I said. My mouth had turned so dry that talking was hard.

"I'd rather not handcuff you." Marsh's eyes turned navy blue with intensity.

"You don't need to. I won't run or make any fuss," she said. "May I call my attorney from your car?"

"Of course," he said.

All in all, it was probably the most civilized arrest in the history of St. Elizabeth.

Mom, Stella, Althea, and I sat there, stunned.

As they walked toward the back door, Eve turned toward Marsh to ask, "May I speak to our accountant for a moment? I don't want this week's paychecks to be late."

Mom's jaw dropped. So did mine. Eve's ability to think about her employees at a time like this totally astonished both of us.

"If you can make it fast," said Marsh, turning back to glance at me, his expression unreadable.

I shook my head and mouthed, "She didn't do it."

He shook his head and turned away.

"Can you believe that?" Althea found her voice.

"No. He's got the wrong person."

"He'll figure that out. Agent Dillon is a good man," Mom said.

"Does that mean we aren't hired?" asked Stella. "I hate to sound selfish, but I could sure use the money."

"The salon needs you and I'm in charge. Come on, let's talk to Carol. She'll know how to get you onto the payroll."

Carol blubbered like a baby. Snot ran down her nose and dripped onto the computer printouts in front of her. "Sh-sh-she is so brave! I can't believe she did it, can you?"

"No, I can't." I tactfully pointed to the mess she was making of the printouts, and Carol mopped up after herself. Before introducing Stella, Althea, and Mom, I said, "Eve told me that I was in charge while she's gone."

Carol nodded. "She told me the same thing. Said that your word was to be obeyed as if it were hers. She said she had complete and total faith in you."

That hit me like a sock to the gut. I stood there speechless

until Althea elbowed me. I introduced the crew from Violetta's, and Carol began putting together the tax forms and
whatnot that each woman would need.

"I better get out on the salon floor and talk to the troops.
I'll call each of you tonight and talk to you about your
schedule."

"Better yet," said Mom. "Why don't all of us text message you with the hours we're not available? That would
make life easier for you."

I agreed, gave her a hug, and left my old coworkers to
comfort the new ones.

The stylists stood in a clutch at the center of the salon.
Suzee Gaylord sobbed, Vinny looked like he wanted to
bolt, Corina was pale as the tip of a French manicure,
Taffy seemed uncharacteristically rattled. That's when I
realized that Agent Dillon must have walked Eve around
the front of the building to get into his GBI-issued Crown
Victoria.

"Everyone?" I beckoned them closer to me with my
hand. "Agent John Dillon took Eve away, as you probably
saw. I believe she's innocent, and I imagine you do, too. In
the meantime, she put me in charge—"

Vinny interrupted, "She stuck her head in the front door
and told us that."

"Okay, so I know it's tough on you, but we need to carry
on. It's bad enough that Eve's, um, under suspicion, but if
we do our jobs, the business won't suffer, right?"

I expected Suzee to give me grief, but she didn't. "That's
right. We can't help Eve. Not right now, at least. But we can
do our jobs the way she expects us to."

With that, the group broke up and meandered off to
their workstations. Mom came up from the back. "We've
signed everything. Is there anything I can do?"

"I have no idea how to cope with this, Mom."

She put a hand on my shoulder. "Be honest. Be fair. Be patient."

"Okay."

"And I'll go get donuts."

"Donuts?"

Her soft blue eyes winked at me. "Can't hurt."

# Chapter Fifty-one

WITH THE NEWS OF EVE'S ARREST, EVERYONE IN town suddenly needed a haircut. We were booked solid for the next two days within the first half hour—and the phones continued to ring.

"This isn't working," I said to Corina as I hurried through another call. "I have an idea."

Racing to the back room, I found Carol. "Can my mother, Althea, and Stella start work right away? We really need the help."

"Sure. I can process their paperwork later," said Carol.

Once I explained the situation, Mom and Stella offered to pitch in. Althea had a doctor's appointment in Savannah and would be gone all day.

"But I can probably come early tomorrow," she promised me as she gave me a good-bye hug.

Racing out to the salon floor, I stopped by Suzee Gaylord's station and explained to her what I'd done. She agreed with my decision, her scissors flashing as she texturized a woman's hair. "You can put someone at the station next to me. That way if there's any question about supplies, I can help out."

Whatever animosity she'd harbored toward me, she'd put behind her. I admired her professionalism, and as soon as I had the chance, I planned to tell her so.

I took the one other empty station and soon had Becky Yoder in my chair. Mrs. Yoder had been a regular at Violetta's. Once she recovered from the shock of seeing me here at Snippets, she started yakking a blue streak. "It's all over the news, Grace Ann. So that Eve woman killed poor Lisa Butterworth? I hope she fries for it. I really do. The Bible says an eye for an eye."

"I don't believe for a minute that Eve hurt Lisa," I said. "You want your roots touched up?"

"Yes, please. The police must think she did it, elsewise why did they take her in?" demanded Mrs. Yoder as I combed through her hair.

"Should I trim up the ends for you? People are innocent until proven guilty. I assume they had probable cause to arrest her, but probable cause isn't the same as a conviction. They might very well decide to let her go after they question her."

"Do the ends and tidy up my neckline, please. I like it shaved into a point, remember? If she didn't do it, who did?"

"If I knew, I'd tell them," I said. "Let me grab some coloring from the back."

When I got to the back, Mom was there, so I joined her in the search for the proper product.

"Grace Ann! Where is Eve? I've been calling her for hours!" Wynn sounded frantic.

"Mama, I'd like you to meet Wynn Goodman," I said.

My mother had never met Wynn, but the sight of him brought her up short. You'd have to be dead and in your grave two weeks not to get all excited by a man that good-looking. If the situation hadn't been so dire, I would have been rolling on the floor laughing at her expression.

"How do, ma'am? You have the most beautiful, talented daughter!" Wynn's face changed in a heartbeat as he grabbed her hand and kissed it gallantly. "I am so happy to meet you. What brings you here today? You visiting?"

"Mom's here to help out. Wynn, we need to talk," I said. "Mom? Becky Yoder's out there. Would you go get her roots started for me?" I tossed my mother the coloring solution. "There's a smock for Mrs. Yoder on the hangers in the closet to your left."

Once Mom was on her way, I took Wynn back to the manager's office. "Special Agent John Dillon came by."

"Not him again!" Wynn groaned.

"And arrested her for Lisa's murder."

"No!" Wynn wailed.

"Hush! Eve told me to tell you not to worry. She was going to call the attorney, and I'm sure he'll be able to—"

"No, no, no!" bawled the big blond hunk sitting across from me. "Don't you see? This is all my fault. What am I going to do? I'm lost without her."

"Get your head on straight. If you really want to help your wife, stop thinking about yourself. Think about what you can do for her! And your baby!"

Wiping his face on his sleeve, he nodded. "You're right. I should have called the attorney the minute they came to the door."

"Came to what door?"

"Of our hotel room. The manager was with them. They had a search warrant."

"When was this? Today?"

"No, yesterday. But I didn't want to worry her."

"Did they take anything?"

"Yes. A black hoodie."

# Chapter Fifty-two

✄

BY TWO O'CLOCK MY BLOOD SUGAR HAD PLUMMETED, and I felt woozy. Mom took one look at me and said, "Go get something to eat. Bring back a sandwich for me."

I hated to leave my chair, but I wasn't thinking clearly, and that's not a great idea when you've got a sharp pair of scissors in your hand. "Let Suzee know if you need anything."

Mom frowned. "Where did Wynn go?"

I sighed. "I don't know. He went back to talk to Carol for a minute, and then he was gone."

"Grace Ann, I have to say that he is the handsomest man I've ever seen in my entire life."

"You've got that right," said Mabel Flanders, who sat beneath my mother's nimble fingers as she put curling rods into the customer's hair. If Mabel felt at all embarrassed about leaving my mother after twenty years of service, she hid it well. "I saw that young man's photo on the TV when they was reporting about arresting his wife. Whooee. He sure is pretty!"

I shot Mom a "let's not talk about this right now" look and hightailed it for Subway.

As I counted out change for the cashier, Agent Dillon stepped up behind me. "Got a minute?"

"How'd you find me?" I followed him to a back table. "My mother?"

He chuckled. "Yes, ma'am."

I took one seat and he sat down across from me. "She didn't do it."

"I figured you say that."

"So she owns a black hoodie. Big deal. I bet half the people under forty in this town have a dark-colored sweatshirt with a hood."

"Right. But hers happened to have hairs from Lisa Butterworth's head on it."

"So? If you didn't notice, Eve owns a hair salon. Coming home with stray hairs on you is part of the gig!"

He cleared his throat. "Grace Ann, I bet very few of the hairs on your clothes have follicles attached to them. I seriously doubt you yank them out of your client's head in a clump, do you?"

"Oh."

"Eat your lunch. Your mama also told me to make sure you ate before you came back. If you don't mind, I'll grab a sandwich and join you."

My turkey tasted like paste in my mouth. Usually, I love pickles, but today, they held little appeal. By the time Marsh sat back down, I'd pretty much given up on my food.

"You have to eat to keep up your strength. You can't

help your friend if you aren't thinking clearly," he said as he bit into a meatball sub.

"Be careful. You're going to get that on your tie." I reached over and moved the silk, pressing it gently against his chest. Even without touching his flesh, my fingers started tingling.

His smile was kind. "I know you believe in her. Trust me, I had good reason to take her in."

I nodded. "You know about her borrowing Carol Brockman's car?"

"She neglected to tell me that when I first questioned her." He chewed with his mouth shut. I like that in a man. "Worse yet, your ex-husband's interviews were of little help. I can't decide whether they are hard to decipher because he's nearly illiterate or because he was purposely trying to withhold information from me so he could look like a hero."

"Take your pick. Either is plausible. Hank wouldn't have graduated from high school if he hadn't been on the football team. As for how he made it through the police academy, well, you're looking at his personal tutor."

"That doesn't surprise me one bit. It also explains why you seem to get in the thick of these investigations, and you always have a better handle on what's happening than he does."

I nibbled on my pickle. "So let me guess what you're thinking. You're betting that Eve arranged to meet Lisa at the salon. Maybe even text messaged her after she and Wynn parted company. Once Lisa was in the building, Eve confronted her. They got into a hair-pulling match. Eve hit Lisa between the eyes, and whammo, she fell into the tank. Eve left, not realizing Lisa would drown."

"You know I can't discuss this with you, Grace Ann. Let's change the subject. I saw that the salon was super busy."

"Ghouls. I guess everyone wanted to get the scoop." I used my index finger to smash a potato chip into smithereens. I got up, refilled my sweet tea, and sat back down. "I'm happy for the business, it's true, and I've been able to find work for the entire crew from Violetta's, but there's something about acting like a flock of turkey vultures picking at roadkill that turns my stomach."

"Sorry about that. People can be disappointing." His brow furled, and it seemed as though a weight bowed his shoulders. "Believe me, I struggle every day against becoming cynical. I became an agent because I wanted to help people. I know that sounds incredibly corny, but it's true. The times when I feel I've been able to help are few and far between, especially when I make an arrest like this. I can tell you think a lot of Mrs. Goodman. I'm sorry this is distressing to you."

"That's okay, Marsh. It's going to be a lot more distressing to you when you discover how wrong you are."

# Chapter Fifty-three

✂

MY BRAVADO FADED QUICKLY AS I TRUDGED BACK TO the salon. The sugar maple next to Snippets wore only a sparse sprinkling of its red leaves. They crunched underfoot as I walked back from Subway, their sharp autumn essence stopping me in my tracks. I took a deep breath and tried to wish myself away from here. Maybe I could tumble along like one of those fallen leaves. Who knows where I'd land? Maybe underfoot or in a gutter. The fact that the leaves were dying didn't escape my notice.

My mother took the Subway bag from my hand gratefully and said, "Thanks, hon. I hope you don't mind about me sending Agent Dillon your way. He's such a nice man."

"Nice but wrong."

"Grace Ann, he's got access to all the facts, and you don't," she whispered while her customer used the hand mirror to examine the back of her cut. Mom had shaped it perfectly so it lay flat at the woman's neck, and from where I stood, I could see she'd also managed to work around a nasty cowlick. My mom was still the best hairstylist I knew, even if she did say I was more talented. Her years of experience gave her the ability to tackle tough problems, like cowlicks or overprocessed hair or hair that was too thin or thick, and solve them so that her clients always looked great.

I bent my head close to hers so the customer couldn't hear us. "I know. I know. But I still don't believe she did it, do you?"

My mother's voice was sorrowful as she watched the client examining herself. "Hon, people do things for the darnedest reasons. She is pregnant. Hormones can make you crazy. There was talk on the radio, I guess, about it having been an accident."

"Maybe." I turned my attention to the customer and said, "That's very becoming on you."

Watching the customer pick up her purse and amble toward the cash register, I turned to Mom and whispered, "Here's the thing: Eve was more than ready to take the blame for what Lisa did. She apologized to you even though she hadn't been involved. When she hired me, she also told me she'd give us back our customers. Why would a woman who's so upright not take responsibility for an accident? Hmm? All she had to do was call her attorney and tell him what happened."

"There's a lot of difference between confessing to your employee's misconduct and confessing to murder," Mom said as she wadded up the used cape and pushed it into the soiled-linens bin.

"But if it was an accident? I mean, doesn't that change everything?"

"You tell me." Mom's eyes reflected sadness. "Maybe she's covering up for someone."

"Wynn?" I couldn't keep the skepticism out of my voice.

"They say that Lucifer was the most beautiful of all God's angels. That man could wrap anyone around his finger. I see now why you fell for him even though he's such a snake. I swannee, he's enough to make an old woman like me weak in the knees." She chuckled and set the comb, brush, and pins she'd used inside a towel to take over to the sterilization unit.

"But he came to me all worried that she'd done it! Mom, he's not real bright. I can't see Wynn keeping his mouth shut if he was to blame."

"Surely he isn't that dumb."

"Mom, he would give himself away. Trust me. I know he would. He doesn't think things through very well. He's a totally impulsive person."

She pursed her lips. "If neither of them did it, who did? Grace Ann, I know you want to believe in this young woman, and I'll be the first to admit she could charm the birds out of the trees, but maybe she just snapped. Maybe you ought to quit playing detective and leave the job to Agent Dillon."

Her words hurt because they echoed my own doubts. Was it possible I was wrong about Eve? Okay, so she was vulnerable and sweet. Not at all what I had expected. That didn't necessarily make her innocent. Under the circumstances, who could blame her for Lisa's death? Hadn't Marsh said it could have been an accident? Perhaps a confrontation led to a struggle, complete with scratches and hair pulling, and then to a smackdown, with Lisa landing in the fish tank.

Or was it possible that Eve was covering up for Wynn? Knowing that he was claustrophobic, and that he wasn't particularly bright, did she decide to take the fall? Given her sterling track record as an entrepreneur and her pregnancy, wouldn't a judge and jury treat her with leniency? And if they knew her father was losing it, might they not suspend her sentence? Was she counting on them being compassionate? Had she weighed her chances against Wynn's and decided that she was more likely to be given a short sentence or a suspended one?

*Maybe Marsh is right. Mom, too. What business do I have playing detective? And as for being a good judge of character, look at who I'd married!*

Trying to shake off my gloomy thoughts, I did a quick check on all the stylists. My rounds took me past the front window. A horn honked and brought me back to the present. Two cars, a Honda and a Camaro, fought for the last available parking space in front of the salon. The media attention to Eve's arrest continued to bring customers to our doors.

The irony of this situation did not escape me. It had all started with me wanting more business for Violetta's. Now, it was ending with a lot of business coming our way, but certainly not as I had planned.

"Lisa Butterworth, you are some marketing genius. You got yourself killed, Eve arrested, and more foot traffic than you can shake a stick at."

Carol appeared at my elbow. "Eve's on the phone."

"Eve? Are you all right?" I asked.

"Yes, and I don't have much time, so please listen carefully. Steven Clifford can't get out here until tomorrow. He's in Montana and the airport is socked in with a freak early snowstorm. I'm fine waiting here. They gave me a cell by myself and I'm okay, but I'd like for you to come pick up my personal effects. I don't want my rings sitting here overnight."

"Sure, I'll come get them."

"Thanks, Grace Ann. I knew I could count on you." A voice in the background hurried her along. "Got to go."

# Chapter Fifty-four

✂

I DROVE TO THE SEPD AND SPOKE TO THE TRUSTEE at the jail.

"Hey. I'm Grace Ann Terhune. My friend Eve Sebastiani Goodman asked me to stop by and sign for her personal possessions." I craned my neck around the hulk of a man in uniform, trying to catch a glimpse of Eve.

"Yes, ma'am. I have the paperwork right here."

A clipboard was offered to me with a pen pinched under the clip. Scanning the document, I quickly found the spots for my signature. The trustee exchanged the papers for a manila envelope with an inventory sheet stapled to the front.

"Mind if I check to make sure everything's here?" I asked.

"Suit yourself." The trustee feigned boredom as Eve's huge rings tumbled out along with her iPhone, her Italian leather wallet, her Gucci sunglasses, and her Patek Philippe watch. The manifest stated she had $4,523.25 when apprehended. I did a quick count of the cash, and the figures dovetailed.

"Who walks around with that sort of money on her?" The trustee stared at the bills in my hand.

"A very wealthy woman," I said. "And a nice one, too. She's innocent."

"That's what they all say."

I slipped the envelope into my purse and walked out. As I did, I felt bad knowing that Eve was back there in a cell. I just couldn't believe she was the one who killed Lisa Butterworth.

With a long afternoon ahead, I drove through the McDonald's on my way back to work and bought two sweet teas, one for Mom and one for me.

"Thank you so much, honey. I just saw Suzee walking toward the employee lounge. Let's go sit in there. You've been on your feet all day. Why don't you join me for a spell?"

Suzee watched my mother take a load off in one of the big stuffed chairs. "Mrs. Terhune? There's a remote control in the side pocket if you want to start the massaging action."

"You don't say? Please call me Violetta," Mom said.

"I was so hungry, my stomach was growling," said Suzee as she dipped a fork into a Tupperware salad bowl. "It took me forever to concentrate. I kept thinking about Lisa and that oversized fish bowl."

"I wanted to thank you for how you pitched in," I said to Suzee. "You've been great."

She shrugged.

"Even so, I know you were next in line. It has to be a disappointment."

"Look, I'm not a morning person and I wasn't sure I could work here after what happened. I admit I wasn't very friendly to you this morning. But I might as well tell you, Eve's promised to make me the manager in Savannah when the old manager leaves next month. Please keep it quiet until she can announce it."

"Good for you," I said sincerely.

"Yeah, well, good news if she makes it out of jail."

"I'm sure she will," I said.

"I hope so, but she had plenty of reason to be mad at Lisa." Suzee cut her lettuce into smaller pieces and doused it with dressing.

"Were you two friends? You and Lisa?" I figured I had nothing to lose.

"I thought we were, until I realized she was dumping all her grunt work on me. As time went on, she got more and more nasty. I don't care for bullies, and she certainly was one. Carol and I have known each other for years. I'm the one who recommended her for this job. I hated seeing how Lisa browbeat Carol. I mean, Carol's got her issues, who doesn't? But she's a hard worker and she's eager to please. Lisa rode Carol like she was a brand-new sled at Christmas."

"What do you think happened? Could Eve really have killed Lisa?" Mom asked. "I bet finding Lisa was a nightmare."

Suzee pushed her salad to one side. "You better believe it. I've been coming in at eight after I drop my daughter, China, off at school before anyone else is here to get my station ready for the workday. I have to pick her up promptly at five at aftercare or they charge me a bundle. The back door was unlocked, which was my first clue there was a problem. I shouldn't have walked in, but my first thought was that we'd been robbed, so I raced from the back room to the front. At first glance, I thought I was dreaming. I mean, it looked like one of those Weeki Wachee mermaid shows they do down in Florida. Her hair was streaming, covering her face. Then I realized it was Lisa and I saw how the step stool was knocked on its side. The light fixture from the hood was under water, too. I knew she was dead. I mean, you could tell."

"Child, I am so, so sorry." My mother reached across the table and took Suzee's hand, which caused the other woman to offer a weak smile of appreciation.

"Who do you think did it?" I asked.

"Beats me. I'm glad I was at a preschool meeting so I have an alibi. Forty parents and two teachers were there with me."

One more person off my list.

"I've seen women act like Lisa because they misunderstood what it means to be in charge. Is that possible? Sometimes women think they should act like men, and they totally overshoot the mark." Behind her rimless glasses, Mom's periwinkle eyes perked up with a possible reason for Lisa's bad behavior. Mom was like that; she always tried to give people the benefit of the doubt.

Suzee shook her head. "No, I think it had to do with her living at home. Her parents didn't have any respect for what she did. What we do. Lisa could never live up to her sister. Bit by bit, it ate away at her. Turned her mean."

"Tell me about Vinny," Mom said. "I haven't had the chance to talk to him yet. Isn't he the only man in the salon?"

Suzee played with a carrot coin before popping it into her mouth. "I don't know how else to put it, but Vinny bats for the other team, you know? Moved here from Atlanta after a bunch of creeps beat the crud out of him. Making him cry was Lisa's idea of a good time."

"Could Vinny have snapped?" I wondered out loud.

"He lives within walking distance of the salon. I suppose he could have come back by that night. There wouldn't have been a car in the lot to give him away. But I believe he had a date for homecoming."

"What about Wynn?" Mom chewed a piece of ice from her drink. "We heard he planned to break up with Lisa. Is it possible they got into a fight?"

Suzee lifted an eyebrow at me. "I heard a rumor that you once dated him. Is that true?"

This was the way of conversation. You exchanged information in a barter system. If I ignored Suzee's question, she'd quit talking, and I owed it to her to be forthcoming. Especially when she'd been so generous in sharing.

"Yes, I did. I was young and stupid, and he betrayed my trust."

"So you've got a grudge against him?" Suzee's eyes brightened with interest.

"I don't have any use for him."

"Could he have done it?" Mom asked me.

I shook my head. "I don't know, but here's the thing: Wynn doesn't know when to shut up. If he killed Lisa, I think he would have confessed already." I sipped my tea. "But then again, he is claustrophobic. Maybe the fear of being locked up has made him careful. What do you think, Suzee?"

"We all know he carries a gun," said Suzee. "If he wanted to do her in, why didn't he promise Lisa a romantic drive, take her out to the inlet, shoot her, and toss her into the ocean? No one would ever have found her body. Plus, there wouldn't have been any mess."

"Wow. You've really give this some thought!" I said.

She grinned. "I read a lot of murder mysteries. I find it relaxing."

# Chapter Fifty-five

✂

I TIMED MY NEXT BREAK TO COINCIDE WITH VINNY'S. After he walked to the back of the shop, I carefully folded my work apron and followed him. While he searched inside the refrigerator, I took my time examining the offerings in the small vending machine. The choices included colas, fruit juices, healthy protein bars, pretzels, and trail mix. Inserting a dollar bill and a quarter in the vending machine, I watched a bag of pretzels hit the retrieval bin. I still had a bit of sweet tea in my plastic cup from McDonald's, so after he sat down, I got my drink from the fridge.

"How's it going?" I said to Vinny as I took the chair across the table from him. He poured a tall glass of green liquid into an insulated cup. "Better yet, what's that?"

"I'm doing a twenty-four-day cleansing fast. It's supposed to clean the toxins out of your body, rejuvenate all the old cells, and rid you of poisons."

"Yeah, but can it make you grow hair?" I asked.

"Make me grow hair?" Vinny was puzzled.

"Kidding, just kidding. When I was a kid and I wouldn't eat my peas, my grandmother used to say they'd make my hair grow. Of course, living in a salon, I wanted pretty hair."

Finally, a smile. "My new boyfriend is a health-food nut. He's been after me to change my diet. Says it will keep me healthy and build muscle."

"It's nice to have someone who cares about you," I said. "How long have you two been dating?"

"A couple of months."

"I heard you two went to the homecoming game. I can't believe I missed it! The first time the Sabertooths won in ten years, and I decided not to go. I guess that last touchdown was a doozy."

"We didn't stay for the whole game."

"No?" Tingles ran up my spine. If he didn't stay, he could have come by the salon.

With a sigh, he said, "A couple of jocks saw Timmy take my hand. One of them pointed at us, the others turned around. It was clear there was going to be trouble."

"I am so sorry to hear that. I guess St. Elizabeth isn't as evolved as I was hoping it would be."

"Yeah, well, I've talked with Eve. She's going to see about transferring me to a salon in Miami. If she gets out of jail, that is."

"I'm sure she will. Was Lisa in favor of letting you move on?"

He set down his drink clumsily and a bit of green liquid

splashed on the tabletop. I jumped up, grabbed a paper towel, and handed it to him.

"Lisa Butterworth. May she rot in hell."

"Whoa! That's a pretty potent curse." I walked back to the sink, wet a paper towel, and handed it over so he could properly wipe the table clean.

"I'm not usually like that, but she made my life miserable."

"Why?"

"Who knows? Maybe she hated gays. It got so bad that I had to go get a prescription for Xanax. I couldn't function otherwise. I was having anxiety attacks here at work. When she found out, she stole an entire bottle of them from me."

"I am sincerely sorry," I said. "No one has a right to treat another person that way. I can see how that might make someone snap."

"Yeah." He kicked at the table leg. Because he was wearing a pair of black Converse All Stars, it didn't make any noise.

"I've been told that Lisa's death could very well have been an accident. The person who smacked her in the head probably didn't realize she wasn't going to climb out of the fish tank."

"Is that what you're doing? Being nice to me so I'll confess?" He jumped up. "Well, I didn't do it! I swear to you, I didn't!"

"Calm down," I said, gesturing with both hands that he should lower his voice.

"Is someone saying I did?" He looked terrified.

"No. No one has said any such thing," I said. "And I'm not accusing you. I'm simply trying to figure out what happened. I hate the fact that Eve is in jail."

Finally, he sat back down. For a while, he said nothing

as he fingered the seam on his black jeans. "I'm sorry she's in jail, but it might be for the best even if I don't get to go to Miami."

"Why?"

"Because I'm pretty sure she did it."

This was not what I wanted to hear. "What? Eve? Why?"

He glanced around and leaned in to talk quietly. "The Blockbuster Express machine is outside that convenience store down the street. Timmy and I decided to watch a movie. You know, to get our minds off being harassed."

"Walk-Inn Foods," I supplied. "That's where the Blockbuster Express machine is."

"Right. But first, Timmy and I drove here. I'd left a jar of this stuff in the fridge. Mixing it up is a pain, and it doesn't stay good for long. So while Timmy sat in the car, I slipped in through the back door, expecting to see Carol because I recognized her Camry. Instead, I heard Eve confronting Lisa."

"What did she say?"

"She told Lisa that she had enough evidence to send her to jail for a felony. Lisa laughed. She said if she wanted to steal from Snippets, she wouldn't have taken such a paltry amount. 'The real problem here is that your husband is in love with me and I'm going to have his baby,' she said. Then I heard them screaming at each other, calling each other names, and I left."

I chewed thoughtfully on a pretzel. "I would have left, too."

Vinny pushed his chair aside. Carrying the empty container to the sink, he rinsed it carefully, squirted in a bit of dishwashing liquid, sloshed that around, and rinsed his glass jar again. "Lisa wasn't stealing from the shop. I know who was taking the money."

"Who?"

"Taffy."

"And you know this how?" My sweet tea cup was empty, so I put it in the recycling.

Vinny had dried his container and tucked it under his arm. He turned to me, a look of defeat coming over his entire person. "It's a bad habit she has. On her way to work, she stops by that Chevron station with those slot machines? The ones that give you a credit card if you win? If she loses money, she takes some from the till to tide her over. She's convinced that one day she'll win big."

"How do you know this?"

"Before Timmy and I got a place together, I lived outside of town, not far from Taffy, so we'd carpool. At first, she was really sneaky about what she was doing, but later, she trusted me. Now I wish I'd told Eve, because keeping Taffy's secret might have gotten Lisa killed."

When we went back to the salon floor, the crowd had thinned out. Many of our walk-in customers had children to pick up after school, others simply didn't feel like waiting any longer. My mother looked tired but happy.

"Mom, I can take it from here. You can call it a day. How long is Stella staying?"

"She has to pick up Jess after soccer in an hour."

"Are you okay?" I said.

"Never better. I really enjoyed myself. This salon is so nice. So modern!" She gave me a hug and fairly skipped out the front door. Humming to myself, I trimmed a customer's bangs.

All the while, I was turning what I'd learned over and over in my head. Did someone in the salon kill Lisa Butterworth? Was it Eve? Was there a struggle that escalated?

The person with the most to gain was Suzee Gaylord. But Suzee said she had an alibi. Marsh would have checked on that.

Could it have been Vinny? No. He, too, had someone who could vouch for him.

Carol? But Eve had dropped her off at home. How did she get here? How far away did she live? And what was her motive?

The contractor, Roy Jasper, also had a great alibi. Or did he?

I dialed Vonda's number. "Hey, you. Got a question."

"Shoot," she said.

We were like that. We'd fuss at each other one day and forget it the next. Our friendship was stronger than any disagreement. Besides, she'd gotten bent out of shape because she loves me—and I would have been just as upset if she'd put herself in jeopardy.

"Do you remember the name of the football player who made the block so the Sabertooths' quarterback could score with the winning touchdown?"

"Of course I do. What's it worth to you?"

"Movie, next Friday, I treat."

"The new Quentin Tarantino flick?"

I laughed. She knew how much I hated violent films. "You drive a hard bargain, but you're on."

"Troy Jasper. Squatty kid, built like a spark plug. His dad's a builder or something like that."

"Thanks, Vonda"—I hesitated—"and thanks for being my pal."

"Best friends forever. Love ya!" And she hung up.

Could Wynn have done it? Maybe he had learned to keep his mouth shut. Or maybe fear of being locked up had caused him to wise up.

Or could it really have been Eve?

As I walked my coworkers to their cars, I wondered. Maybe Marsh was right. I'd seen the scratches on her neck. She hadn't been honest with me about coming back to the salon. Certainly, Lisa had provoked Eve, and bested her by getting pregnant easily by the same man. Maybe her father's illness was the last straw.

"Friendship is something we write on our hearts, one letter at a time," I mumbled.

How hard would it be to erase it?

# Chapter Fifty-six

CHANGING INTO A PAIR OF SOFT YOGA PANTS AND A tee, I curled up on my sofa and flipped through the channels on the TV. Suddenly a *ding-ding-ding* sound came from inside my purse. I dug down and pulled out the envelope full of Eve's belongings.

Ripping it open, I let the cell phone slide into my hand. A text message appeared in the window:

*Eve, I am so, so sorry. I have brought you nothing but grief. I am to blame for everything. By the time you read this, I'll be gone. Good-bye—Wynn*

With shaking hands, I dug for my cell phone and called Marsh.

"It's me, Grace Ann. Wynn Goodman is going to kill himself."

"What?"

"I signed for Eve's cell phone and personal effects. He just sent her a text message."

"Any idea where he might try this?"

"The hotel?" That was all I could think of.

"I'm on my way. You sit tight." And he hung up.

I paced my living room. Sam watched me nervously, hopping from perch to perch easily now and talking to me. Then it hit me. Wynn wouldn't go to the hotel! He would go to the salon!

I pulled on a pair of shoes. Ran into my bedroom and grabbed a hooded sweatshirt, which I dragged over my head as I trotted toward the front door. In a panic, I climbed into the Fiesta and turned over the engine.

I didn't have a plan. I thought about calling Marsh again, but if Wynn was at the hotel, Marsh would have the best chance of stopping him. He'd flash his badge, get the manager, and they could break down the door to Wynn's room.

There are only six traffic lights in St. Elizabeth, and I hit two reds on my way to Snippets. As soon as I drove to the back of the lot and around the building, I saw Wynn's car. With shaking hands, I called Marsh.

"Wynn's car is here."

"Your place?"

"No, the salon."

"I told you to stay put."

"Got to run." No way was I going to let him boss me around. I hopped out of my car and sprinted to the back door. I realized that if I unlocked it, but didn't hit the security code, help would come right away, so that's exactly what I did. Except that my hand was shaking so badly, it took forever to get the key into the lock.

I pushed open the door.

That's when I remembered—Wynn had a gun.

There were two choices: yell out (and give my position away) or sneak along (and give myself a chance to see what was happening). If I called out, Wynn might panic and shoot himself. Or me. If I crept along, I might be able to see what was happening, access the situation, and then call out.

I chose option B, creep and crawl. I'm no superhero. Besides, what if I came upon Wynn having another romantic rendezvous? If I was sneaky, I could back out.

And, yeah, I wasn't feeling particularly brave. My knees were knocking. My pulse sounded like a bass drum, thumping away. In fact, as I crouched down and moved along the back wall, I thought I'd throw up.

*Get ahold of yourself, Grace Ann! You told Eve you'd watch over him!*

The logical place for Wynn to be was at the desk where Eve spent most of her time. Carol's office was at the back of the building, but the manager's office was right off the salon floor, basically a cubicle without a door, right around the corner from the hall leading to the employee area.

I kept low, which was hard on my thighs, but I figured I would be less noticeable and harder to hit if Wynn got spooked. But that crouching position is tough to hold. Especially when you are shaking with fear. Finally, I gave up and got down on my hands and knees and crawled.

Am I stupid or what? Here I was trying to save a guy who was your basic pond scum. No, lower than pond scum. He'd betrayed me, cheated on his wife, and maybe, just maybe I should let him "off" himself.

Okay, that thought lasted all of a half second. No way could I let Wynn shoot himself. First of all, how would I explain that to Eve? Secondly, how could I live with myself? And third, what would my mother say? That one really shook me up.

As I got closer to the manager's office, I realized Wynn wasn't there. I stopped, rolled onto my bottom, sat there, and listened. I could hear mumbling, and it was coming from the salon floor. I got back onto my knees and crept forward, which hurt like holy heck. After clearing the hall, I inched my way up the side of the wall so I was in a standing position and peeped around the corner.

There stood Wynn, facing the big framed poster of Eve, talking to her. The outside sodium-vapor security lamps cast an orange glow that glinted off something in his hand.

A gun.

"Baby, I am so, so sorry," he said as he tried to embrace the poster. "I never meant to hurt you. Honest! I know I shouldn't have screwed around. She came after me, and it was too easy, and I'm a creep and a louse and . . ."

"Wynn?" I spoke softly from behind the corner. "Don't shoot! It's Grace Ann."

He turned. "Grace Ann?"

"Eve asked me to get her personal effects from the jail. I saw your text message. Can I come out? Please don't hurt me."

"I'm not going to hurt you. I'm going to kill myself," he sobbed. "I'm no good, Grace Ann. You know it."

As my vision adjusted to the half-light, I watched him wipe his eyes on his sleeve.

"I'm going to step away from the wall, okay? Please don't shoot me." I could barely walk for how hard my legs were shaking.

"I wouldn't hurt you. I didn't hurt Lisa. I swear it. I think Eve killed her! And I drove Eve to it!"

Saying a prayer, I stepped out onto the salon floor. "Wynn, Eve asked me to take care of you. You can't hurt yourself. She'll be mad at me! Think of the baby!"

"Who needs a dad like me? A no-good cheat?"

I took a step closer. "Could you put the gun away? It's making me nervous."

"I should do this, Grace Ann. If I were any kind of a man, I would pull the trigger and be done with it. All I've been to Eve is trouble."

"That's not true and you know it. Listen. I grew up without a dad. I would have given anything to have my father. Even if he wasn't perfect." I was within fifteen feet of him.

"You mean that?" His shoulders, silhouetted in the security light, slumped. "Honest?"

"Yes, I mean every word of it. Look, if you kill yourself now, Eve doesn't have anyone. She told me about her dad. Is it fair for you to skip out on her? She needs you!"

Wynn was so quiet that I could hear his labored breathing. I was so close that I could almost touch him, but I stopped to give him a bit of space.

"She needs you," I repeated.

Finally he said, "I hadn't thought about that."

"Her attorney couldn't get out of Montana. The airport is socked in. Don't you think there should be somebody in her corner? Why don't you hand me the gun?"

He sighed. "Yeah, I guess—"

I reached for the gun.

Glass shattered behind me. Wynn and I both flinched. "What the—" he started, as we turned toward the source of the noise.

"Hold it right there! Police! Got you covered!" Hank yelled from the front door. Rotating red lights flashed and disappeared on the wall behind me.

"Hank? What the hell are you doing?"

"Drop it!" Hank screamed.

"Hank, stop it. Wynn was giving me his gun."

"I'll shoot!" screamed Hank.

"Hank, I mean it! Stop! Wynn isn't going to hurt me. Everything is under control! Would you put down that gun?" Desperation welled up inside me. Hank had never been a good marksman. In the strobing red light, his arm was shaking visibly.

"Was this a trick?" Wynn whined to me. "I trusted you, Grace Ann."

"No! I have no idea where he came from! Wynn, you have to believe me!"

"I said put down that gun or I'll shoot you where you stand!" Hank hadn't moved from the front door. At that distance, no way could he fire off a shot with any accuracy. I'd been to the gun range with him enough times to know he had barely qualified.

"See? I told you, Grace Ann. This is my case. I'm going to bring this creep to justice!"

"Oh, crud." Taking a shot at Wynn would fulfill every one of Hank's twisted fantasies. He would brag that he was defending me, the woman who scorned him. If he killed Wynn, we might never know who really murdered Lisa Butterworth.

Hank's arm continued to bounce around wildly. In the distance, sirens shrieked. If I didn't do something, fast, Hank would pull the trigger.

I took a deep breath and stepped between Hank and Wynn. "You'll have to shoot me to get to him, Hank."

"Ah, crap, Grace Ann. Move the hell out of the way. How can I defend you if you—" But his complaint was cut short. A shadow moved behind Hank, grabbing his gun, twisting it out of his hand, and causing my ex-husband to turn a somersault in the air. Then I heard the clink of metal and saw the shadow reach down toward where Hank had landed.

"Got him." The faceless form straightened.

Officer Qualls.

From the corner I'd previously occupied, came another sound. A throat being cleared. "Mr. Goodman? Special Agent John Dillon here. Please put your gun down. We have Officer Parker under control. He can't hurt you. I won't hurt you, and I know you don't want to hurt Ms. Terhune."

# Chapter Fifty-seven

✂

FORTUNATELY, WYNN LET ME TAKE THE GUN OUT OF his hand. Holding it pointed down, like a pair of scissors, I stepped to the nearest station. There I did as I'd been taught. I carefully set the gun on its side, facing away from me, so that Marsh could pick it up, which he did with lightening speed. A click told me he had the magazine open, and the *chink-chink-chink* of bullets as they hit his palm further reassured me.

"Officer Shepkowski?" Marsh called. "Get the lights."

Suddenly, the room was bright, and my eyes struggled to adjust once more. Wynn's face was wet, as was his shirt-sleeve where he'd wiped it across his eyes. Shep Shepkowski stepped out from behind the corner. "Yes, sir? What should I do now?"

"Let's take Mr. Goodman in."

"Right," said Shep, and with a bashful nod to me, "Hey, Grace Ann."

My mouth went dry as Shep took Wynn's elbow. "B-B-But he didn't do anything. I mean, he was trying to kill himself, not to hurt me! All this is Hank's fault!"

"Ms. Terhune, please control yourself." Marsh sounded cold. "We will take Mr. Goodman in so he can see his wife. I have a feeling she's not going to be happy that he tried this. And I'd bet my badge that after she scolds him, he won't try anything like this again."

"O-O-Okay." I sighed and rolled my head on my shoulders. "Got it."

Shep started forward with Wynn, but they didn't get far before he planted his feet and turned toward me. "I suppose I should thank you, Grace Ann, for talking sense into me."

"You're welcome." I didn't really mean it, so I added, "I did it for Eve. Tell her, please?"

Qualls and another officer, someone I'd never met, got Hank to his feet. "I'm bleeding," he squealed. "You traitor! Qualls, you're supposed to be my partner!"

"Right. Come on," she said as she marched him toward the police car.

# Chapter Fifty-eight

I CALLED HOKE'S LUMBERYARD'S EMERGENCY NUM-ber and took a seat while Marsh talked to crime scene investigators. Of course, they had to take photos and make notes. Larry Hoke showed up in less than fifteen minutes, carrying a big sheet of plywood and a drill. He went back to his truck for a circular saw. Using two chairs in the waiting area as a makeshift sawhorse, he cut the plywood down to size.

As Larry sank screws into the front door, I nearly dozed off in the stylist's chair. You wouldn't have thought that possible, but the whole situation, the surge of adrenaline and the let down, was exhausting.

"Grace Ann? I'm done here." Larry stood over me. "I'll send along a bill. You're okay, aren't you?"

I nodded and thanked him. His timing proved perfect, as the crime scene guys were packing up, too.

"Can I go home?" I asked Marsh.

"Yes, but I still need to talk to you, and take your statement, so I'll be right behind you." Noticing my sleepy eyes, he cocked his head. "Better yet, I'll drive you home. You can get your car tomorrow."

I nodded. Since I could barely keep my eyes open, that sounded like a good plan.

I remember him scooping me up and carrying me from his car into my place. I remember mumbling, "It's not locked."

When I woke up, I was in my own bed. It was ten in the morning, and sunlight streamed through my window. The smell of coffee encouraged me to pad out to the kitchen.

"Morning," said Marsh.

"Morning."

"I called your mom. Told her what happened and gave her the key to the salon. I found it in your purse. She told me to tell you she's got the situation covered. Would you like eggs? Toast? Bacon? I went out and bought a few groceries."

"Yes, please." An odd feeling of domestic tranquility came over me. Marsh bustled around, clearly at home on the range.

"You still think Eve did it?" I asked.

"I can't comment on an ongoing investigation."

"You're a party pooper."

"And you, Ms. Terhune, are a danger to yourself and society. What in the blue blazes got into you? I told you to stay put." A bit of testiness crept into his voice, but he wasn't really angry.

"How could I sit there and wait for the big boom? Huh?

Come on, Marsh. If that had been you, would you have sat in the parking lot and waited?" I wondered how bad I looked. Yesterday's makeup had probably gotten smeared all over my face. Fortunately, I use Mally eyeliner and eye shadow. That stuff never drifts.

"We're not talking about me. We're talking about you," he said with his back to me. Then he craned his neck so he could see over his shoulder while scrambling the eggs. "Couple of things we need to get straight. First of all, my name is John, not Marsh. Second, I am always going to err on the side of keeping you safe. And third, you didn't even lock your door!"

I groaned and buried my face in my hands. "I was in a hurry, all right?"

"I thought about raking you over the coals for being so reckless, but I bet it wouldn't do me any good, would it?"

"No good at all. Geez. Don't I get any kudos for being brave?"

"Foolhardy."

"Brave."

He stepped around the counter, picked up a copy of the local news, and tossed it down in front of me. The headline read: "Courageous Local Girl Saves Life." Underneath it sat a shot of Special Agent Dillon and a photo of me from when we held a party to celebrate Violetta's twenty-fifth anniversary of being in business. The rest of the article bored me, until I got to the last line: "Officer Hank Parker has been suspended pending an investigation."

"Woo-hoo! Hank's tie is in the wringer now. Who'd'a thunk that Qualls would turn on him?"

"I did. I set her up to watch him. Do you know why he arrived right after you did? That sorry SOB put a GPS tracking device on your car."

"He said I was getting a flat!"

"No, he was tracking you. Stuck the tracker under your car."

I shook my head. "He almost shot Wynn."

"And you." Marsh—I mean John—stepped around the counter and folded me into his arms. "Grace Ann, I've never been so worried in my life."

"I have morning breath."

"Go brush your teeth. I'd like to kiss you properly before I wring your neck for scaring me out of my wits."

# Chapter Fifty-nine

BEFORE WE LEFT MY APARTMENT, I BLEW THE OLD seed husks out of Sam's dish. At the bottom were only a few lonely whole seeds. "Sam, I'm so sorry. I'm a loser as a parakeet mother."

John laughed. "Tell you what. We can swing by the pet shop over by Snippets and grab more seed. I'll come back and feed him, if you'd like."

"Perfect!" I said and I stood on my tippy toes to deliver another kiss. Our necking nearly caused me to toss in the towel and spend the day in bed. With company. But John and I both had work to do.

Instead, I showered quickly, dressed in a pair of black jeans, topped that with a black-and-white striped tee shirt

I'd bought at Cracker Barrel, of all places, and put on my makeup. He pronounced me "adorable," and the blush on my cheeks was more due to passion than to powder.

After John parked the car, we walked hand in hand from the municipal lot to the shop.

"Does this mean we're going steady?" I giggled.

"Steady as a rock," he said with a smile. His gorgeous blue eyes were misty with affection and his hand felt comforting and safe as it held mine.

"Hey, Petey," I said as we walked through the door.

The young manager glanced up from the hamster cage he was cleaning and turned white as a sheet. "Wh-wh-what?"

"I said 'hey.' I need more bird seed."

"S-S-Seed?" Petey glanced around nervously. "Th-th-this way." And I followed him, staring into the hood of his dark sweatshirt. John leaned against the front counter, pecking out a text message on his cell phone.

"When are you leaving?"

"T-T-Tomorrow. I was going to go today, but our paychecks came in late, and . . ." He sounded as if he'd run a mile or two.

"You okay?"

"Y-Y-Yeah. Sure." He tugged at the neckline of his jacket. "This be all?"

"Yes." At the register, I paid for the seed. Petey didn't ask me if I wanted a sack. After handing over the receipt, he walked with amazing speed toward the back of the store.

John turned over the engine and put his car in reverse. "Get everything you needed?"

"Uh-huh." Something nagged at me. Something I couldn't quite—

"That's it! Petey did it! That kid! He's the one who killed Lisa!"

"Explain it to me," said John, putting his car into park. "I have no idea who that kid is or why you're convinced he's involved."

"The night I went to buy Sam, Petey—he's the kid we just saw—told me he had a meeting with a client. Snippets has a contract with Fur, Fin, and Feather to maintain the big saltwater aquarium. Petey was paid a bonus for loss prevention, but Lisa had killed all the fish. Don't you see? She let him into the salon because she was his appointment! They quarreled and she must have climbed onto the step stool to make a point about the fish being dead—" I popped my hand over my mouth. "Petey carried around a sack of glass pebbles! He was playing with them the night I bought Sam. The kind you put in the bottom of a fish bowl. Was Lisa struck in the forehead with something like that?"

"Yes, she was. And he's tall enough, and we know he wears a hoodie."

"He told me that he's leaving town. Said something about going while the getting was good."

"That's enough for me. I think I'll bring him in for questioning," John said as he picked up his car phone and requested backup from the St. Elizabeth Police Department. "This time, do you think you could stay put? I really don't want a repeat of last night."

"On my honor!" I held up three fingers. "I was a Girl Scout, and I wouldn't lie. Better yet, I'll walk to work while you handle that."

John smiled. "I guess a couple of blocks won't hurt you."

With a quick kiss, we both climbed out of his car.

The glazier bent over the front door of the salon, fitting the new glass to the hole that Hank created during his faux rescue. "Excuse me," I said, stepping around him.

The minute I walked in, the whole salon erupted with applause. "What?" I marveled at their response. Suzee Gaylord was on the elevated area with the stylists' chairs. "Way to go, Grace Ann!"

Everyone hooted and cheered a bit louder. I laughed. "Okay, pizza is on me for lunch."

My mother spoke to her customer and hurried over to hug me. "Honey, I can't believe that stupid Hank Parker. He nearly got you killed."

"Actually, he nearly killed me himself, but that doesn't matter now. How's everything going?" I glanced around and saw that we were busy as ever. Corina had the phone under one ear and her hands on the computer typing in reservations.

"Fine. Everyone has been so helpful. Suzee particularly. Mr. Martin has the front door almost finished."

I nodded.

"Althea and Stella will be in at noon and Rachel is coming after school." Mom's grin stretched from ear to ear.

"You sure look happy." I admit that my mind was on Petey Schultz. I hoped I hadn't led John on a wild-goose chase. Worse yet, I hoped I hadn't given Petey a reason to be even more nervous or upset than he clearly was. But it couldn't be helped. In my heart of hearts, I felt certain that Petey was the killer. I bet when that Band-Aid came off his face, there were scratches underneath.

Mom laughed. "I am. This floor is wonderful to stand on. The customers keep coming. My daughter is fine, after a narrow miss, and a heroine, too. Oh, and your sister called. Owen will be fine. They tested him. He's evidently not much of a talker."

"That's a relief!" I glanced around at the happy hum of activity. Soon every member of the Violetta's crew would be here, except for Beauty. We'd have to work on that.

**TWO DAYS LATER . . .**

"Poor Petey. Growing up like he did, he didn't know which way to turn. Didn't have anyone to run to. No one who had his back." As Mom spoke, her hand slid under the table to find mine and give it a squeeze.

"With Lisa attacking him, all he wanted was to get away," I said as I squeezed hers back before letting it go.

"I've recommended that he get a reduced sentence," John said. "He had no idea she wasn't going to crawl out of that tank. You know, there are two kinds of crimes: one where the perpetrator intentionally causes harm, and the other that's what I call a 'stupid crime'. When somebody quits thinking. You can guess which category Lisa Butterworth's death is. In my mind, at least."

"On a brighter note, the contractor says he can get started on Violetta's next month," Mom said. In her pink sweater and gray slacks, she was the picture of good health. Her periwinkle eyes twinkled from behind her glasses.

Walter reached over and patted her arm. A short, plump man with a full goatee and a mustache he waxed into rigid loops, Walter's interest in Civil War enactments guided his hairstyle and beard choices. Tonight, he wore a gray jacket that reminded me of his Confederate uniform. I was glad he'd left his sword at home. Didn't seem appropriate for a family outing, especially since Logan and Owen were both fascinated by any sort of weaponry.

"You're sure you can quit Snippets at any time? They'll give you all your old clients?" Alice Rose's brows wrinkled with concern.

"That's right." I said. "You can't believe how grateful Eve is. She's so happy we've cleared her name—"

"And her husband's," added John. "After all, it was looking really bad for her."

I nodded. "Especially because she had scratches on her neck from a cat fight with Lisa."

"They'd also pulled each other's hair," said John. "In fact, there was plenty of circumstantial evidence we could have used to convict Mrs. Goodman."

Our waitress distributed dessert menus as the busboy at Denny's started clearing our table. We'd billed this as our "celebration" dinner, because I wanted my sister to meet John, and we all had so much to catch up on.

"That's right. But tell Alice Rose the news." I nudged Mom. Beneath the table, John reached over and took my hand. He's sweet like that.

"To thank us—Grace Ann, really—Eve offered to let us take over her salon. We'd sort of be business partners. We can buy everything from her at her prices. Grace Ann can run Snippets as long as she wants. We get the benefit package that Snippets' employees enjoy. All that's necessary is for us to pay rent and utilities." Mom smiled happily. "It's the best of both worlds. Her lease is good for a year. That'll give me plenty of time to get the mold out of my house, and to deal with the historic register people."

"I don't think I heard about that," John said, withdrawing his badge from his inside pocket and handing it to my nephews for them to ooh and aah over.

"Before all this happened, I received a letter from the historic register saying my house had been proposed for inclusion on their list," Mom said. "Naturally, I have all sorts of questions. Mainly, I'm worried that I might have to undo all the changes I made to the first floor when I turned it into a salon."

Alice Rose nodded. "I bet that mean old Lisa Butterworth turned in the paperwork."

"I agree. She said something in passing about it being a travesty, what you did to the house and all." I sipped my sweet tea. "While I have sympathy for her situation with her parents, I don't see why she wanted to disrupt Mom's life. She'd already ruined our business. Why force Mom out of her home? Why cause Mom all this stress?"

Walter's mouth turned down and he fingered his napkin, running his hand over it nervously. "Um, Violetta, I, uh, I'm the one who contacted the historic register."

"You!" Mom's eyebrows shot up. "Why, Walter Highsmith! Whatever possessed you? Was this a trick to get me to travel with you?"

Walter hung his head. We all sat there, stupefied.

"No." He sighed, closed his eyes, and then turned to Mom. "See, I was doing research on my own Victorian, and I came across information pertaining to your house. Did you know there are grants available? There are. I sent in your proposal for inclusion at the same time I did mine. I thought that if Violetta's was in the historic register, it might mean money and publicity for you."

Mom worked her jaw, a sure sign that she was mad as a wet hornet. Fortunately, both her hands were palm side down on the tablecloth, because I was pretty confident she wanted to smack Walter.

I couldn't blame her.

All sorts of scenes jumbled together in my head. I saw Mom working alone. I remembered how she never dated. I thought about how lonely her life must have been. And I made a decision to speak up.

"Mom? Have you forgiven me for pushing you into hiring Lisa Butterworth? Because if you have, surely you can forgive Walter. He didn't mean any harm, just like I didn't, either."

"I thought I was helping, Violetta. I was wrong. At the very least, I should have consulted you before I moved forward. Can you forgive me?" He reached for her hand.

She stared at his as he tried to wiggle it under hers.

We collectively held our breath. I mean, even the nephews stayed quiet. Under the table, John gave my fingers a tiny squeeze of encouragement.

"Walter, I forgive you." She leaned over and kissed him lightly as she looked soulfully into his eyes. "Now what do you want for dessert?"